He's Lying About Everything

ALSO BY ROBIN MAHLE

HE'S LYING ABOUT EVERYTHING

ROBIN MAHLE

JOFFE BOOKS

Joffe Books, London
www.joffebooks.com

First published in Great Britain in 2025

© Robin Mahle 2025

Cover art by Nick Castle

ISBN: 978-1-80573-137-5

To my husband.
Thank you for your support, dedication, and for
having no part in this story's inspiration.

PROLOGUE

So this is how it ends — water pressing against my lungs, the domed corrugated ceiling above me rippling as though it, too, is drowning. I've barely started my life, and now it's over. My mind flashes to the countless hours I've spent in this pool, training, exhausting myself. Forgoing parties, dances, homecoming games. My entire collegiate career hinged on my success in this pool.

Now, it's where I die.

It's strange, the clarity that comes in these final moments. Every sound, splash, and muffled cry distorts into a dull echo. It's as if the world is underwater. For me, I suppose it is.

When I left here only hours ago, after an argument with a man I loved, I didn't expect to return so soon. Tomorrow is the season's most important swim meet, and I intended to return first thing in the morning. But I had to know. I had to get to the truth. That's how I ended up here.

Talk about regrets.

Returning to the building at such a late hour, I sensed something was off. That feeling you get when the tiny voice in your head tells you to run — I should've listened. Instead, I walked inside. The pool shimmered amid the hazy green light.

The rest of the building was dark. The familiar chlorinated scent surrounded me as it always had. I swear I must have chlorine in my blood. But that won't save me now.

This place is my second home.

After the revelations came the push. Panic overtook reason, and the water swallowed me whole. Did I struggle? Of course. But it wasn't enough. As an expert swimmer, I would've expected more from myself . . . fought harder, kicked and thrashed, clawing my way to the surface. Instead, the surface slipped farther and farther away, and my strength right along with it.

The cold surprised me the most. Not just in the water, but a deeper, penetrating chill, as though something — someone — wanted this.

With what little consciousness I have left, I see the blurry silhouette looming above the water's surface. Watching. Waiting.

An accident, they'll call it. A tragic mistake. She trained for too long, too hard. Her body exhausted itself, they'll say. But the truth is sinking with me.

CHAPTER 1

Derek

The mild burning sensation in my nose is the chlorine. Immediately recognizable, it hits me first. As I draw closer, my footsteps echo inside the vast building that encloses the pool. Above me, fading rays of light scatter through misty windows.

Bleachers flank three sides of the pool. I walk past them, my hands tucked into my pants pockets. I don't want to be here to say the things that must be said — to say them to her.

In front of me are the diving boards, each one higher than the last. This isn't just any pool — it's one of the best Olympic-sized pools in all of New England, funded by obscene amounts of money from the university's annual endowments.

The tiled edge shimmers blue and green as I peer into the water at an indistinct figure moving beneath the surface. Her movements are graceful and hypnotic. As the figure rises to the top, my heart skips, and a smile spreads across my face. "Nicole," I call out to her, my voice echoing off the masonry block walls.

She turns toward me with a seductive grin. Water drips down her face. Her hair, wet and slicked back, highlights her sharp cheekbones and firm jawline. Nicole paddles toward the steps, and as I reach for her towel, she climbs out. Water clings to her flawless figure, clad in a one-piece swimsuit emblazoned with the school's emblem.

"What are you doing here?" she asks.

I wrap the towel around her shoulders and peer into her brown, deep-set almond eyes. Their color matches her skin. "I finished grading papers and thought I'd stop in to see how you were doing. Tomorrow's a big day." As a professor, I've learned that beginning on a positive note before introducing a negative one yields the most effective results.

She blots the water from her face. The hairs on her arms rise in the cool air, and I try not to stare at her breasts as her suit outlines them. "It is a big day. If I win, I'll draw the eyes of Olympic scouts. I can't afford to screw this up."

"You won't," I assure her before returning my hands to my pockets. "Listen, uh, I won't be able to make it—"

"What?" Nicole lowers her towel. "You're not coming to the most important swim meet of the season? Why?"

I scratch my eyebrow with my middle finger, a familiar gesture when I'm faced with saying things I don't want to say. "Well, not only could it draw attention, but I also happen to have a family thing going on."

A frown replaces her previous smile. "Of course you do." She scoffs. "Damn it, Derek, why do you always do this? How many times have you promised you'd end things and yet here you are, letting me down once again. I'm sick of it, you know that?"

I raise my hands to calm her as her voice echoes around me. I can't risk anyone overhearing our conversation, though I'm uncertain whether anyone else is here. The risk is too great. My job, my family. "Nicky, please, you know how hard this has been for me, but Evelyn and I share a child."

"Oh, I'm perfectly aware." She tosses the towel onto the chair and reaches for her T-shirt, pulling it over her wet swimsuit. "I'm also well aware that I'm not the only one."

"Excuse me? Look, whatever you've heard . . ."

"Really?" she cuts in, hands on her hips. "You know what? You can't make it tomorrow, Derek, that's fine. I don't need you there. In fact, I don't need you at all."

Her face heats with anger. Only a moment ago her eyes held affection, but now I see only contempt. "You must think I'm stupid. You think I don't know I'm not your only side-piece? You think we don't talk to each other?" She stops, her expression changing as her mouth tilts into a calculating grin. "I'll bet Evelyn would like to know about your extracurricular activities. I'd probably be doing her a favor."

The warning echoes in my ears, igniting a fire in my gut. Whatever my purpose was on arrival has now morphed into self-preservation. I take her shoulders, my fingers digging into her soft skin. "Don't threaten me, Nicky. I don't respond well to threats."

The sound of wheels on concrete echoes in the distance. Someone's coming. The janitor with his cleaning cart? Maybe. I can't afford for anyone to see me here — not with her.

I release my grip, drawing in a calming breath. "Look, Nicky, it doesn't have to be this way, all right?"

She drapes the towel around her neck. "They warned me about you. I should've listened. Get the hell away from me. I don't ever want to see you again."

It takes me a second to register it all. But there's nothing left to say. Hearing that cart approach, I turn to leave. "Just keep your mouth shut, Nicky, and neither one of us will have to face the consequences."

I slip out the side exit, unseen. Now, to head home to my family. Home to my wife and child, who've done nothing to deserve this. I love them, and I won't let anyone destroy my life.

I arrive just in time for dinner. Evelyn will have made something nice for us. She always does. And as I open the door, the waft of roasted chicken brings me comfort and relief. It returns me to a sense of normalcy. I can ignore that I've

5

betrayed the beautiful woman who now stands at the stove, her brunette hair pulled back in a low bun, strands brushing against her cheeks. Her statuesque figure is no longer flawless but striking in a way that reminds me she is a mother. Warm and soft. Kind and gentle.

"Just in time, honey," she says, smiling at me. "Dinner will be ready in ten minutes."

I slip my arm around her waist, breathing in her soft vanilla fragrance. "Perfect." I kiss her cheek. "Just like you, Evie. Perfect."

CHAPTER 2

Evelyn

A thin blade of light slices under the guest bedroom door, the only sign of life in a house that seems to shrink around me. Derek's snoring — relentless and guttural — drove me from our bed an hour ago, but it isn't the snoring that rattles me now.

I strain to hear his footfalls. It's late, almost midnight. What's he doing up? Is he coming in here? A thoughtful gesture to check on me, or maybe he has something more romantic in mind? My optimism is relentless.

The windows in here are draped by heavy curtains, sealing me in this darkness. That thin strip of light under the door is my lifeline.

I outstretch my hand, touching the nightstand in search of my phone. Grabbing hold of it, the screen lights up much too brightly. I squint to see the time, and when it comes into focus, my guess is close. It's 12:15 in the morning.

A shadow crosses under the door. He's tiptoeing past our son's room now. The stairs creak. He's descending them. My hope for a passionate encounter dwindles. Does he want a glass of water? A bite of food?

Yet when I hear the rumble of the garage door opening and the slight vibration of a car's engine, it hits me . . . he's leaving.

Derek and I have been married for eight years. We share a four-year-old son, Ben. We live in the most beautiful Cape Cod home in one of the best neighborhoods in Medford, Connecticut. He's a professor at Medford University — with tenure, I might add.

What can I say about Derek other than he's brilliant? It was obvious from the moment we met in college. He's witty and passionate about his work. I'm still not sure why he chose me when he could've had any woman. These days, I try not to pull at that thread. I've always considered myself to be an attractive woman. I'm mindful of my appearance and do my best to stay in shape, though I could probably do more. But my husband? He's the Superman of English professors. No doubt he could pull off the blue tights if necessary. Tall, broad shoulders. Perfect wavy black hair. Admired by all who encounter him. And I mean — all.

The thing is, I love my husband, and he loves me. That is something on which neither of us wavers. No matter what. On the outside, we have the perfect life. I've worked tirelessly to render our impeccable image.

But don't look at it too closely — the cracks are beginning to show.

* * *

At first, the thumping noise seems nothing more than a figment of my subconscious, a muffled echo escaping my dreams. Construction workers — that's what it must be. Their hammers and drills banging away as they remodel my neighbor's house.

But when a slight touch grazes my cheek, soft and feather-light, the distant thumping isn't so far away anymore. The sensation yanks me into the waking world, and my eyes snap open. "Ben," I whisper into the semi-darkness, recognizing the tiny hand still lying against my face.

The soft glow of dawn filters through the gaps in the drawn curtains. I turn my head to look at him. "What is it, sweetheart?"

"The noise," he replies, standing next to the bed. "Someone's banging downstairs, and it woke me up."

I look around, forgetting for a moment that I'm in the guest room. "Did you wake up Daddy?" As my focus on him grows clearer, Ben shakes his head with resolve.

I rise onto my elbows, then toss my legs to the floor as Ben backs up. "It's probably the people fixing Mrs. Johnson's house." I get to my feet. "I'll go see."

The first thing I notice is the cold — like the heat's been turned down. I grab my robe at the end of the bed and pull it around me. "You want to come with me to check?"

"Okay. I'll be brave."

I pull him close. "That's my boy."

As we enter the hall, I glance down to the end. My bedroom door is closed. The noise didn't seem to awaken Derek. Lucky him. As we reach the top landing, I hear the thumping again and immediately recognize it. This isn't the sound of hammers and drills. Someone's at the door. It's much too early for that, so now I'm on high alert. I turn to Ben. "Sweetheart, why don't you go back to your bedroom, and I'll see what's going on? Then I'll make you a special breakfast. Would you like that?"

"Yeah. Can it be pancakes?"

"Sure." I pat his shoulder. "Now, go on." I wait a moment until he disappears into his room. I glance again at our bedroom door, wondering if I should get Derek up. But when the knock sounds again, there's no time. Whoever's there is impatient. And at this time of morning, I don't think they're here to sell me solar panels.

Securing my robe around my waist, I head downstairs, smoothing my hair in the process. God knows what I look like right now. As I reach the foyer and peer into the small mirror next to the door, I shudder at my appearance.

"Just a minute," I call out, peeking through the security lens. *What the hell?* I pull back, quickly unlocking the door to open it.

A man in a suit, flanked by two uniformed police officers, stands on the other side. "Mrs. Evelyn Moore?"

"Yes. Is something wrong?" Is this about my parents? Derek's parents, or maybe his sister? A million scenarios run through my mind as I stare at this man presenting a badge.

"I'm Detective Bartz. Is your husband, Derek Moore, at home?"

One thing I haven't mentioned is that I was once a lawyer, having given it up after the birth of my son. Not a defense attorney — it seems that might come in handy right now — but I know my way around situations like this. "Yes, but he's still asleep. May I ask what this is about?"

"Do you know a Miss Nicole Peterson, ma'am?"

My pulse rises, and I become acutely aware of my heart beating in my chest. The name doesn't ring a bell, but she's most likely a student in one of Derek's classes. Has she lodged a complaint against him? That would hardly explain the early morning pounding on my door. "No, I can't say I recognize the name. What does this have to do with my husband, Detective?"

He pockets his badge and tilts his head. "Well, ma'am, she's dead, and we think your husband was closely acquainted with her."

"Dead?" I repeat the word because it suddenly sounds foreign to me.

"Yes, ma'am." The detective peers over my shoulder, and I instinctively shift my weight so he can't see inside our home. "Is your husband available? I'd like to ask him some questions."

CHAPTER 3

I envision her wide-open eyes staring into the pool's depths. A terrified expression, frozen on her face forever. A bubble rising to the surface; the last vestige of air escaping her lungs. My mind's eye conjures these images as the police talk to my husband. Meanwhile, I hover in front of my coffee maker, waiting for it brew.

According to Detective Bartz, Nicole Peterson was a beautiful girl. Strong. Athletic. His description is designed to evoke guilt, no doubt. She was the top swimmer on the university's team, having led them to a national title last year. Set to graduate this spring, but that won't be happening now.

The coffee's done, and I pour myself a cup. Taking a sip, I watch them in our kitchen nook, sitting on the oversized chairs. Derek and I don't eat breakfast together much anymore, so I decorated that spot with a couple of comfy chairs and a small table. The two armed officers loom over them like hired muscle.

"Can I get anyone a cup of coffee?" I cut in, raising my mug. "I just made a fresh pot."

Bartz turns his attention toward me. "Yeah, sure. That sounds great. Black, please. One sugar. Appreciate it."

11

"Okay then. Any other takers?" I ask, glancing at the officers, who both shake their heads. I prepare his coffee and walk over, setting it down on the table. "Here you go."

"Thank you, Mrs. Moore," he says, taking a sip. "Perfect." Bartz pulls out a recorder from his suit jacket. "You don't mind, do you, Mr. Moore?"

"No, sir," Derek says.

Normally, I'd object to the use of a recording device, but it's best I keep my mouth shut. If I push this detective, he'll insist Derek go into the station to make an official statement. That would make things far more difficult. At least this way, I can attempt to control the narrative if this thing starts to tilt. Though, we may already be capsizing.

"I understand you and Miss Peterson were in a relationship," Bartz says, tossing a glance my way as if I'm somehow still unaware. It's safe to say I've connected the dots.

"Yes, sir. That's correct, but it had recently ended," Derek glances at me.

"Is that so?" Bartz jots down something in his tiny notepad. "And when did you last see Miss Peterson?"

"Friday evening," Derek says. "She was in the pool — training."

"So, had it ended at that point, Mr. Moore, or before then?" Bartz raises his palms. "I'm trying to get a sense for why, if you'd ended things with Miss Peterson, you would've seen her only hours before we suspect she drowned."

"To be honest, I'd gone there to tell her it was over." Derek glances at me again. "Then I went home and had dinner with my family."

"I stay home with our son, Detective Bartz," I interrupt, assuming Derek's look was a silent request for a lifeline. "So I know when Derek arrived because I had just about finished making dinner. He got home around six thirty."

"So you ended your relationship with Miss Peterson, and then she drowned." Bartz tugs on his jacket lapels as if punctuating the irony. "And did you leave your home again after that, Mr. Moore?"

12

"He didn't." I jump in before Derek can answer. "We stayed in the rest of the evening. Derek bathed Ben and put him to bed while I caught up on some reading. We went to bed around ten o'clock." I'm keeping quiet about hearing Derek leave the house in the middle of the night.

I'm emboldened enough to attempt to put an end to this — a hint of the confidence I once possessed returning to me. Bartz seems to have no other reason for being here than the fact Derek and this girl, Nicole, had a relationship.

"Please forgive me, Detective, but do you have specific evidence you'd like to discuss with Derek? Because it's starting to feel a little like a fishing expedition right now."

Bartz raises the corner of his mouth in a half-smile. "Are you his lawyer, Mrs. Moore?"

"No, sir, but I am a lawyer."

He snickers. "Of course you are." The detective licks his lips, resting his elbows on his knees. "Look, Mr. and Mrs. Moore, I'm just trying to figure out how an experienced swimmer, a star swimmer, such as Miss Peterson, managed to drown in the university's pool. She didn't suffer an external injury. That much we know. And given what we've learned about Professor Moore, well, it seems he gets around."

"Excuse me, Detective," Derek cuts in. "Is that necessary? You're in my home with my family."

Bartz raises his hands. "You're right, Professor. My apologies. But you'll forgive me for wanting to find out exactly what happened to Nicole Peterson. You two had a thing for a while, so, of course, it makes sense for us to come speak to you. To get your side of the story."

"And unless you have evidence to suggest my husband played a part in a death that could very well have been accidental, then I don't think it's necessary to continue this conversation." Now I worry I've pushed too far, but there's no turning back. "People make mistakes, Detective. Derek isn't perfect, and neither am I. I imagine you aren't, either. So, if there's nothing else . . ."

"No. Nothing else. We'll be on our way." He stands and offers Derek his card. "If you do happen to think of anything . . . you or your wife . . . feel free to contact me."

As Derek shows them out, my mind claws through the timeline, frantic to pin down the details of Friday night, but the specifics slip through my grasp. I can't recall the precise time Derek came home or when we finally went to bed. Everything I'd said to that detective was a best guess. The only thing I *do* remember — clear and unshakable — is him leaving the house at 12:15 on Saturday morning. When did he return? I have no idea. A knot twists my gut at the implications. Could he have had something to do with that girl's death? My hand trembles as I lift the coffee cup, and I blink back the sting of tears.

A soft thud reverberates through the house as the front door closes. They're gone, but the relief is fleeting. This isn't over. Derek shuffles into the kitchen, his footsteps dragging like dead weight. His head hangs low, hands buried deep in the pockets of his sweatpants, but when his eyes finally rise to meet mine, the silence between us screams at me.

"I'm sorry you had to find out this way," he says, his voice a ghost of itself.

The lack of remorse in his words astounds me. "*That's* what you're sorry for? If I were you, I'd be sorry for the fact that a young woman is dead."

"Of course I'm sorry." He walks toward me, arms open, ready to pull me into an embrace.

"Don't," I whisper, flinching at his touch.

He takes a step back, swallowing hard. "I didn't do this, Evie. Please believe me. Whatever happened to Nicole had nothing to do with me. I love you, and I love our family."

I take in a deep breath, letting his words settle around me — words I've heard before. Finally, I put down my mug and leave the kitchen, brushing past him without another glance.

After this morning, everything will change. Regardless of whether this girl's death was an accident, the affair will come out. There's no denying that. Our standing at the school will come into question. My charity work. The volunteering I do when Ben is at preschool. I've prided myself on helping our community.

Meanwhile, Derek helps himself to whatever and whoever he wants. A fact I've conveniently ignored because those cracks I mentioned earlier? I've done my best to plaster over them.

This life of respect and admiration, of dinner parties with meaningful discussions about important things, is over. A girl is dead.

Do I blame Nicole Peterson for screwing my husband? Well, as the saying goes, it takes two to tango. But no, I don't blame her, especially now. Derek can be very persuasive.

One thing is certain — that detective doesn't believe she died as a result of accidental drowning. If he did, he wouldn't have come to my home at the crack of dawn on a Sunday. It was a tactic to catch us off guard. And it worked. The only problem is, in the event he's right, I can't be sure Derek didn't kill Nicole Peterson.

Strange thing to think about one's spouse — whether they're capable of murder.

CHAPTER 4

Derek's phone has been ringing nonstop — an incessant reminder of what to expect in the coming days until the police reach their conclusion. I've yet to draw my own out of fear of what it would mean.

An hour ago, Derek finally silenced the damned device. He claimed the calls were from his co-workers, the other members of his English Department, including the department head. He muttered something about them being worried, making it seem they expressed genuine concern.

I guess I shouldn't be surprised. Derek's always been a popular figure among his academic peers, his charisma and intellect drawing them in, just as they had me.

I've tried to keep Ben ignorant of the mounting unease. I took him to the movies. We wandered aimlessly through a bookstore, where I let him choose whatever he wanted. All these attempts at diversion were simply to avoid confronting Derek about where he'd gone in the midnight hour of Saturday morning. I didn't dream it. I'd heard him leave. But the truth terrifies me.

Now, Derek and I sit side by side on our comfortable couch where we've shared so many moments of intimacy and happiness. Our bodies are only inches apart, but he couldn't be farther from me at this moment.

The television drones on in front of us, its flickering images — irrelevant. The warmth of his hand as it rests on my thigh does nothing to assuage the chill in my bones. Yet I let it remain because I still love him.

"Babe," he whispers.

I know what's coming, but I don't know if I can face it. As I turn toward him, the dam restraining my emotions crumbles. My lips tremble, and my eyes sting.

"I'm so sorry for what I've done, but I swear to you, I didn't hurt that girl."

The words come across as hollow to me. I want to scream, to tear into him, to demand why my love wasn't enough — why he had to shatter our illusion of happiness. I could've continued to overlook his affairs because I loved our life. But this isn't about me anymore. This is about Nicole Peterson, a young woman whose life ended before it even began.

As a mother, my son is my greatest strength and my biggest weakness. He holds my heart, every beat, every breath. But as a wife? My devotion has made me weak. I've chosen to see the man I *want* Derek to be, not the man he truly is. I've ignored the warnings, dismissed the doubts, and now I'm standing on the edge of a cliff wearing a blindfold. Did he kill her?

I look him in the eyes. Can I tell him what he needs to hear? Ignore the raging thoughts in my head?

"I believe you."

Turns out, I can.

* * *

Three days have gone by with no answers. Plenty of speculation, of course. And Derek remains under the watchful eye of Detective Bartz, who still awaits the autopsy results.

Meanwhile, today is the weekly boosters' meeting. I've been a member of the influential group for years. They're responsible for raising money for the university. I considered skipping out on it but wondered if it would make me look like I believed my husband was guilty.

It's the first time I've been out on school business since it happened. Maintaining my composure is a must, so I'm dressed in a long skirt and my best fall boots. My hair is pulled back in a sophisticated bun, and my scarf complements my blouse. But will anyone notice? No. No matter that my outfit accentuates my best features, all they'll see is a killer's wife.

The atmosphere on campus is subdued. Walking across the university grounds, I ignore the whispers. The looks. I know what they think. It's all I can do to keep my knees from buckling as I push ahead, finally reaching the door of the building. Taking a steadying breath, I raise my chin and enter the room.

All eyes land on me as I make my way to the conference table. It seems I'm the last to arrive. Something I could've planned a little better. They all know what happened. What Derek is suspected to have done. His popularity among the students has gotten him far, but I don't think it'll prevent what awaits us.

I sense the shift in attitude as I sit down, politely nodding to everyone. "Good morning." They're looking at me as if I'm the guilty one. As if I held Nicole's head under the water until she stopped breathing.

"Good morning." Ainsley Jennings begins the meeting without another word of acknowledgment to me. "As you all know, we have a fundraiser on Saturday. We could use a couple more auction items, so if you guys can reach out to a few more people and see what you can do."

I raise my hand. "I have a friend who's a chef. She's written a new book, and I could get her to sign—"

"That's not really something we'd be interested in, Evelyn," Ainsley cuts in. "Anyone else have something in mind?" Her gaze falls on the others in the room.

I sit in silence while they carry on without my input. Their occasional glances, judging me, reveal their disdain. I'm humiliated and want to fade into the baroque-papered walls. If I could slip away unnoticed, I would. It isn't like they didn't know Derek's history. They knew, too. All of them. Yet they'd wanted to be in his presence. Soak up his charm and wit, wishing they could be him.

"Okay." Ainsley closes her little binder. "If there's nothing else, we can close out this meeting." She smiles, locking eyes with everyone else but me. "Then I'll see you all next week."

They stand and gather their things, each one in a hurry to leave before I have a chance to stop them and plead my case. I have no intention of doing any such thing because they don't matter. The only one who does is the only one left in the room now it's finally cleared. I have to say something to her. "Look, Ainsley, I understand what you must think . . ."

"Evelyn." She walks around the table toward me. "We all appreciate what you've done for the school over the years, but with everything . . . maybe it's best—"

"Yeah," I say, cutting her off, knowing I've lost her. "You're probably right. Once this is over, I'm sure things will get back to normal and we can . . ." I trail off when I see her expression. She has no intention of moving on or moving forward, not with me.

"Take care, Evelyn." Ainsley walks out.

This is it. I see it now. No matter the outcome, they'll think I'm protecting him. They've canceled me right along with him without a shred of proof or the truth of what happened. They'll pretend Derek and Evelyn Moore never existed.

* * *

As we sit down to dinner tonight, Derek's phone rings. I close my eyes in frustration, not only because we've always had a 'no phones at the table' rule, but because I can't take hearing him reiterate his innocence to whoever is on the line this time. The more he insists on it, the less convinced I am. As his wife, I'm supposed to be on his side, and I am. But it's hard to ignore how we got here, and why.

"Derek Moore," he says into the phone.

I smile at Ben, who's busy playing with his food. I pretend I'm not trying to hear what's being said, but I glimpse Derek's expression. Is that relief? A hint of a smile?

"Thank you, Detective. Yes, sir. Very tragic. Good night." He ends the call and sets his gaze on me.

He wears relief, and I anticipate good news. I pray for it. "Well?"

He shrugs, and a tear pools in the corner of his eye. It's the first sign of emotion I've seen in him since this started. "That was Detective Bartz. The coroner pronounced Nicole Peterson's death an accident."

For a moment, I feel like I can breathe again. I glance at Ben, then turn back to Derek, and in a low tone, continue. "What do they think caused the accident?"

Derek seems mindful of Ben's presence and leans over the table. "The autopsy didn't show outward signs of injury, so they think it was something called underwater hypoxic blackout. Guess it happens from holding your breath for too long, and it's not unusual for swimmers who are training." He takes a breath. "It's over, babe. It's over."

So he didn't kill her. I should be relieved. I should be happy I'm not married to a killer, though I couldn't bring myself to believe that in the first place. "This part of it might be over for you, Derek. But this is far from over. The damage is done."

* * *

Any meetings scheduled for this week have already been canceled. They all offered one excuse or another. So-and-so's out sick. Too many conflicts with other meetings. Whatever. I stopped asking.

Derek is at work, and I'm home with Ben after picking him up from preschool. Word travels fast because even the staff at the preschool had heard what happened. I assured them the police had cleared my husband. Nevertheless, they all looked at me like I killed Nicole Peterson myself. This isn't going to go away like Derek thinks it will.

Preparing dinner, I hear his car pull onto the driveway. He's home earlier than usual. When he walks in, his expression is downcast, and bourbon seeps from his pores. I can smell him from here. Never mind that he drove like that. "You're home early. Is everything okay?" It's fair to say that it isn't, and now I'm waiting for the other shoe to drop.

He lowers his laptop bag on the bar stool and walks to the fridge. Popping open a bottle of beer, he takes a long swig.

I step away from the stove, folding my arms because I'm already pissed that he's been drinking and chose to drive home. Now, he's having a beer. "What is it, Derek? What happened?"

He wipes his lips with the back of his hand and sets down the bottle hard on the kitchen counter. "We have to leave."

I spin around, searching for someone else he might be speaking to because I'm certain I didn't hear him right. "What? Now? We have to leave now?"

"No, I mean, we have to leave this place. Leave the school. Our home. They want me gone, Evie. It doesn't matter that the police cleared me. The powers that be know I'm innocent, but they want me gone regardless. They say my behavior has come into question."

My hand covers my mouth, though this comes as no surprise to me. However, I am surprised it didn't happen sooner. "They're firing you? You have tenure. They can't do that, Derek."

"They're offering me early retirement," he says, laughing. "Can you believe that? I'm thirty-six and they're offering me retirement." He uses air quotes to make his point.

"And if you don't leave?" I lay down the wooden spoon I'd been using to stir the saucepan.

"They'll force me out," he replies. "Cut my classes. Remove me as a senior professor. I'll have nothing left to do but sit in my office all day."

I think about how the people around me have acted in a similar manner — practically forcing me out of my various charitable positions. "I understand you're upset, but Derek, after what happened, I'm not surprised. Nicole's family has money. A lot of it."

He has no idea I've looked into this young woman's life. How could I not want to know what made her special enough that Derek would've risked setting fire to his entire life? In the end, I found nothing other than she was loved by a family who would never see her again.

"I doubt they believe their daughter's death was an accident," I continue. "I'm sure threats were issued if the school didn't act in the best interest of its students. I know that's not what you want to hear—"

"Fuck." Derek runs a hand through his thick dark hair. "Where the hell are we going to go?"

For a moment, I want to throw all of it in his face, but I don't. I won't let my anger at his actions cost me my marriage. He's innocent in her death. That's now been proven. Maybe now . . . maybe now he'll see the consequences of his actions, and this will change things for us. For the better. The terrible truth is that a young woman drowned. Yes, Derek had an affair with her, but he didn't kill her. I draw in a deep breath. "We move on. We find another school that will hire you. That's what we do, Derek. It's all we can do."

He walks toward me, gently taking my arms. "Evie, I'm well aware you don't deserve any of this. Let's get the hell out of here, then. They don't want me, well, I don't want them. We'll start over, and I swear I'll be the husband you deserve."

22

CHAPTER 5

Under the fall skies, our new neighborhood appears pictur-
esque as I stand outside our door. Golden-red leaves are still
falling, with most having already drifted into the nearby river.
Chrysanthemums bloom on front porches. A few Halloween
decorations remain, although it was last week. And we still have
half-unpacked boxes scattered throughout our new home.

The so-called early retirement package Derek received
was enough for us to quickly secure this house while we were
still selling our old one — the house where Ben was born. It
was a hard move to make, but we had no choice.

Derek called around, looking for another school that
would hire him. He finally found one after calling in a favor.
I didn't ask who owed him or why.

So, here we are in Beaufort, Connecticut, living in a
home I'm fairly certain we can't afford and pretending as
though nothing has happened. As though a young woman
hasn't died. A young woman he'd slept with.

I only know that now we're anonymous. It's the best part
about this place. No one knows who we are or why we're here.
We have a chance to remake our lives and our marriage. It's
our fresh start, and I intend to take advantage of it.

Derek seems to like his job, though the money and prestige are a far cry from where he left. As I return inside, closing the door to the chilly air, Ben stands before me, ready to start the first day at his new preschool. "Looks like someone's excited to meet his new teacher and make new friends."

He nods and smiles a little, but he's struggling. Just four years old, and he misses his friends and the only home he's ever known. Still, I hope he'll come to love it here. That goes for all of us.

We arrive at school on time, having to drive a mile or so to get here. It might've been a nice walk if it wasn't so cold.

The friendly faces of teachers and staff wait for us at the entrance. Knowing these people have no idea about my life or my marriage brings me relief. I don't have to look at the students who fawned all over Derek. I don't have to hear the whispers of his deceit all around me. I'm starting to feel normal, as though this is how things are supposed to be.

"Good morning, Ben." The woman who runs the preschool leans down to him. "Are you excited for class today?"

He shrugs, tucking himself behind my leg. I regard her with a polite smile. "He's excited, just a little shy."

"Well, how about I walk him to class?" She offers Ben her hand.

I squat to meet him. "Would that be okay? Can Mrs. Babcock walk you to your classroom this morning?"

He nods with reluctance.

I kiss the top of his head. "Have a good day, sweetheart." I glance at Mrs. Babcock. "Thank you."

"Of course." Ben takes her hand, and she ushers him inside.

I can't help but fix my gaze on him as he walks down the hall. I'm a little worried about how he'll get through the day.

"He's adorable."

I turn around at the voice behind me and see a blond woman. Hair down past her shoulders. Slender, but with full hips. Pretty, with kind brown eyes. And she's young

— younger than me, anyway. Around her neck hangs an ID badge attached to a lanyard. But it's flipped over, and I can't see her name. "Sorry?"

"Your son. He's absolutely adorable."

"Thank you. It's his first day. He's nervous," I say before offering my hand. "I'm Evelyn Moore."

"Summer Burton. Nice to meet you. So you're new?" she asks.

"Yes, we are. We moved here a few weeks ago. Took us a while to find the right place for Ben, but I think we've found it," I say, taking in the surroundings.

"I'm sure he'll be happy here," she replies. "I'm new here, too."

"You are? Well, I guess we have something in common, then, Summer." I thumb back to my car. "I should get going, but it was so nice to meet you."

"Of course. It was nice meeting you, too, Evelyn."

I head toward the parking lot and grab the remote to unlock my car. As I stand in front of the driver's door, it slips between my fingers, falling onto the asphalt. "Damn it."

I squat down to pick it up, and when I return upright, I glance at the school's entrance and see the woman who'd just introduced herself to me — Summer Burton. She's standing with another teacher, eyeing me. Wait, is she? I narrow my gaze. Yes, she's whispering to that woman, looking my way as though I'm the subject of their discreet conversation.

We lock eyes for a moment, and then she darts inside, the door closing behind her. "What was that?"

No. No way she knows anything. No one here does. But is that true? Ben's records have been transferred. Is it possible these people know exactly who I am? Who my husband is, and where we came from? Fumbling to unlock my car, I throw myself inside, trying to shake off the anxiety building in my chest.

I press the ignition, reversing out of the spot when someone lays on their horn. Startled, I slam on the brakes and

25

glance into the rearview mirror. "Shit." A car is stopped inches from me. "Sorry." I wave into the mirror, mortified I almost hit this lady on my first day here. I deserve the look she's giving me, and I wave again until she drives on. "Really sorry," I repeat as if she can hear me.

Never mind that now, my thoughts have been taken over by paranoia. The drive home passes by in a blur. I can think of nothing else but the look on Summer Burton's face. Her slight lean toward that other woman, her whispered conversation. Her raised chin as she looked out at me in the parking lot.

The approaching traffic light turns red, pulling me back into the moment, and I press hard on the brake. My tires screech as I come to a stop. "Snap out of it, Evie. For God's sake."

I decide it's best to pay attention for the remainder of the drive home. Turning into our neighborhood, our house is the third from the end. I pull onto the driveway and cut the engine. With my hands still gripping the steering wheel, I slow my breathing to calm my nerves. "It's nothing. Forget it. She doesn't know you. You don't know her."

Having convinced myself, I step out of the car. The sun feels warm on my face, but the wind raises the hair on my neck. The neighborhood is quiet, and I dart my gaze as though I'm a trespasser here. But this is my house. My family.

What had started out good and hopeful has already spiraled into suspicion and fear. Inside, I drop my purse on the foyer table and head into the kitchen for a glass of water. I'm here alone with my thoughts. The dark cloud that is Nicole Peterson's death still hangs over me. I have to get past this.

A knock on the door rattles me out of my stupor. "For God's sake, who is that?" Setting down my glass, I make my way to the door.

Standing on the other side is Josie Brewer, our next-door neighbor. She's older than me, probably in her mid-forties, though I haven't asked. Looking slightly frumpy in her long black cardigan sweater, she thrusts a casserole dish at me.

I take a step back. "Josie, hi. What can I do for you?" The polite thing to do would be to invite her in, but I'm embarrassed because the house is a mess. I don't know Josie and her husband, Stuart, well enough to be okay with that. Not to mention, she strikes me as the nosy type. It's best to keep her at arm's length for the time being.

"I wanted to bring you and your family some dinner. I thought it would give you a break from cooking." She peers around me, her puffy brown eyes scanning over the chaos inside. "Looks like you've still got your hands full with getting settled in."

With some reluctance, I take the casserole dish. "Oh yeah, still lots of boxes to unpack. But this is so very nice of you, Josie, thank you so much. Things have been hectic, as I'm sure you can see. Our preschooler, Ben, started school today as well, so it's been busy for sure."

"I've seen your son out playing. He's just the sweetest. You and your husband — Derek, if I recall?"

"Yes, that's right."

"You and Derek must be so proud. I remember when mine were that young. Of course, they're grown now. Off in college and such."

A forlorn expression masks her face, and now I'm obligated to indulge her. "Well, I suppose that means you did a good job raising them."

She seems to shake out of it, her cheeks plumping above her smile. "You're very kind to say that. Anyway, given the state of everything, I'm glad I brought this over. You be sure and let me know if you need anything else, all right?"

"I will. Thank you again, Josie." I begin to close the door, but she steps forward, stopping it with her hand.

"Oh, one other thing, I noticed last night you had a light on downstairs — I assume it's your husband's office. Forgive me, but our houses are very close, and I could see the light from my side window. It was very late if I recall. I'd gotten up in the night to get a glass of water. Just wanted to make sure you knew it was on. I thought maybe it had been left on all night. Shame to waste electricity."

I want to tell her to mind her own business, but the woman brought dinner, and I need to get in good with the neighbors, so what can I say? "I'll go check on that. I appreciate the heads-up. And I'll bring your dish back tomorrow, washed up and ready to go."

"No rush." She swats her hand. "You take your time. Enjoy the rest of your day, since your boy's off at school for a while. Everyone needs a little me-time now and then, don't they?"

"Absolutely. Take care, Josie." I finally close the door as she turns away. Marching to the living-room window, I pull back the curtains just enough to see her returning to her house. But she stops and glances back. "Shit." I let go of the panel, praying she didn't see me watching her.

After a few moments, I muster the courage to check again. And when I pull back the curtains this time, she's gone. "What the hell business is it of yours if Derek's office light was on? What else can you see in my house?"

I return to the kitchen and put the dish in the fridge, not bothering to inspect the contents under the tinfoil. I've let what happened at the school get to me, that much is clear. As I stand at the kitchen island, I wonder if Derek's light is actually on, so I head toward the back of the house.

He's converted the bedroom at the end of the hall for his office and often grades papers after Ben and I have gone to bed. But working into the night, well, I don't know about that. I don't recall when he came to bed last night. We sleep in the same room now since we don't have a guest room anymore, but I must've been tired. I heard nothing.

When I arrive, all the lights are off, so there's that. Flicking on the switch, I peer inside at the stacks of papers and books littering his desk. My gaze drifts to the bookshelf along the far wall, which overflows with textbooks on English literature. Some of his boxes aren't yet unpacked, though his degrees and accolades are already hanging on the wall.

I move around and take a seat at his desk. From this vantage point, the window on the right wall reveals Josie's house, so I rise again and walk toward it. Twisting open the blinds a little, I see she's right in that her exterior mirrors ours. That's the window she spoke about.

A fleeting figure vanishes from that window as I gaze out. "Well, well. Guess I'm not the only one who's curious, huh, Josie?"

CHAPTER 6

On my way to pick up Ben, I stop by the university to see Derek. I can't decide whether to tell him about Josie's somewhat alarming meddling or to keep it to myself. It's possible I'd imagined a figure in her window. However, that doesn't excuse her familiarity with what's going on in my own house. But this day has given rise to old feelings I thought I'd left behind. What about those whispers from this morning I can't seem to shake — were they about us?

The idea is ridiculous, of course. That woman doesn't know us. She was kind and welcoming, and here I am being petty and paranoid. Yet I know firsthand how quickly rumors spread through small college towns like this, and it's difficult to let down my guard. Derek and I are rebuilding our relationship and can't afford our past to creep into the present.

I've only been on this campus once since arriving in Beaufort. The university is stunning. Smaller than Medford, this school is old, steeped in tradition, and teeming with history. As I walk through the commons, the paved pathways lead to the various brick buildings. Students wander, mostly alone and staring at their phones. Nothing like when I was a student.

Derek and I met at school. He was a grad student. I was in my senior year as an undergrad. He was so different in those days, lacking the self-assurance he has now. Then again, I was different, too, having since lost most of my former confidence. I'd scraped my way through law school, landing a job with a mid-sized firm. I was stronger then, but that strength chipped away over time. I can't even pinpoint exactly how or why it happened, but it did.

As I enter the English Department's building, I search for Derek's office at the far end of the hallway. My sensible flat shoes reverberate lightly on the wood floors as I make my way back. And there it is, but I stop on a dime.

His door is ajar, and leaning against the frame is a striking woman with dark hair flowing over her shoulders. Her cream-colored silk blouse lies perfectly over her form and is tucked neatly into her black suit pants. The black high-heeled pumps add a couple of inches to her height. Her posture is relaxed, her face lit with a smile.

The woman laughs, and the sound floats down the corridor, fading as it reaches me. Derek's familiar voice follows, though I can't make out the words. She tilts her head, her hand brushing against the edge of the doorway seductively.

I step back, pressing myself against the wall just out of sight. My breath hitches, and an irrational need to leave overcomes me. But my feet stay planted, my eyes fixed on the scene before me. Others walk by, seemingly oblivious to me or the world around them.

Who is this woman? A colleague? A student? No, she's too old to be a student. She must work with Derek. He hasn't mentioned anyone this beautiful working with him. Then again, would I have expected him to, given our past? Yet here she is, standing in his doorway as if she belongs there. My stomach cramps as worry takes hold.

The woman flicks her hair, and for a brief moment, I catch a better view of her face. Her features are delicate and soft, with the kind of beauty that requires little effort. She

31

looks at Derek with a familiarity that sends my anxiety even higher.

I've been here before — not this hallway, not this exact situation, but this feeling. That gnawing, insidious voice whispering that I'm not enough. That I never have been. I thought things would be different here.

"This is ridiculous," I mutter. I'm standing here, hiding from my own husband. But the sight of the woman, the intimacy of her posture, the ease of her laughter . . . it all feels like a sharp jab to my ribs like I'm the intruder.

I step out of the shadows, finding the courage to approach Derek's office. As I make my way, her gaze drifts toward me, though I imagine she has no idea who I am.

"See you later," the woman says as she steps out of Derek's doorway.

We meet each other in the hall, and I smile at her. "Good morning."

"Morning."

I keep my head held high and continue past her. I don't dare chance a look back. Instead, I stand in the doorway of Derek's office. "Hi."

He looks up at me with a smile. "Oh, hey, hon, what are you doing here? Everything okay with Ben?"

Do I ask who she was, prompting him that I haven't forgotten his past mistakes? We're supposed to be starting with a clean slate. Whoever that woman is, I'm forced to remind myself she's not important.

"Fine, yeah. I was just on my way to pick him up and thought I'd stop by." I walk inside and take a seat. The smell of old wood and books surrounds me. "Listen, uh, I wanted to get your take on something that happened today."

"Oh yeah? What's that?" he asks, pulling off his glasses and offering me his full attention.

I hesitate, trying to play out how this will go. Will he be dismissive? Tell me I'm worrying over nothing? That's typically how it goes when I bring up my suspicions. He's an

32

experienced gaslighter, so I take another approach, one that doesn't aim a guilty finger at him. "I met someone I think could become a friend, and I'm wondering if it might be weird because she's a younger teacher at Ben's school."

"Why would it be weird? Is she *his* teacher?" he asks.

"No. I don't know why, but . . ." I trail off, doing my best to think on my feet. "Maybe we wouldn't have much in common. Her name is Summer, and she seems nice."

"That's great, hon. I'm happy for you. It'll be fine. Don't worry." He tilts his head. "Is that why you came to see me?"

"Yeah, it's just, well, it was on the way, and I wanted to see how your office was coming along." I glance around, nodding my approval. "It's looking good in here."

"I think so, too. But it's nice you dropped by, and I'm glad you met someone."

I stand up. "Me too. I guess I should go. I'll see you when you get home."

"Okay, babe. See you tonight. Give Ben a kiss for me." He slips on his glasses again and returns to his work.

I head back into the hallway, craning left, then right. No sign of the beautiful brunette. The slippery slope of old patterns tugs at me. I want to search for her, find out who she is, and why she seemed so comfortable around my husband when he's only worked here for a couple of weeks. But to do so would be to admit that I haven't forgiven Derek. That I didn't believe him when he claimed he'd be the husband I deserved.

Rather than compound my own doubts, I head back to my car with mixed emotions. I'm relieved that Derek seemed happy I dropped by, but I'm uneasy I didn't mention Josie or the whispers I'm sure were directed at me. Oh well, neither is important, so I push the seed of doubt from my mind.

It doesn't take long to make it to Ben's school. At the entrance, he stands beside his teacher, and his gaze lands on me. A toothy grin appears on his face before he dashes over.

"Mommy!"

I scoop him up into a big hug, looking into his beautiful, pure brown eyes. "How was school today?"

"Good. We made art with noodles and glue."

"Oh wow! I can't wait to see it." I set him down and take his hand as we turn toward the exit. From the corner of my eye, I glimpse the teacher from this morning standing a few feet away. Summer.

For a moment, I'm not sure what to do. I know what I saw earlier, but the rational part of me realizes it doesn't make sense. The amount of baggage I carry is enough to sink me to the bottom of the ocean. The only way to leave it behind is to let it go. So that's what I'll set out to do.

"Hello. It's Summer, right?" I ask her as we approach.

"That's me. Hi, again." She leans toward my son. "How was your first day, Ben? Do you like it here?"

He nods with enthusiasm.

"Do you want to come back tomorrow?" she adds.

He nods again, squeezing my hand this time.

"That's good to hear because Miss Payton said you were so good in class today. She can't wait to see you again tomorrow."

I look at her, a smile tugging at my lips. "You're good with kids. You must be a mom, too?"

She stands upright again, wearing a solemn expression, and now, guilt overcomes me. I've said too much. Great start, Evie.

"Maybe someday," she replies.

"Mommy?" Ben asks, drawing my attention. "Can I go say goodbye to my friend over there?"

Behind me, a young boy stands with his mother. "Of course, but hurry back. We have to get going soon." He runs off, and I return my attention to Summer. "Listen, this might seem a little forward, I guess, but since we're both new around here, how about we go and grab a coffee or have lunch this weekend? If you have time, of course."

Her smile widens, and her eyes soften. "Oh my gosh, I would love that. It's been hard making friends here, so I — yeah, I think that would be fantastic."

"Great. We'll figure out the details tomorrow." Ben returns, and I rustle his hair. "Let's get you home, kiddo." We walk away, and I'm feeling better now, my anxiety subsiding. Summer's earlier whispers — all but forgotten.

If I focus on the present, the past will soon be forgotten, too. It's a notion I must cling to if I hope to get my life back.

* * *

It's Derek's turn to get our son ready for bed tonight, so I finish cleaning the dinner dishes and then grab a cup of tea to enjoy out on the front porch. Stepping outside, the light breeze raises the hair on my arms. Two wood rockers sway under our front window, and I take a seat on one of them, draping a blanket over my legs.

The mug warms my hands as I raise it to my lips, sipping on the hot tea. Stars shine in the clear night sky, and for a moment, my tension releases. I forget about my worries and troubling thoughts to focus on the good in my life. I'll come to like it here. I just need to give it a chance.

The stillness on our street is soon broken by muffled voices arising from the Brewers' house. It sounds like an argument. I can't help but smile knowing I shouldn't take solace in this but happy we aren't the only ones with marital problems.

Still, I'm curious about them — about everyone in this neighborhood. Who are these people? Besides being rich, I don't know much else about them. They must wonder about us, too. Where we came from. If we have money too. That's an easy one — no, we don't. Not anymore.

The people we bought this house from apparently left in a hurry. Our realtor didn't say much, but now that I've met Josie Brewer, I'm beginning to think they left because of her. We'll have to keep up our guard around them, I suppose. At least until we can form our own opinions.

As I raise the mug to my lips again, a crash sounds from next door. "Oh my God." My cup tumbles to the ground, shattering around me and sending hot tea onto my lap. I look at the Brewers' house. Was that glass breaking? Maybe. Do I check it out? Ask if they're okay?

I stand up, the blanket soaked, my legs stinging. The voices have gone quiet, but the silence around me is broken when my front door opens. Derek appears in the doorway. "Did you hear that?" I ask him.

"Yeah. I'd just come downstairs." He glances next door. "What the hell was that?"

"I think it was the Brewers. I heard them arguing, then the crash."

Derek steps out and joins me on the porch, looking me up and down. "What happened to you?"

"The crash startled me. I dropped my cup." I gesture at my legs. "It's okay, it wasn't that hot."

He gazes at the house next door. "Should I go over there?"

Before I can answer, Josie steps through her front door. "Uh, oh." I turn to Derek, panic masking my face.

He raises his hand. "Relax. We haven't done anything wrong. We're just standing here on our own property."

Josie's stare bores into the back of my head, so I turn around, wearing a smile. She's standing on her top step, out from under the overhang. "Evening, Josie. Is everything okay?" I play dumb, though she must realize we heard everything. "Derek and I were just enjoying a hot drink out here, and we heard a noise."

She eyes me, and even from that distance, seems to notice my stained clothes, yet says nothing. "Fine. Yeah, everything's fine. Stuart dropped a box of our best china. Needless to say, I'm a little ticked off about it."

"Oh my gosh. Yeah, I'm sure. What a shame. Oh, and by the way, that casserole was delicious." That was an awkward sidestep, but I don't want to pry.

Something in her eyes suggests she's more than a little ticked off. We aren't yet well-acquainted, but it's obvious her face is heated. It must've been a fight, but of course, I'm not going to say one damn word about it. Instead, I offer a wave. "Well, good night then."

She waves at us. "Good night. Glad you liked the food. It's the least I could do."

After she returns inside, I look at Derek. "Least she could do? What was all that, anyway?"

He keeps his gaze on their house, hands planted on his hips and chin raised. "Your guess is as good as mine, but I doubt it was over a box of china."

It occurs to me this might be the time to bring up Josie's peculiar interest in what goes on in our house. "I forgot to mention that, earlier, when Josie dropped off the casserole, she said your office light had been left on. She'd gotten out of bed during the night for a glass of water and noticed it."

He raises his brow. "Are you serious? What, was she spying on me?"

I shrug. "Couldn't tell you. And I swear, when I went in there to check if you'd left on any lights, I opened your blinds and saw her standing in her window staring right at me."

"Wow, okay. That's not strange at all." He shakes his head. "You ready to go back inside? You should get changed."

He steps back inside, and after a final glance at the Brewers' home, I follow him. Before he closes the door, he turns to me. "Before . . . whatever that was . . . I was coming out to tell you there's a faculty party on Saturday night. I'd really like for you to come with me."

In recent years, I'd come to despise those events. Derek often turned into someone I didn't recognize. But he insists things will be different now. Do I give him the chance to prove it? What would I be saying about our marriage if I didn't?

And then I remember the woman in his doorway. Maybe I should be there, after all. "Okay, sure. Sounds great. I'll arrange for a sitter."

CHAPTER 7

As a woman in my thirties — a wife, mother, and former lawyer, there is no reason I should be as nervous as I am, walking toward the restaurant where I'm about to have lunch with Summer Burton. Yes, she's a little younger than me. Admittedly, prettier. But I can't allow my insecurities to tear me down. I would tell any woman the same thing, so why can't I convince myself?

She's sitting outside under one of the red umbrellas. It's chilly out, but heat lamps are spaced around the outdoor dining area. The place is busier than I expected, but I admit that this feels nice — being out again. My first lunch with a new friend. As involved as I was in our old community, I'd known everyone there for years. Starting fresh isn't easy for me, but I'm here, and I intend to make the most of it.

"Hi, there." I take a seat across from her. "So nice to see you again, Summer. I'm thrilled you could fit this into your schedule."

She sets down her Kindle and regards me with a smile. "Are you kidding? We're in the same boat, remember? I'm so happy for the invitation. So, how are you? How's Ben doing?"

"Great, yeah. He really enjoyed his first week at school. It was a good decision." The server captures my attention.

"Good afternoon, ma'am. What can I get you to drink?" he asks me.

First of all, I don't like that he called me ma'am. I'm not that old. And I can bet he didn't call Summer 'ma'am.' "How about a cup of coffee to start?"

"Okay." He looks at Summer. "And you, miss?"

Figures.

"Actually, I think I'll have a glass of wine," she says. "How about your house red?"

"Sounds good. I'll be back with your drinks soon and will be happy to take your food order."

Just as he's leaving, I call out. "Make that two, please. I'll have the wine. Scratch the coffee."

"You got it." He winks at me and walks away.

Summer presses her lips into a thin smile. "Good for you. You deserve a glass."

"After this week, yeah, I guess I do." I laugh.

"Oh. Is everything okay? I thought you'd said it was a good week."

I won't bother her with my unsubstantiated fears. Unloading that sort of baggage and blame this soon will guarantee her abrupt departure. "Yes, it was. Still busy getting settled in, is all." I glance at her left hand. Her ring finger is bare. "You're not married?"

"No," she replies, rubbing her finger as though she'd worn a band before. "I'm single. I needed a fresh start after breaking up with a guy a while back."

"Ah, I see. New town. New start. I get it." More than she knows.

The server returns with our drinks and takes our order. When he leaves again, I raise my glass. "Here's to new friendships."

"To new friendships," Summer replies, raising her glass to meet mine. "Cheers, Evelyn."

The food arrives and my glass of wine disappears quickly. "I really like this place. You chose well," I say.

"Thanks. One of the girls at the school mentioned it. I was a little worried about sitting outside, but it's not too cold."

"The heaters help." The conversation flows as we continue getting to know each other. I'm becoming more and more at ease around her.

She places her empty glass of wine on the table. "You didn't mention where you guys moved from."

It's a reasonable question, one I should've prepared for. "Oh, just a small town north of here . . . in New Hampshire." And I've just lied to her. Perfect way to start a friendship.

"Really?" she asks. "Did you come here because of your husband's work?"

"Uh . . ." The question rattles me, and I check the time on my phone. "Oh my gosh. Is it that late already?" Relief sweeps through me because I had almost forgotten about tonight.

"Oh, do you have someplace you need to be?"

"I do, actually." I take out my wallet. "I completely forgot about my husband's staff mixer tonight. It's at the school. He's a professor at the university and I promised I'd go since we're new and everything."

"Oh, yeah, don't worry about it." She swats away my concern. "And I'll pick up the tab. You can get the next one."

Holding my credit card, I narrow my gaze. "Are you sure? I can wait for them to bring the check."

"Please, no. Let me get it. Honestly. You should go. Get ready for your night out." She sets her napkin on the table. "Sounds like it'll be fun."

"Thank you. I'm so glad we did this." I get up and gather my things.

"We'll do it again," she replies. "This is the start of a wonderful friendship, Evelyn."

I smile. "I think so, too, Summer."

* * *

When I enter the house, Derek is in the kitchen, holding his phone and pacing a tight circle. I sense imminent disaster, but over what I have no idea. "What's going on?"

He lays his phone on the counter with a resounding thump. "Our sitter just bailed."

"What? I thought Simone said her daughter was available. I confirmed it myself." Simone's our neighbor on the other side. Her teenage daughter often sits for others in the community, so we thought she was a safe bet.

"She was," he continues, "but apparently, something better came along, and she told her mother she couldn't do it."

My shoulders sink. "Really? Her mom was okay with her backing out of a commitment?"

"I guess so." He shrugs. "Looks like we can't go to the mixer tonight."

Disappointment clings to him like a wet blanket. We both know he shouldn't miss this, but that means he'll go alone. "I'll stay here. You go. It's your work. Your people. Being the new guy, you can't miss this." The doorbell rings and I glance into the foyer. "Are you expecting someone?"

With a drawn brow, he peers around. "No."

I head toward the door and open it. "Josie, hey. What can I do for you?" There's an awkwardness lingering between us after the events the other night. Her gaze is downcast as though she's embarrassed. I almost regret opening the door at all.

She raises her sights and returns a small grin. "I was wondering if I could get that casserole dish back from you."

"Sure, of course. Come in. Right through here." I lead the way to the kitchen and lock eyes with Derek. "Josie's looking for her dish. I think I might have put it in the cabinet by mistake."

"How are you, Josie?" he asks, rubbing his forehead.

"I'm doing all right. And you?" She tilts her head. "You seem . . . irritated. Did I come at a bad time?"

I swear her eyes just glinted at the idea she had done exactly that.

"Oh, no, not at all. Sorry." He swats away her concern. "It's nothing. Well, not nothing. Evelyn and I had plans for

41

this evening, and Simone's daughter was set to babysit Ben for us. Unfortunately, she just backed out."

Josie clutches the small gold pendant around her neck as though this is the worst news she's heard today. "That's awful. I'm so sorry. How disappointing."

"These things happen." I walk toward the lower cabinet and retrieve the dish. And on my way to hand it over, I can almost see the wheels of her mind turning.

"You know." She aims her index finger at me. "I don't have any plans this evening. I could look after Ben if you'd like."

I shoot a glance at Derek and see a glimmer of hope in his eyes. *No. No. No.* I have no idea who this woman is, and she's already left a bad taste in my mouth. Something about her raises the hair on the back of my neck. If given the chance, she'd sure as hell go through our things while we were out. Maybe worse.

"That would be amazing," Derek says with a sigh of relief. "Thank you so much for the offer." He turns back to me wearing a strange smile I don't recognize. "Isn't that great, hon?"

"Yeah, yeah, that's great. You're an absolute lifesaver, Josie. Thank you." Now I get it. He wants me to go along with this. To keep my mouth shut about any concerns over this woman who I've already caught watching us. Then again, I was watching her, too, so who's the guilty one?

"Okay, great." Josie takes the dish from me. "What time?"

Derek glances at his phone. "An hour?"

"Perfect. I'll see you both in an hour."

I show her to the door. "Thanks again, Josie. See you soon." Closing it, I march back into the kitchen. "Really?"

Derek turns up his palms. "What? She's harmless. Nosy, but harmless."

"You're only saying that because you're desperate." I glance out the window as though I might see Josie, face plastered against it, peering at us. "There's something about her, Derek. I don't know if I want her around Ben. She's . . . she'll go looking through our stuff. I'm sure of it."

"And what is she going to find, huh?" he asks. "Nothing. Nothing of interest to her, okay?" He walks toward me. "Please, Evie. I want you with me tonight. I need you." He takes my hands.

Looking into his eyes, I see his sincerity is real. Now I feel like the bad guy. I have no real evidence to prove Josie's out to get us. Just more paranoia. "Fine. Yeah, maybe you're right."

Derek kisses my cheek. "Great. Now, hurry and get changed. The clock's ticking."

"All right." I walk upstairs to our bedroom. Despite my suspicions, I want to have a good time tonight. This is our chance to meet new people and make some friends in our new town.

I don't want to admit that it's also an opportunity for me to size up my competition, certain the gorgeous brunette will be there. As much as I want to believe Derek when he says he'll be the husband I need, my former life has been obliterated, and I won't let that happen again.

Rifling through my closet, I search for something nice to wear and settle on casual dress pants paired with a light sweater and scarf. As I'm touching up my makeup in the bathroom, Derek knocks on the door.

"Come in," I call out.

He enters, wearing black dress pants and a gray button-down shirt. "You look nice."

I meet his reflection in the mirror. "Thanks, so do you."

"Oh, I meant to ask, how was your lunch with — Summer, was it?" Derek asks.

"Yep. It was nice." I put in my earrings. "She's very sweet, and we got along really well. I think we'll end up being good friends."

"I'm happy to hear that." He checks the time on his phone. "We should get going soon. Don't want to be late. Oh, and Josie's here. Boy, we got lucky with that, huh?"

"Yeah, we sure did." I'm certain my expression is betraying me, but I follow him downstairs where Josie is sitting on the couch next to Ben. I stop Derek a moment before we reach the bottom. "Are we sure about this?"

"It'll be fine, hon. Don't worry. We'll only be gone a couple of hours. You know how these things go."

"Sure. Okay." We continue down the steps, and I plaster a smile on my face. "Hi, Josie, thanks again for offering to watch Ben tonight."

"Of course. I'm more than happy to help out," she replies. "Ben and I have a fun evening planned." She looks at him. "Don't we, Ben?"

He shrugs.

"All right then." Derek pulls on his sports coat. "We'll see you soon, kiddo."

"Bye, baby." I kiss Ben on the cheek. "Be good for Mrs. Brewer."

We walk outside, and Derek opens the passenger door of the Mercedes for me. "Thank you." I slip onto the seat, my thoughts consumed with the prospect that tonight isn't going to go as I hope. I don't tell Derek this, of course, but I don't know anyone in his department, and somehow, I always feel inferior to them — the academics. Obviously, I shouldn't. I'm a lawyer, after all, but I do.

He slides behind the wheel of our luxurious car, which we could afford before he was forced out of his job at Medford. And then I remember Nicole, and now my thoughts spiral before the night has even started.

"You okay, babe?" Derek presses the ignition. "Don't worry about Ben. Come on . . . I wouldn't leave him with just anyone. He'll be fine. You have to trust people sometimes."

For a split second, I want to reply with something cruel, but I don't. I keep it in, as always. Instead, I glance up at our living-room window to see Ben peering out. He's waving and smiling. I'm not sure what Josie's angle is or whether she's looking to stir up trouble for me and my family, but that won't happen. This is our second chance. I won't let anyone take it from me.

44

Arriving at the university, Derek and I step out into the chilly evening air. The earthy scent around me makes me wonder if rain is imminent. I didn't bring a coat.

"You ready to go in?" he asks, wrapping an arm around me.

"Sure am. Let's go." I don a smile and push the negative thoughts from my head. It's easy for me to fall down that rabbit hole. Instead, I try to remember that I'm here to show my support for Derek and maybe make a friend or two. Screw the competition.

Chatter fills the room as we enter. The faculty lounge is far nicer than I imagined. Dark wood tones. Beams across the ceiling. Elegant light fixtures shower us with radiance. While the mood is casual, an air of sophistication predominates. Just beyond the lounge is an adjacent dining hall, where several people are mingling.

Derek hooks his arm around mine as we continue inside. Golden-red flames crackle in a stone fireplace along the back wall. High-top tables draped in white linen dot the room. When Derek entered the world of academia, I was swept away by the romance of it all. Lost in the brilliance of their ideas, their words. Meanwhile, I swam in a sea of arrogant, flashy lawyers whose level of sophistication was outpaced by grade schoolers. Something changed along the way.

We make our way into the dining hall, where Derek introduces me to a few of his colleagues. They seem friendly enough. Their wives eye me curiously. Do they know what happened and that we're here because Derek had no place else to go? Regardless of his innocence, not a single school wanted to get within a hundred feet of him. He pulled strings, that much I know. What I don't know is the cost of those strings.

Ahead of us is a circle of people who all seem acquainted with Derek.

He gestures toward me. "Everyone, I'd like you to meet my wife, Evelyn."

I smile and shake hands, immediately forgetting names as they come at me in a flurry.

However, one woman stands out from the rest, with long, chestnut hair that tumbles over her shoulders in loose waves. It's her — the one who was standing at Derek's office door when I came to see him, though I'm not sure she recognizes me. Do I look so different with hair and makeup?

Her emerald cocktail dress accentuates a petite frame and brings out the green in her hazel eyes. She wears a pleasant smile, but I sense something beneath it. Maybe she does recognize me after all. Now, my instincts kick in.

"Evelyn, this is Shana Foster. She started teaching English 101 here last year," Derek explains.

Shana gives me a little wave, her bracelets jingling. "Nice to finally meet you, Evelyn. Derek's told us a lot about you, and I feel like I know you already."

Funny because he's never said a damn thing about you. "Oh, well, thank you. It's so nice to meet all of you. Derek has told me wonderful things about his co-workers." I smile at her, trying to ignore the uneasiness in my gut. Something about the way she's standing so close to Derek bothers me. I think back to her standing in his doorway, sharing laughter and free-flowing conversation with my husband. "How are you enjoying teaching here so far?"

"Oh, I just love it," Shana gushes, lightly touching Derek's arm. "The students are so bright and engaged. It makes my job easy."

"Wonderful." I clench my jaw, feeling the icy grip of suspicion around my throat, threatening to pull me under. At that moment, a lifeline arrives. A waiter walks by with a tray of wine. I snatch two glasses, handing one to Derek.

"Cheers," I say, clinking my glass against his. "To new beginnings."

Derek offers a reassuring smile, seeming to sense my discomfort. He seeks forgiveness, and I do my best to grant it. "Should we get a bite to eat, Evie? The crab cakes look delicious."

"That sounds perfect," I reply, eager to pull him away from Shana. "It was a pleasure meeting you all."

46

As we walk to the hors d'oeuvres table, Derek puts his arm around me. "Don't worry about her," he whispers. "I'm not that man anymore, Evie. I need you to believe me."

I want to believe him, more than ever. And I want to enjoy the night. Looking out, the room hums with chatter and the clinking of glassware.

With food on our plates, Derek leads me to a small corner by the bar. He's almost finished with his wine, while I cradle my half-full glass.

"Have I told you how amazing you look tonight?" he asks.

I know what he's doing, and I appreciate the gesture. Maybe we aren't a lost cause, and it isn't too late for us to fix things. "You have, but I don't mind hearing it again," I reply.

He leans closer, and I inhale the scent of his cologne, woodsy with a hint of warm black honey. "You're the most stunning woman here, Evie. And I'm including that guy's trophy wife over by the canapé table."

I laugh, soft and genuine, forgetting all about Shana Foster. "Well, you're not looking too bad yourself." I flick an imaginary speck from his lapel. The knot in my chest finally loosens.

Derek reaches out, brushing a stray hair from my face. "We're going to be all right, Evie. Just give it time, that's all I ask."

"I know, and I will." My gaze drifts beyond him to a blond figure who emerges from around the corner. "Is that?"

"Sorry?" Derek peers over his shoulder. "What are you looking at, hon?"

I return my attention to him. "Oh, uh, nothing. I'm just going to run to the restroom. It's down there, right?" I gesture toward the hallway.

"Down the hall and the third door on the right is the ladies' room. Do you want me to get you another drink or more food?"

"No. I'll do it when I get back. I won't be long."

He smiles. "Okay. I'll be here waiting."

I head toward the hallway, navigating the dining hall and the people inside it. When I reach the wide corridor,

47

branching out in several directions, I glance left, then right, but I'm alone in the vast space.

"Third door on the right," I say to myself as though I might get lost otherwise. Arriving at the ladies' room, I open the door. "Summer? Are you in here?" That blond hair, even though I'd only caught a fleeting glance, I'm sure it belonged to her. But why would she be here? Is she a guest? When I get no reply, I take a step back but catch sight of a woman emerging from one of the stalls. "Shana, hi." Now I'm embarrassed.

"Hi." She walks to the sink. "It's Evelyn, right?"

"Yes." I stand there a moment, having no idea what to say to her. I came in here because I was certain I'd seen Summer, as odd as that would be. "Sorry, I was just looking for a friend . . ."

"Summer?"

I tilt my head. "Yes. Do you know her?"

She turns off the faucet and reaches for a paper towel. A small chuckle escapes her. "No, I just heard you call out the name."

"Oh . . . well, sorry to bother you. I should be getting back." I open the door.

"Derek's a great guy," she says.

With my back to her, I close my eyes, trying to settle the annoyance growing in my gut. "His son and I think so, too." I walk back into the empty hallway, that same old feeling creeping in once again.

48

CHAPTER 8

While I don't believe I made any new friends last night, things had gone better than expected at the staff mixer. After a while. I'd quickly forgotten about seeing Summer, realizing I'd only done so because of Shana Foster. It wasn't her fault, but mine. Everything she'd done made me suspicious, and I'd quickly spiraled after that.

Derek had spent the evening doing his best to douse my concerns over Shana, and I tried hard not to let the past color the present.

When we returned home to find Ben fast asleep and Josie reading a book on the sofa, I realized I'd been worried over nothing, just as Derek said I would be.

Now, on this crisp Sunday morning, Ben and I are out shopping. He's outgrown last year's winter clothes, and with harsher weather coming, I don't want to be caught off guard.

As he and I browse the racks of coats, my thoughts drift back to last night. Not to Derek or his valiant attempt at making me feel like the woman of the hour, but to Summer. I feel foolish for believing she'd been there when it was just a random blond woman I'd seen. Turned out, as I made my way back toward the dining hall, the blond woman re-emerged. I followed, and she caught up with a man who seemed to be her husband. That's all it was.

My thoughts are interrupted by Ben's gleeful shout as he grabs a puffy blue coat off the rack. "Mommy, look!" he says, excitement on his face. "It's just like the one from my favorite show."

"Is that so? Well, we should see if it fits." I help him try it on. It's a little large, but he'll grow into it. As I'm zipping the coat, shadows cross on the floor in front of me, capturing my attention. There, only feet away, is Summer. Looking pleasantly surprised, she heads toward us. I call out to her. "Well, hello there."

She offers a subtle wave, her eyes flicking between Ben and me. "Evelyn, hi. Fancy running into you here." She reaches out for me, her fingers brushing my forearm. "Oh my gosh, how did last night go? The mixer?"

And there it is. As usual, I let my imagination run away with me. If any doubt remained that I'd seen Summer at the mixer, it's now been laid to rest. "It went well. Better than I thought."

"That's great. Oh, I'm so glad to hear it. You seemed a little anxious about it yesterday." She looks over at my son. "Hi, Ben. Are you getting a new winter coat?"

"Uh-huh. Mommy says my other one is too small cause I keep growing." He flexes his biceps.

I let out a chuckle, patting him on his back. "Yes, it's time to get him some new clothes." I return my attention to her. "What are you doing here?" That came off more accusatory than I meant it to.

"Oh, I — uh — just ran out of laundry detergent. But of course, I can never buy just one thing when I come here."

"Me either." I study her and see nothing but kindness and sincerity. My wariness gets in the way of new friendships, and I'm doing my best to put Medford in the rearview. Maybe that starts with introducing Summer to Derek. Maybe that's how I prove I can trust her, though I try not to think too hard about what that says about me. "Hey, if you don't have any plans for next weekend, why don't you come to the house for dinner? You can meet Derek. He can invite someone from work."

Summer reveals a cunning smile. "Evelyn, are you trying to set me up?"

I shrug with a sheepish grin. "Maybe. If nothing else, it gives you a chance to get to know Derek. I can't guarantee he'll bring anyone, but it might be nice if he did."

A slight tilt of her head, a raised chin. She's considering my offer. "You know what? Yes. I'd love to come for dinner. I need to get out there, just like you have, and get to know more people around here. And I would love to get to know your family, Evelyn. It would mean a lot to me."

"Then it's settled," I reply. "I'll text you the details once I get them ironed out. This is great. It'll be fun."

"Mommy?"

Ben tugs on my shirt, and I gaze down at him. "What is it, honey?"

"Can we go now? I'm bored."

"I guess so." I regard Summer once more. "Better get going. See you soon."

After we finish the shopping and check out at the register, Ben and I head outside and walk to the car. As I help get him buckled into his car seat, I catch a glimpse of something on the windshield. Looking back at him, I double-check the straps. "Okay. Let's head home."

Walking around to the driver's side, there it is — a slip of paper wedged between the wiper blade and the windshield. I look at the other cars parked next to mine, wondering if this is just a random flyer, but none of the others have one.

I snatch the paper from under the blade and unfold it. Scribbled in almost illegible print, it reads:

You can't hide. I know what your husband did.

I lose my breath, like the wind has just been knocked out of me. My head grows light as I spin on my heel, scanning

51

the rows of cars. Nothing but people loading bags, pushing carts, and walking into the store. No one looks my way. No one notices me at all. "What the hell?"

I climb behind the wheel and peer at Ben in the rearview mirror, doing my best to control the panic that surges in my chest. "All good?"

"Yep."

"Let's go home, then." I press the ignition and back out, carefully, this time. As I drive between the rows of cars, I stop on a dime.

"Mommy, what's wrong?" Ben asks, jolting forward.

Crossing in front of me, I see her — Josie — walking toward the store. She sees me and smiles, rushing to my door. I roll down the window.

"Well, hello there, neighbor," she says, peering into the back seat. "Hi, Ben."

"Hi." His voice is small and shy.

"Looks like we just missed each other," I say as light-heartedly as I can. "We're heading home."

"Well, I got a list a mile long, so I'll be here a while. Take care, Evelyn. You too, Ben."

She continues into the store and a horn beeps behind me. I start on again, keeping an eye on the store's entrance. "Were you following me?" I whisper, glancing at the note that lies unfolded in my center console. "Did you leave this?"

"What did you say, Mommy?" Ben asks.

"Oh, nothing, honey." I take a breath to calm myself, not wanting to let Ben sense my unease. Driving home, my eyes dart from side to side, checking the mirrors. The streets feel frightening now, as if someone could be lurking around every corner, watching our every move.

Tears prick my eyes as the tenuous grasp of my emotions begins to slip. Someone left this note. Someone knows about us. "Stop."

"Are you okay, Mommy?" Ben asks.

I clear my throat. "Yes, sweetie, everything's fine." Still, my mind races. Summer showing up, Josie arriving just as we were leaving, and, wait . . . Shana. The way she clung to Derek's side last night. Does she know who we are and why we're here? Did she follow me? Is this how she hopes to take my husband from me — with threats of spreading her lies? I grip the steering wheel tighter, feeling like I'm drowning in a sea of mistrust.

Arriving home, I realize there's no way I can keep this from Derek. Has he experienced similar instances? Are we being threatened in our new home? I get Ben inside and wait for him to go upstairs to his bedroom.

Derek is in the living room, and he sees the fear that must be written on my face. Yet, he says nothing until Ben is out of ear-shot. "Are you okay?" He stands from the sofa and approaches. "What happened?"

It's all I can do not to break down in tears. My hands tremble as they reach into my purse. "When we were leaving the store, I found this on the windshield."

Derek's forehead creases as he takes hold of it, unfolding the paper. His eyes widen as he reads the single line — the ominous message that thrust me into a panic. "What the hell? Who wrote this?"

"I don't know, Derek, but I saw Josie there — at the store. As we were leaving, she was going in. That can't be a coincidence." She's the most logical person. She knows my car, and she probably watched me leave home for the store. That has to be it. "It's her. I told you there was something off about her."

Derek's jaw tightens, his eyes flashing with anger. "No. There's not a chance in hell she knows anything. No one does."

"Clearly someone does." I step back. "Someone knows who we are and what happened. They know what you did."

"What I did?" Appearing indignant, he presses his fingers against his chest. "I had nothing to do with it, and you know it. The cops know it too."

"Josie was in our house. Is there anything here, in your office, or someplace else, that she might've come across?"

Derek spins around, raising his eyes to the ceiling. "Jesus Christ, Evie, you think our neighbor scoured through our things when she was babysitting and figured out I worked at Medford U? Even if she did, there's nothing about Nicole Peterson around here."

But he's wrong. We were given copies of the police statements we'd made. I'd filed them away, just in case. In case of what, who knows? Proof, I guess. Proof Derek didn't do anything wrong. I look up, Ben catching my attention at the top of the stairs. "Honey." I let out a sigh. "Do you need something?"

"I'm hungry." He stands on the landing, looking afraid to come downstairs. He overheard us arguing.

"Okay, sweetie. Come on down, and I'll get you some lunch."

I usher him into the kitchen and make him a sandwich. Derek and I say nothing more for the time being. Josie did this, I'm convinced of it. Arriving at the store moments before I leave. The way she seems to turn up, bringing us food, offering to babysit. The crash I'd heard at her house. And I saw her in the window that day. But why would she care? What does she want from us?

* * *

I can't sleep. Derek snores next to me, seemingly unbothered by what's happened. I'm sure that's not true, but he doesn't see what this could do to us. Maybe that's because it's happening to me. Why leave the note on my car? I had no part in what happened in Medford.

I turn onto my side and see a sliver of moonlight cutting through the gap in our curtains. My alarm clock displays the time. Dear God, it's only one a.m. It seems much later.

I might as well get up because I won't sleep until I see for myself. Quietly slipping out of bed, my feet turning cold on the wooden floor, I tiptoe out of our bedroom and into the hall. Ben's door is partially open, and I peek in on him because I worry. He's buried under his covers, just his little head poking out.

I walk downstairs and into the hallway toward Derek's office. What I'm about to do isn't new to me. Nevertheless, I thought that part of my life was over — checking up on him. I guess I was wrong.

As much as I don't want to find out, I have to check whether he has emails or text messages from someone in his office — Shana, for instance. He said I didn't need to worry about him because that's not who he is anymore. But do I have to worry about her?

Might he have said something to her? Grown closer and confessed his sins, arming her with information that would ruin this family? I can't put it past him. He's always been eager to show his emotional side to a woman with a poor-me sob story. If it isn't Josie, then it must be her.

Walking inside, I reach his desk. Guilt grips me. I don't want to do this, but what choice do I have?

I turn on his laptop and enter his password. He hasn't changed it, so that's a good sign. He'd agreed, after Nicole, to allow me access to everything. Phone, computer. It was his way of asking for forgiveness.

His emails populate the screen, and I lower myself onto the chair, already studying them. My lips quiver as I see — nothing. Nothing that suggests he and Shana Foster are flirting or setting up covert meetings. No hint of anything unprofessional at all. I've allowed myself, once again, to be sucked into this vortex of suspicion.

Ashamed, I close the lid and get up from the chair. How is this happening again? We've done nothing wrong. Derek has done nothing wrong.

In the darkness, I return to the hall, stopping at the staircase. Before going up, I glance into the kitchen, thinking how I could use a drink of water. Amid the shadows, I navigate toward the cabinets and retrieve a glass. As I prepare to fill it with water, something in the breakfast nook window captures my attention.

"What is that?" I set down the glass and move toward the nook. The curtains that cover the window are mainly for show and don't block out much. The outline of my front yard, the bare tree in the center of it, all fairly visible. And then . . .

I lean forward, pressing my eye to the opening of the curtain. "Josie?" She's walking away from my house, toward hers. Why on God's earth is she out at this time of night? Why was she over here?

I take a step back and firm my stance. "What are you doing?" I weigh my options. I can either march to her house and ask her why she was here or go back to bed and ignore it.

Too late. I'm already at my front door, heading outside in my pajamas. The bitter air clings to my skin, and my bare feet burn on top of the icy concrete. My breath floats into the sky as I stand like an idiot in the freezing cold. Looking over at her house, I see she's gone. Already inside. Do I go over and knock? Do I set off a firestorm that may have been her intention all along?

"No. Screw this." I make a beeline toward the Brewers' front porch. Something's going on because no one walks around their neighborhood at one in the morning. Then again, that's exactly what I'm doing.

Just as I'm about to knock, a light upstairs illuminates through the window. It's her. She's warning me. She sees me right now. "Goddam it."

Losing my nerve, I turn around, cutting through our side yard, and head back to my house. Inside, I stand in the foyer, cold and out of breath. "Jesus. What the hell is going on? What am I doing?"

CHAPTER 9

The earthy richness of freshly brewed coffee hovers in the kitchen. Its comforting aroma helps to settle my anxiety while last night's events still spin in my head. I spent the last few hours of the night attempting to make sense of them. Wondering what I'd done to bring back our troubled history.

Ben waits patiently at the breakfast counter while I pour milk into his bowl of cereal and spread jam on a slice of toast. "Here you go, sweetheart."

Derek appears from around the corner, dressed and ready to leave for work. His curt smile and slight nod convey what I'd done. He must've opened his laptop to see that I'd already read all the new emails showing up in his inbox. I've seen that look before — disappointment mixed with guilt. "Morning, kiddo." He kisses Ben on the head and walks toward the coffee maker.

"Busy day?" I ask him, hoping to gloss over my actions that have once again widened the chasm between us.

"Nothing out of the ordinary," he replies, pouring himself a cup of coffee. "You?"

"No. I'll probably just finish unpacking those last few boxes we have lying around." I want to talk about what happened.

The note, checking his emails, Josie skulking around in the night. But Ben is here, and we can't get into it. And something tells me we won't.

"Good." He takes a sip from his mug. "Well, I better head out. Don't want to hit traffic." He kisses my cheek in a perfunctory manner before turning to Ben. "Have a good day at school, kiddo. See you tonight."

"Bye, Daddy."

* * *

I walk Ben to the school's entrance where Summer is talking to another parent. She smiles at us and meanders over. "Hey, there," she says. "Hi, Ben. Are you excited to be back?"

He smiles and nods.

His teacher stands just inside the corridor, and I lean down to kiss his cheek. "Go on over to Miss Payton, okay? You see her?" I aim my finger ahead.

"Uh-huh. Bye, Mommy." He skips off.

"Bye, sweetheart." I wait for him to be ushered inside before turning back to Summer. "So, are we still on for this weekend? Dinner at my place?"

She folds her arms and tilts her head. "Is your husband bringing someone?"

After what happened yesterday and last night, I haven't mentioned to Derek about hosting dinner at all. "I'm not sure, but I'll find out. Either way, I'd love to have you there."

"Of course. I wouldn't miss it." The bell rings. "I should head back inside. Catch up with you later?"

"Yeah, sure."

She turns to leave, but stops and looks back at me, eyes furrowed. "Are you doing okay?"

"Yeah, of course." I smile. "Just a busy day ahead. So, hey, I'll keep you posted about Saturday. See you later."

Returning to my car, my smile fades. While Josie is my main concern, I won't dismiss the notion that I need to put

Summer to the test — to confirm that she's an ally, especially if Josie turns out to know things she shouldn't.

Today is a good day for that — finding out more about Josie Brewer. I won't be threatened. Not by her, or anyone. People can say what they want about how I've handled my husband's behavior, but they don't know what I'm capable of when it comes to my family. There's no mistaking . . . that note on my windshield? It was a threat.

So, my first task is to figure out how Josie could've acquired information about Derek. Is she connected to the university in some way? Does she know someone who works there? That doesn't seem likely, but I can't afford to overlook anything.

When I get home, the first person who comes to mind is Chuck Ryland. He's an old friend I knew from my days at the law firm. I pour another cup of coffee and take a seat in the kitchen nook.

Grabbing my phone, I make the call. "Hey, Chuck, it's Evelyn. Evelyn Moore. How are you?"

"Evelyn? Well, I'll be damned. It's been a while. I'm doing great. How are you? What's it been? Four, five years?"

"Something like that." I chuckle. "Listen, I'm sorry I haven't kept in touch, but I was wondering if I could ask you for a favor. Assuming you're still a PI." One of the benefits of being a lawyer is knowing people who know how to get information.

"What the hell else would I be doing?" he asks. "Shoot. What do you need?"

"I have the name of someone I'm looking for a little bit of background on. Previous employment, former addresses. Can you get me that?" He goes silent for a moment, and I wonder if I've overplayed my hand. It's a big ask when I'm not a practicing lawyer anymore.

"What firm you with now?" he asks.

I close my eyes, lowering my head. "I-uh-I'm not currently practicing."

"Mind if I ask why you're looking into a private citizen, being an unaffiliated private citizen yourself?"

I have to give him something. He's a licensed private investigator who stands to lose said license if he colors outside the lines. "There's a chance someone's looking to dredge up a past no one wants exposed, least of all, me. And if it comes out, well, it'll do a lot of harm to my family. Our reputation and livelihoods."

All I hear is breathing on the other end of the line. He's thinking about it, but what's he going to do? If I come out and point fingers at Josie, she'll lie to protect herself. This has to be done without her realizing I'm the one doing it.

"Send me the name," he finally says. "I'll get you something as soon as I can."

CHAPTER 10

It's been a couple of days. Nothing else has happened. No new notes. No unusual midnight sightings of my neighbor. In fact, I've hardly seen her at all. Derek and I seem to have successfully buried the entire situation, just as expected. Still, this isn't over.

As I prepare to host dinner tonight, something Derek reluctantly agreed to, I hear my phone buzz on the kitchen counter. Wiping my hands on the dish towel, I pick it up and swipe open my emails. There it is. Chuck came through in the nick of time.

> Here you go, Evie. Not sure it's gonna do anything for you, but I got what I could. Keep in touch, kid — Chuck.

Most people from the old days call me Evie, including Derek. I was a different person then. I miss her.

I open his report.

> Josie Brewer, formerly Haas. Born March 22, 1980, in Madison, Wisconsin.

Skipping down to get to the meat of the report, I can't find anything regarding any criminal record. I suppose that's good. Josie attended the University of Wisconsin. Great, but I don't really care about all that. Nevertheless, leave it to Chuck to be thorough. I can't fault him for that.

I finally reach the employment section. Scanning through it, I shake my head. There's nothing here. Nothing at all that ties her to Medford or Medford University. I lower my phone. "Okay. Now what?"

Nicole's death was in the local news and probably posted to online news sites. Anyone could've heard about it, but Derek was never publicly named as a suspect. "So how the hell does anyone here know he was even involved?"

Derek walks into the kitchen. "Man, something smells great in here, babe."

"Oh, thanks." I've lost track of time, almost forgetting our guests are set to arrive soon. "It's just chicken. Everyone likes chicken, right? Throw in some wild rice and vegetables, and you got yourself a halfway decent meal."

He walks toward me and kisses my cheek. "Better than halfway decent. I'm glad we're doing this. We need it. And Alex is excited."

"I'm glad he agreed to join us. He seemed nice at the faculty mixer. Did you tell him I was bringing a friend?"

"I sure did." Derek plucks a piece of chicken from the pan. "I told him there's no pressure, that this is more of a making-new-friends kind of thing."

"Exactly." I thumb over to the wine fridge. "You mind grabbing a couple of bottles? We should let the red breathe a little."

"You got it. Everything okay?" He retrieves a bottle of red wine from our under-counter fridge. I'm a stickler for keeping our reds at 55 degrees.

"Yeah, fine." He has no idea that I'm looking into one of our neighbors, of course. He's perfectly content to forget all about that note. His ability to block out the past amazes me.

"Oh, you want to know something about Alex?" Derek asks. "I found out he was up for a promotion in my department but was ultimately passed over. They brought in Shana instead."

"Wow. That couldn't have gone over well. Are the two of them friends?"

"He might have a thing for her, I'm not sure yet." Derek opens the wine to let it breathe. "Always a lot of palace intrigue with these private universities. I do hope he and Summer hit it off, though. Could be good for him."

"Yeah, I hope so, too. She's great. I think you'll like her."

Derek glances at the pots on the stove. "Do you need me to take over while you get changed?"

"Yes, please. If you could keep an eye on things, I only need a few minutes."

"Go." He smiles. "Get changed. Everything's under control here."

"Thank you, hon." I head out of the kitchen.

"Oh, and Josie will be here soon to take Ben to her house for the evening," he calls out.

I stop cold, turning back to him. "What? I thought you were taking him to his friend's house — the one from school. I talked to his mother just today to confirm."

"I ran into Josie, funnily enough, at the university today. When I ran back to pick up those papers I'd forgotten? She was there for some sort of fundraising event with one of the clubs. Not sure, but anyway, she asked what we were up to tonight. I mentioned our dinner and she offered to keep Ben at her house for a few hours."

I walk toward him again, hands on my hips. "Why would you agree to that when I'd already set something else up?"

"I thought this would be easier. Neither of us would have to drive anywhere. We could both enjoy a couple of drinks. What's the problem? Can't you just call the kid's mom and cancel?"

If I tell him my concerns, he'll say I'm overreacting. He'll say there's no chance Josie Brewer left that note. Nothing else has happened. And she's already looked after Ben, and what's the big deal?

I play out the conversation in my head. Am I worried about his safety? No. She's been nothing but kind to Ben. And to us. This is me. It's in my head. I've convinced myself she's the problem, but maybe I am. "Yeah. Okay, fine. I'll call and cancel with the other mom."

Upstairs, I make the call to the mom, apologizing profusely. Maybe I'm wrong about Josie. Maybe it was a coincidence she was in the parking lot of the store moments after I found the note. Maybe she wasn't walking around outside my house at one in the morning.

Irritated, I snatch a mid-calf wraparound dress from the hanger in my closet. Black, because it's slimming. I slip on my black pumps and run a brush through my hair before returning downstairs to see Derek talking to Josie.

She catches sight of me. "Well, don't you look gorgeous?"

"Thank you." Mild guilt weighs on me, but something about her still niggles at my brain. "Ben? You ready to go, sweetheart?" He runs out of the living room carrying his small backpack.

"I'm bringing my coloring books."

"Great. And this is only for a few hours," I reply, to reassure myself as much as Ben.

"Hey, Ben," Josie says. "How about pizza tonight, huh? Do you like pizza?"

"Yeah, it's my favorite."

"Perfect." She ushers him to the door.

"Have fun tonight, buddy," Derek says, waving his hand. He closes the door and turns back to me. "Wow. Just. Wow. You do look gorgeous."

I've never been good at taking compliments at face value, especially from my husband. "Thank you. I should get back to the kitchen and get things ready. They'll be here soon."

He turns on the music and it fills the house with a soft melody. I can't remember the last time we hosted dinner. It's nice. Normal.

I've just put the finishing touches on the charcuterie board and set out the wine glasses when the doorbell rings. I don't hear Derek, so I call out, "Hon, are you gonna answer that?" When I hear the water running upstairs in the bathroom, I roll my eyes. "Okay then. I guess I'll get it." I wipe my hands on the dish towel and walk into the foyer.

"I'm coming. I'm coming," Derek says, jogging down the steps.

He meets me at the door, and I open it to see Summer on the other side. "Hey, Summer. Thanks so much for coming." I gesture to Derek. "This is my husband, who I've talked so much about. Derek, this is Summer Burton. Come on in. It's cold out there."

She steps inside, wrapped in a long coat, her eyes downcast. "Let me take that for you." I help her remove her coat and hang it on the nearby hook. And when I look back, I see Derek's face.

At that moment, I get the strangest feeling as I shift my gaze between them. Blinking hard, I finally get the courage to ask the question that burns my tongue. "I'm sorry, do you two know each other?"

CHAPTER 11

Time seems to have stopped. My gaze shifts between Summer and Derek, neither one offering an answer. The soft music in the background is the only sound in the house, giving the aura of a soap opera scene, and the camera has cut to commercial.

How could they possibly know each other? Unless what I'm seeing is a bolt of electricity, an immediate attraction between the two. Neither situation fills me with joy at this moment. *The whispering?* I recall Summer whispering to another teacher on the first day we'd met and looking right at me. Could this have been why? Did she see Derek and me when we'd first come to tour Ben's school? Were there sparks then that I missed?

"Derek?" I ask him again, firm and unwavering.

"No, honey, of course not. How could we?" He offers a handshake. "Summer, it's nice to meet you."

"You too, Derek. Evelyn's told me a lot about you," she replies.

What the fuck? They're just going to stand here and pretend this is their first meeting? Still, I can't see how they would know each other. But I've run out of time to contemplate it because Alex, Derek's colleague, is walking toward the door right now.

"Alex. Hey, man. Thanks for coming." Derek squeezes between Summer and me and greets Alex with a hearty handshake.

"Hey, I'm all up for a free home-cooked meal," he replies.

"Well, come on in." He ushers Alex inside. "This is Summer . . . I'm sorry, what was your last name again?"

"Burton," she replies.

"Ah, right." Derek snaps his finger. "Summer Burton, this is Alex Murphey. He works with me in the English Department at the university. And Alex, you remember my wife, Evelyn."

I shake out of my stupor when I hear my name. "Alex, hi. It's nice to see you again. Thank you for joining us."

He removes his coat. "It smells delicious in here." Alex is young and handsome with a long face and sharp cheekbones. His big brown eyes crinkle a little as he smiles. He would be perfect for Summer, except I can't shake the idea Summer wants my husband instead.

"Let me take that for you," Derek says.

I watch all of this unfold and sense I'm being gaslighted again. What I saw just now? The look was unmistakable. But I have to get through this dinner.

"We should go sit down. I've put out some small bites, but dinner's just about ready." I head toward the kitchen, my back turned to them. I close my eyes, feeling the color drain from my face. *It's just me. It's my insecurities. That's all it is. Derek's been better since we left Medford. He's trying. He is.*

Standing in the dining room, I gesture to a chair. "Alex, why don't you take a seat over there? Summer, if you want to pull up a chair next to him."

"Let me get that for you." Alex hurries and pulls out her chair for her.

"Thank you." Summer takes a seat while Alex joins her.

"Derek, you mind helping me bring in everything?" I ask.

"Not at all."

As we enter the kitchen, I say nothing more. Now isn't the time, and I need to think this through.

We return to the dining room with the food, and I take a seat next to Derek.

He raises his glass. "Here's to my beautiful wife, Evie, for putting together a wonderful meal to be shared with new friends. Cheers."

"Cheers." The rest of us reply in unison.

Pressing on with dinner, I look at Alex, desperate to fill the silence that has settled around us. "So, Alex, how long have you been with the university?"

"Three years now," he says, taking a bite of his roasted chicken. "I work long hours, but I enjoy it." He turns to Summer. "I understand you're new in town, too, like these guys?"

Summer washes down her food with a sip of wine. "I am. I've been here a few months, actually, after moving from New Jersey. Looking for a quieter life."

"A quieter life?" He snorts. "You're what . . . twenty-five, twenty-six years old?"

"Twenty-six," she replies.

"That's the prime of your life. Seems like you'd want to be out there partying all night."

Glancing away, a small smile appears on her face. "That's never been my thing. And luckily, I met Evelyn." She looks at me. "I'm so happy to have met her — and now Derek."

I don't believe her. She's lying, but why? "I'm so happy to have met you too, Summer. It's been a long time since I've connected with someone in this way, so thank you." I raise my glass to her, my mind churning. I glance between Derek and Summer, trying to read their expressions. Derek looks relaxed, chatting casually with Alex. But there's a stiffness to Summer, a wariness in her eyes when she looks at me.

I take a long sip of wine, letting the alcohol warm me. "So, Summer," I begin, "tell us more about yourself. What made you decide to move here?" If I put her on the spot, maybe she'll let something slip. I have to try to get to the truth because, right now, I'm crawling in my skin, with the notion that, at any moment, I'll lash out at both of them. All that will accomplish is destroying what I'm desperate to protect — and it'll be my own fault.

She smooths her napkin in her lap. "I needed a change of scenery. I'm from a tiny town in New Jersey and I thought it would be nice to try somewhere new."

A tiny town in New Jersey? That's awfully vague. She'd mentioned to me before that it was a move she'd decided on after a breakup. Now, it's a tiny town, wanting to try someplace new? Come on. I glance at Derek and find him eyeing me, as if he senses I'm about to reach my boiling point.

"Well, we're happy to have you here," Derek adds. "Right, hon?"

"Of course." I force a smile and refill my wine glass, trying to push down the concern knotting my gut. There must be a reasonable explanation. I need to keep the conversation flowing and see how the night unfolds. I turn to Alex. "How about you? Where did you teach before this?"

Alex dabs his mouth with his napkin. "This is my first teaching gig. I finished my post-graduate work here, then secured a position."

I nod along, only half-listening. My gaze drifts back to Derek and Summer. Her fingers are caressing the indent in her neck as she looks at him, practically begging Derek to take her right here and now. *No. Stop.* I'm reading too much into this, that's all it is. "That was lucky, then." I clear my throat, trying to focus on my conversation with Alex. "Derek, honey, would you mind helping me grab the dessert from the kitchen?"

He blinks as if coming out of a daze. "Oh, sure thing."

As we enter the kitchen, I head straight for the fridge to get the chocolate mousse. Derek's stare is like a laser in the back of my head.

"Everything okay, hon? You seem — annoyed."

"Oh, I'm fine." I place the bowl on the counter and begin scooping the mousse into the dessert dishes. "Just focused on being a good hostess." My hands tremble, and I feel the sting of tears in my eyes. *Don't do this. Not now.*

Derek comes up behind me, his hands sliding around my waist. "Hey," he whispers. "Don't stress yourself out. It's just dinner."

But it's more than that. His patronizing tone makes it seem like I'm the one with the problem, like I'm being paranoid.

"Evelyn, look at me."

With reluctance, I turn. His brown eyes search mine; his expression appears earnest.

"I don't want to do anything to jeopardize what we're building here," he says. "You know that, right?"

I want to melt into his arms, to believe him completely. After all, I still love him. And I know he loves me. "It's just . . ." I falter. "You and Summer seem . . ."

He returns a puzzled frown. "We only just met tonight. Whatever you think you're seeing between us, I promise, it's not there."

Despite his sincerity, my instincts prickle with doubt. "Okay," I whisper. "We should get back to our guests."

As the evening winds down and the conversation fades, I'm desperate to put an end to this torturous evening. I throw back the last sip of wine, setting down the glass a little too hard. "Well, tonight has been a lot of fun. I hope you both had a good time."

"Best evening I've had in a long while, Evelyn, thank you." Alex sips on his drink before placing his napkin on the table. "I should get going." He rises. "Summer, can I walk you out?"

"Yes, please." Summer stands. "Thank you, Evelyn and Derek, for a wonderful dinner. It was such a pleasure getting to know you both better. And Derek, I hope you don't mind, but I think your wife is an incredible woman."

"I couldn't agree more," he replies, taking my hand.

We follow our guests into the foyer. Alex helps Summer with her coat. Regret weighs on me now as they're about to leave. Maybe it's the wine that's calmed my nerves, or maybe I've just given up. If I continue down this road, I risk cutting whatever threads of new friendship I've weaved with Summer.

Whatever wounds have been stitched between Derek and me, tearing apart. I can't think about it anymore tonight.

"Good night, Summer. I'll see you on Monday?" I ask.

"I'll be there. Enjoy the rest of your weekend." She glances at Alex and Derek, who are exchanging goodbyes. Placing her hand on my shoulder, she leans in to whisper. "I see what you mean about him, but I want you to know that I'd never hurt you, Evelyn. I'm not that kind of woman if you understand my meaning."

I pull back. My lips part, ready to ask what the hell that was supposed to mean. Instead, I nod and smile, swallowing my anger. "Good night, Summer."

We watch them drive away. The cold air bites my skin as we stand in the open doorway. I walk to the coat rack, snatching my coat from the hook. "I'll go get Ben."

"You sure?" Derek asks. "I don't mind doing it. It's pretty cold out here."

I close my eyes a moment, steadying myself. "I got it. How about you start the dishes?"

"Yeah, okay."

I walk outside and head down the path to the Brewers' home. My head spins around Summer's parting words. In the short time I've known her, I've been careful not to let her in. Not to tell her about the troubles in my marriage. Yet she knew. Could she sense it? The tension between Derek and me? Had he flirted with her when I wasn't looking? Christ, I'm going crazy trying to figure it out.

When I arrive, I knock on the door and wait only a moment.

Josie opens it, wearing a smile. "Hello, there. I suppose you'd like your son back."

"I would," I reply, keeping my tone light. "Thank you so much for looking after him. You didn't have to do that."

"Don't think twice about it. He's been a pleasure to have around." She turns back. "Ben, your mommy's here. Grab your backpack, it's time to go home." She regards me again. "How was the dinner?"

71

"Very nice, thank you. You and Stuart should join us for dinner soon." Why the hell did I just say that?

"We would be thrilled to join you two. You name the date, and we'll be there."

Ben rushes out to me, a wide grin on his face. I smile in return. "Hey, buddy. You ready to go home?"

"Yep." He's already out the door.

"Say thank you to Mrs. Brewer, please," I tell him.

He glances over his shoulder. "Thank you, Mrs. Brewer."

I look at Josie and shrug. "Sorry about that. See you later." Josie nods as I turn around to catch up to Ben. I hear their door close. "So, how'd it go tonight? Did you have fun?"

"It was fine. We watched cartoons. I had lots of pizza and some cookies. But Mommy, she talks a lot."

"She does?"

"Yeah. Always asking questions. Our old house, where I went to school before." He grunts, shaking his head.

"Is that so?" I ask, my smile fading. "Well, maybe she shouldn't talk so much, huh?"

CHAPTER 12

I wait until he's asleep.

His breathing deepens, each lungful marking time with a familiar rhythm. How I wish, more than ever, I still had a guest room where I could escape him. To be back in this state of anxiety and doubt sends my skin crawling, and I can't bear lying next to him.

I peel back the covers and slide out of bed. He won't notice my movements. He's out cold — too much wine at dinner tonight.

On the bench at the end of the bed lies my robe. I snatch it, slip into the hallway, and walk down the stairs. Heading into the kitchen, I secure the robe around my waist.

The tree in our front yard stands silhouetted in the window. I see it now. Its branches, stretching outward, like the cracks in our marriage. Soon, those cracks will splinter, spreading longer and wider, sending our marriage onto the verge of collapse. After tonight, I can no longer bury these feelings.

Dealing with Josie Brewer is one thing. I still can't prove she was the one who left the note, but Summer? My new friend, Summer Burton? There's more to her, despite what Derek says. So, what do I do to get to the truth? And am I sure

I want to? I've gone this long pretending, ignoring, looking the other way. What's one more time?

No, the real threat here is the possibility that one of these people is out to destroy my family. And that's where I draw the line.

Regardless of my attire, I walk to the foyer and grab my car keys. Unlocking the front door, I step outside, marching straight to my car. I have no idea of the time, so I check my phone. Two a.m.

Derek's Mercedes is parked next to me, and as I press the remote to unlock my car, ready to drive as far away from here as possible, I see it. "No," I whisper, my breath visible in the cold night air. "No, not again." I quietly close my car door, extinguishing the interior light.

Stepping toward the Mercedes, I scan our street. A heavy mist covers the yards and houses. The light from a lamppost cuts through the haze, casting a cone-shaped amber glow onto the pavement. I shoot a look at Josie's house, just to be sure, but I see no lights on inside. No one outside. In fact, there isn't a soul around.

"For God's sake." Tucked between the black rubber seal and the window glass of the passenger door is another slip of paper.

I yank it out. The paper is damp and cold from the outside air like it's been here for a while. Do I have it in me to read what's inside? I'm teetering on the edge, and this could be enough to send me over. If that happens, I might never return. "They're doing this on purpose. To scare you. To rattle you," I tell myself. "They want you to break. To give up. To leave him." But I won't. I won't do that, so I unfold the paper.

Written on it, the words are succinct. The meaning — undeniable.

Are you going to tell her, or am I?

CHAPTER 13

My eyes are heavy as I try to jolt myself awake with a cup of coffee. I've been sitting in our breakfast nook since two in the morning. No sleep came amid the onslaught of 'what ifs' that dominated my thoughts.

The sun is only just rising. The house is quiet. After finding that note last night, I have no choice but to confront Derek. I need the truth. No more notes. No more games.

Whoever sent these messages is trying to tear us apart. Trying to make me question my husband's innocence. But he didn't murder Nicole. The police ruled it an accident.

The steps creak from heavy footfalls. Derek is awake, and he's heading downstairs. Peering through our breakfast room window, I must say something. I will say something.

"Good morning," he says, heading toward the coffee maker. "You're up early."

"Couldn't sleep," I reply, keeping my gaze fixed on the front yard. "Probably drank a little too much last night." I still don't look at him, but his footfalls approach and his hand rests on my shoulder.

He kisses the top of my head. "I suppose I had a little too much as well. But it was a fun night." He sits in the chair next to me, noticing that I'm dodging his gaze. "Are you okay?"

I turn to him and toss the note onto his lap. "I found this last night. It was wedged in the seal of your passenger window."

"You found this on my car? Last night?" He wears confusion in his gaze as though I've somehow betrayed our trust. "When?"

"When I couldn't sleep." I don't mention I intended to leave, though I'd had no destination in mind. And as I glance toward the stairs, I know I would've come back for Ben anyway.

He takes the note, observing it, and now I have his full attention. "This was on my car?"

"Yes." I take another sip of coffee, returning my gaze to the large oak tree in our front yard, bereft of leaves. "Someone left it last night. Couldn't tell you who."

"Probably the same person who left the other note. Someone who knows where we live." He unfolds it, his eyes scanning the words. "What the hell does this mean?"

My shoulders drop. "Jesus, Derek, don't you see what's happening? This is about Nicole. Her name isn't mentioned, but that's who they're talking about. They know exactly who we are and why we left Medford." I study him for a moment, waiting for him to come clean, but he remains silent. "Whoever it is wants you to tell me something. Tell me what, Derek?"

"I have no idea. I swear it. Look, Evie, I have no idea what the hell is happening here, but I've done nothing wrong." He stops as if catching himself. "I mean, of course I did something wrong, but to Nicole? No. Never. And the police—"

"I know what the police said about it, Derek," I cut in. "The only thing that makes sense is that someone found out about Medford. It's either our nosy neighbor, though I have no idea why it would matter to her, or someone you work with. But what concerns me is that this person thinks they know something I don't." I hesitate a moment. "So what do they know?"

Derek shakes his head and creases his brow but can't seem to find the words.

"Alex," I say. "He was here last night. Summer. She was here too." I see his eyes flicker at the mention of her name.

"You were convinced it was Josie, too." Derek grips the arms of the chair. He looks ready to say more but holds his tongue.

I stand up, looming over him. "What are you keeping from me?"

He rubs his temples as though exhausted by the topic. "Nothing, I swear it. I don't know who left this note. Maybe it was Alex."

"And Summer?" I ask, wondering why he hasn't mentioned her yet. "She was here too. You say you don't know her . . ."

Derek's face hardens. "For God's sake, do you hear yourself? Going back and forth . . . You sound . . ."

"What? I sound what? Crazy? Confused? Angry? How about all three?" I take a breath, emotion lodged in my throat. "Please, just tell me the truth. I can't keep doing this. I am losing my mind, Derek. If there was ever a time for you to be honest with me . . . that time is now."

He bolts up from the chair. "I'm done with this conversation. Look, I know I haven't given you many reasons to trust me, but if you can't trust me on this, then I don't know what we're even doing together."

He storms away, leaving me shaken. I sink into the chair, holding back tears of anger and frustration. I want to think this is about Alex or Josie because it makes sense to me and because I don't want to believe my friend has any part in this. But I can't shake the notion there's a connection between Summer and Derek . . . Jesus, I don't know. I press my fingers against my temples. Derek's right. I do sound crazy. "Maybe that's the whole point."

* * *

Derek and I went off to our separate tasks this morning, having no resolution to a problem that threatens to ruin us. He's come to expect me to bury my head in the sand, as I've done so many times before. But things are different now. I'm pushed to my limit, and I will get answers.

Ben and I arrive at his school. Summer is standing just inside the entrance, and I call out to her while Ben darts inside. On my approach, I carry a pleasant smile, hiding the unrest that courses through me. "Hey, Summer. Did you enjoy the rest of your weekend?" My tone comes off casual, surprising me.

"I did, thanks for asking. Lazed around most of the time. It was nice. You?"

"Still working on getting us settled in, so I did a few things around the house." I look into the hall to be sure Ben is with his teacher. "Listen, I was wondering if you could do me a favor, and I hate to even ask . . ."

"Of course. Anything. What do you need?"

I regard her for a moment. The sincerity in her gaze. The friendliness of her smile. Is it just a mask displaying what she wants me to see? "Do you think you could watch Ben for a few hours tomorrow after school? Derek usually runs a little late on Tuesdays, and I need to take care of a few things. It won't be long. A couple of hours, at best. I'd be back before dinner."

She places her hand on my arm. "Of course I can. I'd love to hang out with Ben, are you kidding me? He's a great kid."

"Oh, I appreciate it so much. Thank you." I check the time, pretending I'm rushed, yet having no place else to be. "So, tomorrow afternoon. I'll pick up Ben and bring him home. You can follow me since I've got the booster seat. I'll get you settled in and then head out. And if, for some reason, I'm not back by dinner, Derek will probably be home by that time anyway." I gauge her expression when I mention Derek, but she gives nothing away.

"No problem at all. I look forward to it," she replies.

"Great. Thanks again. I owe you."

"Happy to do it. See you tomorrow."

Returning to my car, I feel somehow vindicated. Derek has no staff meetings tomorrow. He'll be home at his usual time, so I don't worry about her being alone with Ben. Though, in my desperation for answers, I push away the possibility she might want to harm my son.

The idea is to leave them alone together — Derek and Summer. It's the spark that will ignite the flame. Derek will do everything to keep his secret if there is one to be kept.

I consider for a moment what I'm trying to prove with this little scheme. That Summer's attracted to Derek? That they've met before? Or is it that she was the one who wrote the notes? What do I hope to gain from this exercise?

I slip behind the steering wheel, gripping it tightly. "The truth."

CHAPTER 14

The day has arrived, and the stage is set. Now, I have to let the scene play out. Have I just destroyed a budding friendship, or am I finally getting to the truth of who is out to ruin my family? What do they think they know, and what can they hold over Derek's head?

I unlock the front door, Ben next to me, and I step inside. Summer follows us. "Thanks again for doing this. Like I said, I don't expect to be gone too long."

"Take your time, Evelyn. I don't mind at all." She rests her hand on Ben's shoulder. "We'll have fun, won't we, Ben?"

"Yeah."

The urge to swipe her hand from his shoulder overwhelms me. My motherly instincts kick in, but I remind myself that he'll be fine. He's safe. Derek will be here within the hour. "Okay. Great. I'll see you soon." I kiss Ben. "Be good, buddy. Love you."

Walking out to my car, I clench my jaw, wondering what's happening to me. What I'm becoming. But it doesn't stop me, and that's the frightening part. "After this, it'll be over. You'll have your answer."

* * *

A coffee shop in the center of town is where I've chosen to wait out this plan to see if it bears fruit. My foot taps against the leg of the chair. I've been here for thirty minutes, sipping on a coffee that's now gone cold. The place is busy enough that no one notices me, but I can't shake the feeling that they see straight through my little plan. They see what a terrible mother I must be to use my son as some sort of pawn.

The idea sends my emotions to the surface, and I struggle to contain them. My God, am I any better than Derek at this point? *Stop. Just wait it out.*

The wheels are in motion.

It's what happens when I return that will tell me whether I'm right or wrong. Will he say something to her about the note on his car, wondering if she left it? What about the other note? Summer was there at the store that day, a notion I'd previously pushed aside, refusing to believe it. *Of course she was there, but so was Josie.*

If my husband knows Summer from somewhere in the past, will they confront one another about it? All the possibilities race through my mind, and I feel like I'm the wicked one.

The smell of freshly baked goods and strong coffee soothes me as I waver on the edge of sanity. I know how crazy this seems. And I wonder if I've made a terrible mistake, deceiving my husband and friend like this. Maybe nothing will come of it at all, and this game will be over. But the gnawing doubts persist — too many troubling, pointed occurrences; too many unanswered questions. I have to work harder than ever to keep my family together. Is it worth the cost?

I leave a ten on the table and head outside. The brisk air calms my nerves, and I take a short walk to clear my head before going home. I need to kill more time.

As I stroll past rows of elegant boutiques, I think back on how Derek and I met. How we laughed over coffee, took long walks holding hands. How did we end up here with so much mistrust?

But if he has betrayed that trust yet again, I deserve to know. I owe it to myself and to Ben to find the truth, no matter how painful. Steeling myself, I head back to my car and drive home. It's time to face whatever awaits there.

Pulling onto the driveway, I see Summer's car alongside the curb. She's still here. Derek's car is ahead of me. The plan is in motion, and I have no idea what's happening inside. At least I know Ben is safe with his father. I won't easily overcome my decision to dangle Ben in front of Summer like a carrot on a stick. But I swear it won't happen again.

Entering my home, I hear cartoon voices on the television but nothing else. I continue inside, closing the door behind me, and I walk into the living room.

Summer sits on the sofa. She looks up and smiles. Ben is on the floor playing with his Lego.

"Oh good. You're back. I wasn't sure if I should leave," she begins. "Derek got home a little while ago. I guess he was earlier than you thought he'd be."

I look around feeling almost relieved not to have found her and my husband in some tawdry embrace. "Where is he?"

"In his office, I think." Summer rises. "Did you get done what you needed to?"

"Uh, yeah, I did. Thank you so much, but you didn't have to stay once Derek got home." My attention is drawn to the hall as I see him approach.

"You're back. Great." He shoves his hands in his pockets. "Well, Summer, I suppose you don't need to stick around anymore."

Something in his tone sounds off. He's curt with an edge of underlying anger. Am I reading into this? Am I looking for reasons to prove I was right? I pick up on no such tone from Summer.

"Okay great," she says, walking toward the foyer and slipping on her coat.

"Thank you so much. I really appreciate it," I say. "If I'd known Derek was coming home so soon . . ."

"Don't worry about it. It's fine. I'm glad I could help." Summer opens the door. "See you both later. Bye, Ben."

"Bye," he calls out from the living room.

"Talk to you later, Summer. Thanks again." I close the door as she leaves, relief washing over me. This was all in my head. Now, I can focus on the real threat — whoever left the notes. I turn back to Derek. "I should probably get dinner started. Are you hungry?"

As I walk toward the kitchen, Derek clutches my arm and spins me around. Not hard, but not soft, either. "What's wrong?" I ask.

His nostrils flare and his eyes narrow. "I don't want that woman around Ben anymore, you understand? And I don't want you to be friends with her."

"What? Why?" My heart drops into my stomach, wondering if she hurt Ben in some way.

He peers through the living-room window, watching Summer drive off. "Something about her, Evie. I don't like it." He turns back to me. "Stay away from her. And keep her away from my son."

I don't understand what's happened. Summer seemed fine, but Derek . . . He doesn't rise to anger easily, yet I see it blazing in his eyes. "What happened? Derek, did you two argue or something? Did she hurt Ben?"

He pulls me aside, back into the foyer, and away from our son. "No, he's fine. But damn it, Evie, I think she's the one doing all this to us. Threatening us. The notes. All this started when you two became friends. I don't know why I didn't pick up on it at dinner the other night."

I know why. I recognize the look in his eyes, having seen it many times before when he's felt threatened. He shifts the blame away from himself because he's not the problem. He's never the problem.

"Look, I don't know what happened," I say, my voice rising. "But clearly, something did. So, you'd better tell me right now. Do you know her, Derek? Did she follow us here?"

Ben's looking at us, concern on his face. "Why are you yelling?"

I close my eyes and take a breath. "I'm sorry, sweetheart. We're not yelling."

"Yes, you are. Did I do something?"

"No, honey. You haven't done anything wrong." I walk toward him. "Listen, I have to ask you, did Summer do or say anything to you today after I left?"

"No." He shakes his head. "She gave me a juice box and let me watch TV."

I smile and smooth back his too-long hair, which matches my color. "Okay, baby. You go back to your cartoons. Daddy and I aren't fighting or yelling. I'll go and start dinner now."

I walk into the kitchen, justified in the knowledge I was right. How Summer was able to hide the truth, I can't say, but Derek is doing a piss poor job of it. He storms off to his office, putting a fine point at the end of the conversation. That's what he thinks, but this is far from over.

Fuming, I snatch the meat from the freezer and throw it into the microwave. Why I'm angrier at Derek than I am at Summer, I have no idea. Maybe it's because he's lied to me once again. Summer and I aren't well-enough acquainted, but it's clear our friendship is over — I still have to live with Derek.

I stand at the stove, cooking the thawed meat, my mind racing. As I slide the garlic bread into the oven, I think back over the past weeks. The unnerving sense of being watched while alone in the house, the cryptic notes. When did it all start? And what about Josie? I still have no answers, but I'm positive, somehow, this involves Summer Burton.

Derek walks into the kitchen, and I brace myself for Round Two. Instead, he simply sits at the table, rubbing his temples, appearing exhausted and deflated.

"Look, she came on to me today, okay?" he says. "That's why I got upset. That's why I don't want her around our family." He sets his gaze on me. "We're doing our best here, right? Trying to fix our marriage and move on? I don't know what that woman thinks she'll accomplish, but you need to know the truth. It's best you cut ties with her altogether."

CHAPTER 15

Derek

We didn't even say goodbye to each other this morning. Instead, Evelyn walked upstairs to get Ben out of bed as I walked down, the silence between us thick and impenetrable.

When I make the turn onto the university grounds, a crowd of students hovers near my building. The first thing that comes to mind is that they're probably protesting something or other. Nothing unusual there.

But as I drive toward the staff parking lot, my mouth drops, and I catch my breath. At the back of the English building, flashing red and blue lights swirl on multiple police cars. All of them parked askew at the curb. "What the hell's going on?" My foot slips off the gas and I slow down.

Behind me, sirens blare as an ambulance races up. I spin around, peering through my back window. "Jesus." It whips by me, screaming, heading straight toward the building. "Oh my God. Oh my God." Adrenaline spikes through me as I cut the engine and jump out. Leaving behind my laptop bag, I run toward the entrance. Several feet away, my colleagues huddle, and I rush toward them. "What happened? Is there a shooter? Are we on lockdown?"

Alex's face is blotchy and red, tears staining his cheeks. He says nothing. I turn to James. As the head of the English Department, he must know something. But he too remains silent. "For God's sake, will someone tell me what's going on? Why are you all crying?" I look at the double doors, wide open, police officers coming and going.

I don't wait for their answer; instead, I march toward the entrance when I hear someone call out to me.

"Hey, you can't go in there."

I stop cold and turn around. A police officer with a stern expression walks toward me. "I work here. My office is through these doors."

"What's your name, sir?"

I don't like his tone; it sounds more like an accusation. "Professor Derek Moore . . . sir." That came off sarcastically, and I shouldn't be combative, but the way he's looking at me—"

"Professor Moore, do you know Professor Shana Foster?"

His words land like a right hook, making my head spin. My heart drops into my stomach as I glance at my colleagues again. They already know the answer to the question I'm about to ask. "Yes, I work with her. Why?"

Raised voices sound behind me. I spin around to see two paramedics pushing a gurney through the doors. Someone's going to be wheeled out on it.

"Ms. Foster was murdered, Mr. Moore," the officer says.

I whip back around to him, my face screwed up tight. "What? What did you just say?"

"She's dead, sir. Ms. Foster is dead," he repeats. "Someone murdered her, right here in this building."

His words swirl around me until they find my throat, coiling, choking off my voice.

The officer is studying me, gauging my reaction. "I'm going to need you to stick around, all right? The detective is going to want to ask you some questions."

"Did you talk to everyone?" I return a sideways glance at the other professors. They're looking at me like I've done something wrong. "Why am I being singled out?" I ask, fearing his answer.

"Because she was found in your office, Professor."

* * *

They've said nothing to me — my co-workers — people I thought were my friends. I've been waiting for the detective for over an hour. I haven't called Evie, not yet. I wouldn't know what to tell her. And after what happened yesterday — maybe I've lost her too.

"Professor Moore?"

I turn around to see a balding man, slim but tall, dressed in a suit and walking toward me. A familiar hollowness grips my chest as my mind flashes back to Nicole. Why has this nightmare returned, and how do I wake up from it? "Yes, that's me."

"I'm Detective Langston. Beaufort PD." He peers over his shoulder at my colleagues. "They don't seem to want to be anywhere near you, Professor. Why do you think that is?"

I lower my gaze. "I don't know, sir, but I could venture a guess."

"Yeah, me too." He breathes deeply, exhaling through his bulbous nose. "Follow me."

The detective leads me inside. I'm numb to the moment, but my thoughts drift to Evie and Ben. What am I going to tell my wife this time? Whatever happens here, I have no place left to go.

Langston stops at the door to my office and turns back to me. "This your office, Professor?"

I glance at my name etched on the glass, figuring it'd be best if I didn't state the obvious. "Yes, sir, it is."

He nods, his frown deepening. "I can't let you go inside, but I'd like you to take a look."

Why in God's name would I want to look? What's this guy trying to prove? That I did it? He thinks I'll see her body and suddenly confess to the crime? Jesus. My stomach churns at the thought. "You say you found her in there, but what does that mean, exactly?"

Langston hooks his thumbs in his belt loops, a practiced gesture that seems to confirm his resolve. "I was hoping you might tell me, Professor. How well did you know Professor Foster?"

"Not well at all," I reply, my voice tinged with grief. "I've only been at this school for about six or eight weeks. Came in shortly after the start of the fall semester."

He nods again, opening the door to my office. The smell hits me first. Rancid, stomach-turning. Blood spatters mar my bookshelves and dot the awards that hang on the walls. My desk is covered in trash like the can had been dumped on it. My things — pictures of my family — overturned. And on the wooden floor lies Shana. Face down. Blood pooled around her body. Her hair, wet and matted. Her clothes . . . My gag reflex kicks in. I turn away, puking all over the hallway floor.

I look up to see the detective holding out a handkerchief. "Here. Take this."

I wipe my mouth, desperate to stem the flow of tears that threaten to spill. As I return upright, I look at him. "My God. What happened to her?"

"She was stabbed multiple times." His voice is low and carries the weight of too many similar conversations. "Look, I'm going to need you to stick around a while, okay? Can you do that, Professor?"

It takes me a minute to shift my eyes away from the gruesome scene and back to the detective. A sense of peculiarity clings to everything around me. "Yes, sir. Of course."

He leads me outside again and I see my colleagues, each one with targeted death stares. They think I did this.

I steady my nerves as the detective disappears inside again, and I walk toward them. "Which one of you found her? I can't imagine what it must've been like. You guys okay?" I do my best to make them see I'm one of them. That I didn't do this. I could never do this.

"We didn't," Alex says. "One of the cleaners found her. I was here and he came to tell me. I called the police. I'd just spoken to her yesterday as we were leaving. I can't believe she's dead. Especially like this . . ." His voice trails off, and tears well in his eyes.

I feel like I know Alex better now . . . now that he's been to my house. Shared a meal with my wife and me. *The note Evie found. Was it you who left it?* "You saw her yesterday? Was that after hours?"

He knits his brow. "Yeah, it was. We were both here late." He steps toward me. "You trying to say something, Derek?"

I glance at the double doors again, officers coming and going. A team of what looks like crime scene investigators head inside. My face heats with anger at the idea someone killed Shana, leaving her in my office. For what purpose? Who would do such a thing? "No, of course not, Alex. Unless you were the one who left the threatening note on my car after dinner at my house Saturday night."

He plants his hands on his hips. "Excuse me?"

I move in closer to him, and we're standing only inches apart. "All I know is that someone killed Shana in my office. I was at home last night. Where the fuck were you?"

89

CHAPTER 16

Evelyn

How do I tell someone I thought was a friend that I think she's a liar? Maybe the better question is, how do I continue to trust my husband who has lied to me before? Because I love him, and I've accepted his flaws. But that doesn't mean I want anyone else to uncover his lies.

The nightmare that has been this past year refuses to relent. I'm left to ponder whether I'm able to be the kind of mother I need to be for my son.

"Mommy, we're going to be late for school."

I blink, the kitchen faucet still running, water overflowing my cup. Turning it off, I peer over my shoulder at Ben. "Okay, baby. Why don't you get your backpack? Give me a minute."

He darts out of view.

The timer on my oven beeps. I grab the potholders and open the door, heat blasting in my face. Taking out the casserole dish, I set it on the stovetop. I've made three casseroles. Two last night, and the third this morning. Derek thought I was prepping meals for the week. But these aren't for my family, these are for Summer.

I put them in an insulated bag and grab my things. "All right, Ben. Let's go." Getting into the car, I place the bag in the rear compartment and help Ben into his booster seat. "You ready, kiddo?"

He nods. "Yep."

We drive to school, and as we arrive, we walk hand in hand to the entrance. "Go on and see Miss Payton. Have a good day, baby." Ben disappears inside.

Summer is standing in her usual spot.

"Hey, there," I call out to her, forcing a smile.

She makes her way toward me. "Morning. Where's Ben?"

"Already inside. I wanted to talk to you for a minute."

Summer glances around and I see a hint of hesitation on her face. "Of course. Is everything okay?"

"Oh, yeah. Sure." I dismiss her concern with a wave. "I wanted to thank you for yesterday — babysitting for me and everything."

"No need to thank me. It was nothing, really. I enjoy spending time with Ben."

"That's nice to hear, but I owe you more than that. So, not that it's much, but I made you a few casseroles. You can freeze them and eat them when you're ready, or whatever. No big deal. They're in the car . . ." I look around, acting as if I'm trying to figure out where I can leave these dishes for her. "Hmm. I didn't think this through. I don't suppose I should leave them here." And then I raise my gaze, snapping my finger. "Ah, I know . . . why don't I drop them off at your place on my way home? I can stick them in the freezer for you."

Have I pushed my luck? Am I too obvious? I don't like the look on her face. How do I climb out of this hole? "Although, I'm sure the refrigerator here is big enough, right?" I ask, hoping to recover.

"I don't mind you dropping them off at my place. I mean, don't expect it to be clean or anything, but that would be fine. Besides, if you left them here, I guarantee they'd be gone by the end of the day. I work with a bunch of vultures."

There's her smile and polite laugh. Okay, now I can relax. "I promise I won't judge. You've seen my place, so there you go."

"That's super sweet of you, Evelyn, thank you, even though you didn't have to do that." The bell rings and Summer glances back. When she returns her attention to me, she continues, "I keep a spare key under the flowerpot next to the lawn chair."

"Great. I'll drop them off now. You want me to leave one out for your dinner tonight?"

"Sure. You pick." She turns on her heel. "I'd better go. Thanks again, Evelyn. See you this afternoon."

I return to my car and the smell of the food inside. I head out, taking the road in the opposite direction. I have Summer's address, but I've never been there. Still new here myself, I'm not entirely sure where I'm going, so I use my navigation to guide me.

A part of me wonders how she can afford to live in Beaufort. Even in an apartment, I imagine the rent is quite high. And as I drive on, I consider my plan. What do I hope to find? What will be enough to squelch any notion I have that she's either after Derek or knows about our past?

I thought this would be over, but I guess my brilliant plan didn't go as I'd hoped. I don't buy into Derek's suggestion that she hit on him. If she had, he wouldn't have pushed back. Summer's a beautiful young woman, and I know my husband. No, he's keeping the truth from me, and the one thing I do feel more certain about? Summer had to be the one to leave the notes.

I'd convinced myself it was Josie, but I'm beginning to wonder if her snooping is just part of her personality. After all, why would she care where we came from? We've been the perfect neighbors, giving her no reason for concern. So, now it's time for me to find out what Summer knows and how she came to know it. But the most important thing — what she intends to do with the information.

I see the apartment complex ahead. Several buildings, none more than three stories high. She's in the second one, facing north. I pull into the parking lot and find a spot near Summer's front door. Getting out, I grab the insulated bag and head toward her ground-floor unit, spotting the number on the door.

The flowerpot she mentioned lies beside the chair, and that's where I find the spare key — underneath it, just like she said. So, she trusts me enough to let me inside her place. That should comfort me, but it doesn't.

Inside, gray morning light filters around the closed blinds. I expected a small studio, instead, I see a decent-sized one-bedroom apartment.

The living room and kitchen flow together, with only a small kitchen island separating the two. Her décor is modern yet soft and feminine. The colors are a complementary gray and white. For a young woman who works at a preschool, she has nice things. Expensive things. Red flag number one.

I make my way into her bedroom. Her bed is made, yet when I open the closet, the clothes are hanging haphazardly. Her shoes are tossed around in mismatched pairs. A dresser sits pressed against a wall and I sift through the drawers to see a jumbled mess of undergarments, socks, and bras. Bunched up T-shirts and shorts. "Jesus." Her personal items are in total disarray, while the rest of the apartment appears clean. It seems, outwardly, she's poised and polished, but inside, she's a chaotic mess. The hairs on my neck stand on end as the real Summer Burton reveals herself.

I check the nightstand, wondering what disaster I'll find inside. I open the single drawer, and my heart jumps into my throat.

Reaching inside, I pick up what I'm certain is . . . "Oh my God. These are baby clothes." Several onesies, socks, and tiny shoes. All neatly folded and looking like they belong to a baby girl. "But you don't have kids."

I whip around, searching for anything else that points to a baby living here. A crib. A bassinet. I march back into the kitchen and search the cabinets. No baby food. No formula or bottles in the fridge. No other sign that an infant lives here or that Summer is a mother.

93

My head spins, and I grip the back of the dining chair to steady myself. "Why did you lie about this?" I consider whether Summer had given up a baby or had lost one. "That's possible. But . . ." It occurs to me at that moment. "Is this why you're here? Is Derek the father?"

My head pounds, and I feel sick. Why does she have those baby clothes hidden away? Am I making something out of nothing? Is my tether to reality continuing to fray? I need to confront her, but I must think this through. There is no child here, so either one doesn't exist, or she's given it up. That makes the most sense.

Derek must know about this, which is why he doesn't want her and me to be friends. If he's fathered a child with her . . . my God, I couldn't take a blow like that.

For now, I say nothing, not until I'm certain of what I've seen. I will myself to take deep, relaxing breaths as I try to make sense of this new development. There must be a logical explanation for these baby clothes in Summer's apartment. I need to calm down.

I place the casserole dishes in the freezer, leaving one in the fridge for her later. The thoughts penetrate my mind as I squeeze my eyes shut. The idea that Summer has an agenda involving Derek . . .

What if it's his?

The thought grips my chest. I can't breathe. A small sob breaks away, but I swallow it down, my vision blurring with tears I refuse to let fall. Maybe paranoia has finally taken over. Maybe I'm wrong about all of this.

I walk out of the kitchen, grabbing the insulated bag and my purse, ready to get the hell out of here. As I return to the living room, images from a picture frame stop me in my tracks. It's one of those electronic frames where the photo changes every minute or so. And what I see — even for a moment . . . The image is gone now, but I know who it was. "Oh my God. How did you know Nicole?"

CHAPTER 17

The ground beneath me is giving way. I can barely hear my own thoughts over the rushing in my ears, but one question keeps screaming through the noise: where is this child?

Sitting in my car, I stare at Summer's apartment building, lost as to how I can go home and face my husband. How I can face Summer in only a few hours. *Then don't.*

"What can I do?" I ask myself questions as though expecting someone else to answer. As I see it, I have two options. Confront Summer, asking her if she has a baby, or confront Derek, asking him if he's slept with Summer, as he had Nicole.

The thing is, I'd never seen Summer before moving here. Not back in Medford. Not during the investigation or Nicole's funeral, though I had kept myself at a distance. Her family didn't want Derek or me there at all.

As I consider an impossible situation, I come to the only conclusion that makes sense to me. It's clear Summer is not currently caring for a child. Finding baby clothes isn't the solid proof it appears to be. So, I need to find out who she is and how she knew Nicole Peterson. Eventually, it will lead me to this child.

"I have to leave." Pressing the ignition, I pull out of the parking lot and head home. It seems obvious now that it was Summer who left the notes. She knew Nicole. She knew what had happened and how Derek was involved. But how the hell did she find us?

The more I think about it, confronting one or both of them now might be premature. I need to be armed with more information so neither can squirm their way out of the truth.

I could try contacting some of Nicole's old friends or family, but that seems too risky. If I start asking questions about Summer, word could get back to her. I can't risk her coming out with what she must know about Derek. The school will force him out, not wanting the controversy. Then what? Where will we go?

There is one person I know I can trust. It will require a trip back to Medford, and I'm not sure I can pull that off without Derek raising an eyebrow. But if anyone can help me through this, it's Emily.

As I approach our home, Derek's car is already in the driveway. I'm immediately thrown into panic since he isn't due home for two more hours. Checking my phone, I see he hasn't sent me any texts, and I haven't missed any calls explaining his early return.

My first thought is that Summer knows what I found and told him. My God, were there cameras in her apartment? I didn't even think to look. Was that why she so willingly allowed me entry? "Take a breath, Evie," I tell myself. "It's probably nothing. She didn't have cameras. No one was spying on you."

With each passing day, it becomes harder to ignore how tenuous my grasp has become on reality. Thinking Summer was at the mixer. Believing Shana Foster wants my husband. Certain Josie is out to get us. Christ — now I'm convinced Summer has cameras in her own apartment, ready to catch me snooping?

In my relentless effort to keep up the illusion of a happy home, my own sanity has become little more than collateral damage. How much more will it take before I finally crack?

If I don't go inside now, Derek will wonder what's wrong, so I get out and walk into the house. It's quiet in here. Ben's still at school. I don't hear Derek, but when I enter the kitchen, there he is, staring through the breakfast window. "Derek?"

He turns to me, his face masked in sorrow. "What happened?" My first thought is that he's been fired. That they all somehow found out, and this is the end.

"Shana Foster's dead."

I freeze in place. My head grows light. "What?" My mind's eye conjures the image of Shana, wearing the pretty green cocktail dress, touching Derek's arm, and smiling at him. The very same woman I suspected was trying to take Derek from me. Now, she's dead. "What happened?"

He swallows hard. "She was stabbed to death . . . and found in *my* office early this morning."

My knees buckle. I drop my bags and grab one of the bar stools. "Jesus." I rifle through my memory, attempting to recall exactly where we were last night and whether Derek was home for the duration. And once again, I wonder if my husband is a killer. How many more women need to die for me to be certain?

"Are you a — a suspect?" My voice comes out fractured, and for a moment, I think I might actually fear him.

He raises his hand. "I didn't do this, Evie. You know I was home. Don't fucking do this to me again."

Finding my footing, I take a step back. "Don't do this to you? *You* . . . Derek?"

He moves toward me, and I flinch. "Evie, I'm sorry. Baby, I'm sorry. I'm freaking out right now. For Christ's sake, a woman is dead. She was in *my* office. Everyone thinks it was me. I can't bear you thinking that too. Please, not again. I don't know what's going on. Who's doing this to us? I don't understand any of it."

Do I tell him what I know about Summer? Could she have been there that night at the mixer, and it wasn't my imagination? Maybe I'm not going crazy after all. But why target Shana? I can't even be certain anything was going on between the two of them. If Summer had wanted Derek to herself, why not just take me out of the picture? I'm the wife.

Fear twists his face. Derek's afraid, truly afraid. No . . . I can't believe he did this. Why would he? I wipe a tear from my cheek and firm my resolve. "The police are going to make the connection. Medford. Nicole. It'll all come out."

He nods.

"So, who could have done this, Derek?" I press. "And why?"

"I don't know." He lowers his gaze, hands on his hips. "Alex came at me pretty hard, accusing me. I confronted him regarding his whereabouts, but I don't know . . . It could be that he had something going on with her. Maybe because . . ." He hesitates a moment, glancing up at me. "Maybe he didn't like that she flirted with me."

"Alex Murphey. Your co-worker who was just at our house for dinner?" I ask.

"You weren't there. You didn't see his reaction. They all looked at me like I did it. Even the detective picked up on it." Derek takes my hands. "Baby, someone's out to destroy us. All these goddam notes. Now Shana's dead. She didn't deserve that."

The question I want to ask lies on the tip of my tongue, yet I'm afraid to know the answer. I ask it anyway. "Derek, were you sleeping with her?"

He releases my hands, arms flinging in the air. "Oh my God. You're looking at me just like they did. I'm not going to stand here and listen to this bullshit. I thought you were the one person who would stand by me." He brushes past me and marches upstairs.

I drop onto one of the chairs in the nook. Tears flood my eyes. A woman's dead, and it somehow always seems to go back to Derek. And what I saw earlier at Summer's place? That's nothing compared to this. Earlier, I'd asked myself what else could happen that would finally break me. Now I have my answer.

CHAPTER 18

It was only a matter of time before the police wanted to talk to me. I'm surprised it took them a whole day. Derek and I have been holed up in our home. He didn't go to work today. In fact, the university has halted classes for the entire week.

My plans to look into Summer Burton's connection to Nicole Peterson have been put on hold for the time being. Now, I'm about to be asked questions by yet another detective to solve yet another murder that is somehow connected to my husband.

We've decided to keep Ben home with us, fearing any sort of gossip, or worse — backlash against him. I hope once Derek and I are cleared of suspicion, we can go back to the way things were. Only, I know that's not possible anymore. I'm just not sure what to do about it.

"I have to go, Derek," I call out to him as he sits in his office. "You'll have to keep an eye on Ben. He's in the living room." I shouldn't have to tell him this, but it is what it is.

As I head to the foyer to grab my coat and car keys, he rushes toward me.

"Hang on," he says.

"What is it?" I pull on my coat. "The detective said I have to go alone."

"What are you going to tell him, Evie?"

I knit my brow. "What do you mean? I'm going to tell him the truth." I step back a moment. "Unless there's something you're not telling me, Derek. Is there?"

"No. Of course not." He tucks his hands into his pockets and glances at his feet. "I just wish you didn't have to do this. Especially alone."

"Yeah, well, you're not the only one." I study him for a moment, feeling guilty for thinking he had something to do with this, yet hearing the voice inside my head warning me he did. I don't want to believe it, but a part of me can't help but draw that conclusion. "Look, I'll answer their questions and come right back. Whoever did this, Derek . . . they will be caught. I know what this is doing to you — to us. What your co-workers must think. But the cops will figure this out."

I don't wait for a response. There's nothing left I need to hear from him. Instead, I head out, wondering if I believe my own words.

Once the focus is off Derek and me, I can go back to getting to the truth of why Summer is here. However, it's getting harder to dispute the idea that Shana Foster's murder is connected to Summer Burton. The way she followed us here. The notes. The threats. Coincidences like that don't exist, even I can admit as much.

Standing outside the police station, I gather my nerve. Through the glass doors a few officers are meandering around the lobby. Beaufort is a small town with a small police force that probably doesn't see this kind of thing often — the brutal murder of a university professor. But the cold is getting to me, and I can't put this off, so I go inside.

"Excuse me?" I ask the officer at the front desk. "I'm here to see Detective Langston regarding what happened at the . . ."

"I'm aware," he cuts in, looking serious. "Your name?"

"Evelyn Moore."

"One moment." He picks up the phone, keeping an eye on me as he speaks.

I scan the lobby, noticing how quiet it is. I expected to see criminals and lawyers, cops rushing around. Then again, I watch too many crime shows. And since I practiced family law, I was rarely inside of a police station.

"Ma'am?" he says loudly.

"Yes?" I turn to him, realizing he must've called my name more than once.

"Detective Langston is on his way up. Take a seat over there, please." He gestures to the chairs.

"Okay, thank you." I head over to the two rows of black vinyl chairs with metal arms. Taking a seat, I wait only a minute before I see a balding man, tall and slim, dressed in a black suit. He's heading my way.

"Mrs. Moore?" He offers his hand. "I'm Detective Langston. Would you mind following me back to my office?"

"Sure." After we exchange a brief handshake, I follow him back. My nerves are on edge because I know the things I should tell him, but can I? Will it matter?

"Take a seat, ma'am." He gestures to the chair across from his desk.

I sit down, taking in the nondescript setting. A bookshelf along the side wall. A window behind his desk overlooking the parking lot. Boxes of what appear to be investigation files.

"I appreciate you coming in today," he begins. "You and your husband have been through a lot recently."

What does that mean? Does he already know about Nicole and Medford University? "Yes, sir. I only met Shana once, but she seemed to be a very nice person. I can't believe someone's done this to her." I do my best to remain stoic, but I'm rattled, and if this detective is even halfway decent at his job, he'll see it.

"How about we start with where you were on Monday night?" he continues.

I tell him everything — where I was, where Derek was. What we did and when. I was baking casserole dishes. Derek watched television. I don't know what happened after we went to sleep.

"What time did you and your husband go to bed that night?" He takes notes as he speaks.

"About ten o'clock, I guess. That's around our usual time."

He regards me for a moment, wearing a sort of empathy in his gaze. "I hear you're a lawyer."

"*Was*." I correct him. "I don't practice anymore."

"Why is that?"

"My son. He occupies most of my time, but I hope to return to work in the next few years."

He nods, scribbling in his notebook again. "What can you tell me about Alex Murphey?"

I clasp my hands in my lap. "Well, I met him at a staff mixer about a week or so ago. Derek invited him to dinner this past Saturday night. He seemed . . . on edge."

Langston raises his chin. "How so?"

Now I have to walk through this door I just opened because Alex didn't seem that way at all. But I know exactly what I'm doing. I need Langston to consider other suspects besides my husband. Maybe I should've been a defense lawyer. "I'm not sure, really. It could be because he didn't know us that well. You know how it can be meeting new people."

"Sure. Any other reason why you suspected he felt that way?"

"There's a possibility he'd wanted Derek's job a while ago, before my husband came on board. I understood he was in line for a promotion, but I guess he didn't get it." There's no turning back, but I tell myself I'm doing this for my family.

The detective leans back, folding his arms over his slim chest. "Care to elaborate?"

"From what I understand, Alex has been at the university for a while. Junior professor," I say. "Derek comes in — an outsider — and gets senior status. I can see how that might rub people the wrong way."

He jots down more notes and then rubs his forefinger and thumb over the bridge of his nose. "I'm just sitting here wondering, Mrs. Moore, when you plan on telling me about Nicole Peterson."

His question falls on me like an anvil. Like I'm the coyote and the roadrunner managed to escape again. Of course he knows about her. Any self-respecting cop would. "There's nothing to say, Detective. A young woman drowned in the Medford University pool. They believed it was an accident."

"But your husband knew her — intimately — did he not?" He looks at me like he's got me trapped.

"Yes, sir, he did. I imagine you already knew that, or you wouldn't be asking me the question. It was a tragic event, but it has nothing to do with what happened to Professor Foster."

A tight, closed-lip smile appears on his face. He nods, taking a few more notes. Then he looks at me again, serious, determined to get me to slip up somehow. "We're looking into just how close your husband and Professor Foster were . . . if you take my meaning. It's my understanding, Mrs. Moore, that your husband has a penchant for stepping out."

"Jesus Christ." I turn away, disgusted. "Are you asking me if my husband was having an affair with Shana Foster?"

He tosses his pen onto the desk and leans back in his chair. "That's exactly what I'm asking you, ma'am."

"I don't know." I shrug. "Did you ask him? Do you have proof of an affair you care to share with me?" There's that lawyer logic kicking in again. Only this time, I'm feeling pretty good about using it because how dare this man throw accusations in my face. It's one thing for me to suspect my husband. I won't let anyone else do the same. "Derek was home with me. He didn't kill Shana Foster. That's all you need to know."

CHAPTER 19

Detective Langston was well aware of everything about our lives back in Medford. Of course he was. That's his job. When I walk inside our house, Derek is sitting on the edge of the sofa, an empty beer bottle on the coffee table. He bolts up and walks toward me.

"How'd it go?" he asks, impatience brimming in his voice. Or maybe that's fear.

I pull off my coat and hang it on the hook in the foyer. "Can I set down my things first?" He backs away and I take a breath. "He already knew, Derek. He knew about Nicole."

Derek pushes his hand through his dark hair. "Yeah, I know. Goddam detective is trying to make a case like I'm some damn serial killer or something. He knows I was cleared in Nicole's death."

"Yeah." I walk past him into the living room, saying nothing of the fact that Langston asked me if Derek was having an affair with Shana. I'm sure Derek was asked that very question. "Where's Ben?"

"Upstairs taking a nap."

I lower myself onto the couch, nodding. "Okay. Good." Every muscle in my body tenses as this new reality sets in. "Why her?"

104

He joins me on the sofa. "What do you mean, 'why her?'"

I fix my gaze on him. "Derek, is there something you're not telling me? Look, Langston . . . he clearly thinks you were sleeping with Shana, so, were you?"

"Oh my God. Not this shit again. You do think I killed her." He rises, pacing a tight circle.

His typical reaction. Defensive and deflecting. It doesn't fill me with promise. "I didn't say that. I asked if there's more to this than you're telling me. It would explain the most recent note. 'Tell her or I will.' Maybe that was a warning from Alex." I lower my gaze in defeat. "We're being targeted, Derek. You see that, right? This kind of thing doesn't just happen. Yet it's happened to us twice." I look up to him again. "Why?"

"I don't know, Evie." He squats in front of me, taking my hands. "I love you so much. I didn't do this. I know what it looks like, but I would never . . . I have never . . ." His voice fractures and his eyes redden. "I need you, of all people, Evie, I need you to believe me. Please."

I don't have it in me to say anything about Summer or a baby I know nothing about because, now, I'm not sure what's going on. A woman is dead. I don't believe Derek killed her, so who did? I grip his hands. "Listen to me, Derek. I believe you're innocent of this, okay? And as long as we remain united, the cops will see it too. And they'll find whoever killed Shana."

Relief is evident in his face as I stand beside my husband once again. At the end of the day, I can't stop loving him. He's not a killer. Whatever he did with Nicole, he didn't kill her. And he didn't kill Shana. But I'm beginning to suspect Summer has had a hand in the destruction of my family. I just don't know how or why. Not yet.

A knock sounds on the door. "For God's sake, who is that?" I peer through the opening in the front window curtains. "Josie."

"Leave it," Derek insists.

"No. I have to answer. Who knows what she's already aware of? We don't need her spreading gossip around the neighborhood. I have to answer the door and pretend everything is just fine."

Derek steps back, allowing me to walk to the front door. I glance into the small mirror that hangs in the entry and wipe away the mascara smudged under my eyes. Clearing my throat, I plaster on a smile before opening the door. "Josie. Hi, what's going on?"

She knows. Before a single word comes out of her mouth, that much is clear. She thrusts her hand over her chest; her lips are turned down. "Oh, I'm just so, so sorry about what happened at the school." She glances past me, but I block her view.

"Yes, it's just awful. Derek and I can't believe it," I reply. "As I'm sure you can imagine, Josie, we're pretty upset, if you wouldn't mind coming back another time—"

"Oh, yes, of course. I completely understand."

Somehow, I don't think she does. "Thank you." I begin to close the door, but she inserts her foot to prop it open. "Yes?" I ask, annoyed at her intrusion.

"I just have to ask . . . how's Derek doing? He must be beside himself."

"He is, yes. The entire school is, Josie."

"Well, I imagine the police are doing everything in their power to get to the bottom of what happened. I mean, really . . . finding her in Derek's office like that—"

I narrow my gaze for only a moment, not wanting her to see my concern. Detective Langston said the only people who knew about that were the ones who'd found the body. The school's staff. Sure, they could've talked, but Josie doesn't know any of them. It wasn't in the news story.

I grunt, refusing to say another word.

Josie finally pulls back her foot. "Well, I should go. Please let me know if I can do anything to help. Anything at all."

"I will. Thank you for your concern." I close the door, not giving her another chance to stop me. Returning to the living room, I see Derek drop the curtains. He'd watched her leave.

"I cannot believe that woman," he says, turning back to me.

I'm desperate to know how she knew about the body, but I say nothing to Derek. "Yeah, I can't, either."

CHAPTER 20

The part that made me a good lawyer still lives in me. Talking to Detective Langston the other day reminded me that she still exists. The battle between her and the woman who's afraid of losing everything, afraid of losing her mind, rages on. But for now, one has triumphed and has decided on a plan of action. Because, in the end, she also agrees the family must remain the priority.

In about five minutes, that plan will take shape. As Derek and I finish dinner, Ben having already eaten and gone to bed, my phone rings.

"Don't answer it, babe," Derek says. "It's probably the media again."

"I should at least check." I get up from the table and walk into the kitchen. My phone rests on the counter, and the name on the screen draws a smile. Immediately, I answer. "Hey, Mom. No, I'm not busy. Is everything all right?"

I keep the conversation going for a minute or two, wanting Derek to overhear the bulk of it as he remains in the dining room. But then, I end the call. However, this is where the plan comes into play. I move toward the dining room again and continue, "Okay, no, it's fine. I want to be there. Love you too, Mom. See you soon." I pocket my phone and return to Derek, masking my face in worry.

"Is everything all right? That was your mom?" he asks.

"Yes, she's not feeling well. She's afraid her cancer is back." I drop onto the chair at the head of the table, guilt-ridden because I hate lying about my mother, especially about something like this. She'd battled breast cancer years ago and lying that it may have come back feels like I'm screwing around with Karma. But I have a reason. I just hope it works.

"Has she seen the doctor?" he presses.

"Not yet, but she asked me to come with her this time. She's not sure she can take the news alone if it's bad."

He reaches out for my arm. "Of course, Evie. You should go be with her. I know how hard it's been for her since your dad died." He sighs. "Besides, I have no idea what's going to happen here. With the cops, the school. No point in you sticking around, and I can look after Ben."

"Are you sure?" I squeeze his hand in hopes I'm convincing him. "Leaving at a time like this . . ."

"I can manage, what, a couple of days?" he asks.

"Yes, it'll only be two days. I just need to get her through the appointment."

His eyes search mine. "And if it's cancer again?"

I shrug. "Then we'll figure it out."

* * *

I'm on a plane heading back to Medford, doing my best to get to the bottom of why this is happening to us. It's entirely selfish because I still draw breath. Shana Foster and Nicole Peterson do not. But if I hope to find the truth, it starts at Medford University.

When the plane lands, I check into a hotel near campus. Being back here feels strangely good. I'd had a good life here. My son was born here. I never would've left if Derek hadn't insisted.

I take a drive in my rented car, smiling at the reminders of happier days. The movie theater Derek and I would go to. They always played old black-and-white films, and it was so much fun.

But those days are gone now, and I'm not here to reminisce.

Returning to campus, I make my way through the commons, a familiar place with a familiar scent — coffee. Chilly air, a cool breeze. Bare trees with students sitting beneath them on plaid blankets, draped in oversized hoodies. Makes me almost miss my days as a college student. Almost.

I did well enough as an undergrad to get accepted into a decent law school. Decent, not great. And law school was the hardest thing I'd ever done. Three years, countless papers. Memorizing case law. Don't even get me started on the bar exam. Of course, since the move, and the fact that I no longer work, I haven't bothered to crack open a book to study for the bar exam in Connecticut.

As I look at the students, I see myself. Excited, happy, laughing. It makes me wonder how I got here. I shake off the self-imposed pity party and head toward the administration building. Inside are a few students, as I would expect. My guess is they're interns not getting paid a dime, but that's how it works if one is looking for an academic position, post-graduation.

I step up to the desk. "Excuse me?"

A professional-looking young man in a white shirt and blue tie smiles at me. "Hi. Can I help you?"

"Yes, please. Can you provide me with Emily Harwick's phone number? She works in the English Department, I believe." Emily is the only person I can trust. She worked with Derek, and since I have no idea whether Summer Burton worked here or was a student, or even if that's her real name, Emily will help me.

"That's not public information, ma'am. I'm sorry. I can't give you records like that without proper authorization."

His gaze is indifferent. This isn't going to be easy. He's the gatekeeper, and I need to find a way past him. "Look." I lean in, lowering my voice. "This is . . . about Nicole Peterson. I'm writing a story about her. And I'd prefer not to make the university look bad. Now, I realize you can't give me social security information or anything like that. And that's fine. That's not what I need. I just want her contact information. Email, phone. That's it. Nothing more than any prospective employer would ask."

He raises an eyebrow, still unimpressed. "Um, ma'am, I really don't think I can do that."

I can't leave without this information. I have to find her but going straight to the English Department, where everyone knows me, isn't an option. So, I force a smile and try a different approach. "What would you need from me then?"

"Well, I suppose if it was a prospective employer, they'd have to call to request that information."

"Fine," I say. "I can get one to call you."

"But you just said you were writing some kind of story—"

"You know what? Forget it." I swat my hand. "I thought, after what happened to Nicole, the school might want to clear their name. We've all heard the rumors. No doubt, you have, too. I just need to talk to Emily." I hope I'm getting through to this kid.

He watches me for a moment, sizing me up, weighing whether this is worth the risk. My pulse beats in my throat, my breath catching as I wait for his response.

He sighs, rubbing a hand over his face. He's wavering, so I press my advantage. "I'm not asking for personal life details."

His eyes flicker with something — concern, or maybe guilt. "Fine," he mutters under his breath, glancing around as if someone might be watching. "I'll get it for you. Hang on."

Relief swells in my chest as he reaches for the keyboard and types in a command. Seconds stretch into eternity, and then, finally, he slides a slip of paper across the counter toward me.

I grab the paper and shove it into my bag without looking at it. "Thank you."

As I step outside, squinting in the bright sunlight, I retrieve the paper, studying it for only a moment. "Okay. Good. She's still here."

How do I know I can trust Emily Harwick? How can I be certain she and Derek never slept together? That's easy. Emily prefers women. It's the only logic I can count on at the moment. And she disliked Derek with every fiber of her being because she'd once approached me about him. It wasn't the first time a woman tried to tell me who my husband really was. I listened. Nodded politely. And then turned away, closing my eyes and pretending as I always did.

I'll find Emily. She'll tell me exactly who Summer Burton is.

CHAPTER 21

Derek

Evelyn thinks I don't know that the reason she went home to see her mother was to get away from all this bullshit. The cops, the gossip. All of it. I don't blame her. She's been through this before, as I have. Neither of us wants to face it again. But I can't leave. Detective Langston made that crystal clear.

The school opted to reopen at half-days for the remainder of the week. I'd had to take Ben to preschool, letting Evie know the change of plans. She didn't answer my call, so I left a message.

As I stand outside my office, my mind flashes back to the horrific sight of what happened to Shana. Blood everywhere. Shana's body lying on the ground, in blood-soaked clothes, ripped and torn from the knife.

My heart breaks. Everything's been cleaned out. My things . . . thrown away. The office looks as it did on my first day here.

Whispers sound behind me, and I turn around to see two of my co-workers. The way they're looking at me, I hate it. It feels like it did after Nicole was found. "You two want to say something?" They walk away, and I feel worse now for saying anything at all. They lost a colleague, too.

I finally step over the threshold. A chill crawls up my spine, and I can't shake the horrific feeling. I don't want to be here, but I push on, sitting behind my desk.

For a split second, I wonder if it's possible Evie could do such a thing — commit murder. She'd been jealous of Shana that night. Even disappearing to use the restroom. Was that all she did, or did she track down Shana and warn her off? I'd done what I could to smooth over Evie's concerns, but what if I didn't? I shake my head. No, she didn't do this. I know she didn't. There's no denying our trust in one another hangs by the thinnest of threads, but I can't let my mind go there. I won't.

Waiting for my laptop to boot up, I pull out my pencil drawer.

"The fuck?"

I scramble, heart pounding, shoving my chair backward until I slam against the wall behind me. My throat dries, and I can't catch my breath as I stare at the open drawer.

I look up. Is anyone around? Sprinting from my chair, I run into the corridor, craning in each direction. No one's there. I turn back, eyeing my desk once again. My legs feel like they're encased in concrete, but I force them to step forward — to look again at the drawer. One foot after the other, slowly, deliberately. Could that really be what I think it is? I move closer, leaning over my desk to peek inside. "Jesus Christ. Security!" I dart back into the hall. "Security!"

Students and staff gather around, all with their eyes on me. "Hey, someone call security — now!" They ignore me. "Oh my God. Did you hear me? I need help in here."

James pokes his head out of his office. "What's wrong, man? What is it?"

I aim my finger toward my desk. "There's a fucking body part in my drawer."

"I'm sorry, a what?" he asks, his face screwed up in disgust.

113

"A body part."

James steps into the hall, walking toward me. "Are you serious?"

I push a hand through my hair in frustration. "No, man. It's a joke . . . Yes, I'm serious. For God's sake. Get the goddam police!"

CHAPTER 22

Evelyn

This coffee shop was one of my favorite places to go when we lived here. But, today, I'm not here because I miss their freshly brewed coffee. I'm here to see Emily, and she's just arrived.

I raise my hand until she spots me. On her way over, she smiles, and I remember what she tried to do for me. Only in hindsight do I see it was an act of compassion.

I stand from the chair and extend my hand. "Emily, it's so good to see you." She pulls me into an embrace, and for a split second, I want to melt at her kindness, but I remain firm. "How have you been?"

"Doing well, thanks for asking." She sits across from me. Her short brown hair is neatly tucked behind her ear. A thick scarf is tied around her neck. She has the most beautiful blue eyes, soft and round, almost doll-like. "I have to say, I was surprised to get your call. After everything . . ."

"I got in yesterday. To be honest, I'm surprised to be here, too, but here I am. Thanks for coming. I apologize for the last-minute request." I glance at the server behind the counter. "Can I order you a coffee?"

"Uh, no thanks. I'm okay," she replies. "So, you mentioned in your call that you wanted to talk about someone by the name of Summer Burton."

"And you didn't recognize the name, right?" I say. How to explain this without sounding like a crazy jealous wife, and without mentioning that my husband's colleague was just murdered? "Well, I guess I'm trying to figure out why she's in Beaufort . . . not far from where I currently live with my family. I'm certain she knew Nicole Peterson. So I think she either worked here or she was possibly a student. But given her age, I think it's more likely she was a member of staff." I retrieve a photograph of Summer that I'd gotten from the preschool. Her ID badge. "This is her. Do you recognize her, by chance?"

Emily studies the picture, tilting her head, her short brown hair falling against her cheek. "That's Riley Dittrich. She worked as an aide in the Communications Department. Quit not too long ago. In fact, not long after you and Derek left. She moved to your town and goes by another name?"

"Yep," I reply. "Guess my concerns were on point." I take a sip from my mug. "What do you know about her?"

Emily sits back. "I heard things. Some I'm pretty sure are true, some I'm not so sure."

"How about you start with what you know to be true?" I ask.

Emily nods, hesitating as if trying to figure out where to begin. I have to admit, that frightens me a little.

"What I believe is true is that Riley and Derek . . ." She swallows so hard I can see her throat move. "They were sleeping together."

I've heard those words many times before, but they never stop hurting. What can I say? I'm a glutton for punishment. "Okay." My voice cracks with emotion.

"And when all this stuff blew up about Nicole and her accident, well, I don't know but I think maybe Derek cut Riley loose. Can't be sure, but I assume as much. Just the way

116

she was acting and stuff. I mean, look, I didn't pay that much attention, but Riley was fairly vocal about her personal life."

I force a smile. "Well, I can't say I'm surprised. But do you know if she was friends with Nicole Peterson?"

Emily nods. "Oh yeah. I mean, I don't know how close, but Riley used to be a swimmer. "Anyway, I think she helped Nicole train sometimes. They became friends when Nicole took one of her Comms classes, and Riley was the aide." Emily leans over the table, glancing around. Her full cheeks fall under her grim expression. "And look, Riley — she was a whole handful, right? So, take this with a grain of salt. But I think she's the reason the cops interviewed your husband. I think she told them she suspected him of murdering Nicole." Emily leans back again, shaking her head. "I mean, that's crazy, right? The cops even said it was an accident. But I don't know, Riley didn't seem convinced."

"Or she wanted to make trouble for Derek, given their . . . relationship," I say.

Emily gestures out. "Well, there's that, too."

I take the final sip of my drink and set down the mug again. "There's one other thing . . . did you hear rumors, true or not, about Riley being pregnant? Or did she have a baby that you knew of?"

There's that hesitation again. Emily doesn't want to answer this question, which sends my pulse pounding. "Please, Emily, even if you only heard a rumor."

She licks her lips, casting around her gaze again. "I'd heard from a friend that Riley was going on about how she was pregnant, and a tenured professor was the father. I don't know how far along she was. But I mean, when I saw her shortly after, she was wearing loose clothing, so it was hard to tell." She shrugs. "I mean, look, it could've been anyone's baby." Emily takes a sip of water. "You said she lives in your town now, and the two of you have become friends?"

I nod, closing my eyes, regretting ever meeting Summer Burton, or Riley Dittrich, whoever the hell she is.

"And you haven't seen a baby with her?" Emily presses.

"No," I whisper. "None that I've seen." I don't tell her what I found while snooping around Summer's apartment.

"Well, then, maybe she was lying about being pregnant."

I blink hard to stop the tears that prick my eyes. "Yeah, maybe." We're quiet for a few moments and I see Emily's uncomfortable. "Listen, thank you . . . for coming here, for telling me things I need to hear."

"I didn't do much," she replies with a shrug.

"You did. Today and before." I feel my throat tighten. "I love Derek, there's no mistaking that, but if I'd listened . . . maybe I could've worked harder to fix things. Instead, I ignored them. Pretending they'd go away, and everything would be fine again."

Emily reaches out, taking my hand. "It's easy to judge people for not doing what you think is best for them. But the thing is, no one knows what's best for you, except you. No one else walks in your shoes, Evelyn. Look, I am sorry for all that's going on now. I'm sure it's not easy. But you'll do what's best for you and your family."

"Thank you." I smile.

She reaches around to grab her coat from the back of the chair. "Any time. I do need to head out. You'll be okay?"

I nod. "Of course."

"Good." Emily stands, pushing back her chair. "Take care of yourself, Evelyn."

"You, too." Growing numb, my gaze stays fixed on her as she walks out the door and I try to process everything she told me. Derek had an affair with Summer, now known to me as Riley Dittrich, who also happened to be friends with Nicole Peterson. She possibly told the police she thought Derek was involved in Nicole's death. And Riley may have been pregnant at some point, too.

Now I have more questions than answers. I need to confront Derek, but I know he'll just deny and deflect as he always does. He'll claim Riley/Summer is obsessed with him, and she's causing all this trouble. Maybe even blame her for Shana's murder. Well, at this point, I'm not sure I'd disagree, but the reason behind it isn't clear.

I could confront Summer, but I doubt she would be forthcoming either. I need to know if she has a child and whether that child belongs to Derek. Why come to Beaufort if not to make Derek pay for this child? What I don't understand is why the note? The attempt to be my friend? It seems cruel if nothing else. If Summer wants Derek to take responsibility, then she has a funny way of going about it.

* * *

The hum of the airplane's engines is steady, almost soothing, except it doesn't calm my racing thoughts. Peering through the window at the clouds below, I'm lost, confused, and unsure of how I arrived here.

Could there be a child out there somewhere? Derek's child?

My stomach twists, and a wave of nausea threatens to overwhelm me. How did my marriage — my life — unravel so quickly?

I know why but refuse to admit it even to myself. I let it happen. I ignored the problem, pretending it would go away. I thought the move to Beaufort would give Derek and me the fresh start we needed. Instead, the problem followed us. And so did more death.

I don't even want to consider the worst part of this scenario — that Summer is here believing Derek is responsible for Nicole's death. Perhaps killing Shana Foster to pin it on him, making him pay for all of it. Does she know more than the police?

Tension builds in my chest like a balloon on the verge of bursting. I want to scream, to cry, to grab the nearest thing and throw it. But I can't do any of that. Not here. Not trapped at 30,000 feet on a plane full of strangers.

Instead, I press my fingers to my temples, trying to will away the growing headache. *How am I supposed to deal with this?*

My heart is broken — shattered beyond repair. Derek risked too much this time. Two women are dead. One, I'm certain he'd slept with. The other? I just don't know yet. And now Summer has come for a purpose. Might it be to get me out of the way next?

A flight attendant walks by, offering drinks and snacks, but I wave her off. My throat is too dry for anything to go down, my stomach, too unsettled.

I should leave him, I think for the hundredth time. Forgetting Emily's assurances, these are the pathetic words of a pathetic wife who let things happen while she sat idly by, head buried in the sand.

What if he doesn't know? What if Summer kept this child from him to use as leverage now? If she wants money, she won't get much. Not anymore.

The plane hits some turbulence, jolting me out of my thoughts. I grip the armrests, my body tense, as though the plane's descent mirrors my own life — falling from the sky at breakneck speed toward an unyielding ground, and then bursting into flames.

With the murder of Shana Foster and the possibility that Summer is here with a child and thinks Derek murdered Nicole, I'm left with only one option. Go to her. No threats. No accusations, because I know my husband. His words come out velvety smooth, more persuasive than a lawyer's closing statement to a jury. I don't lay blame at only her feet. So that's my angle. I get from her the truth about why she's come.

But a part of me fears her now. Could this woman be a killer, having taken Shana's life? Is her angle to get rid of me and anyone else she feels is a threat to her love for Derek? Regardless of the risk, there's only one way to find out. And it's the only way I can be sure to protect my family.

120

CHAPTER 23

I have now opened my eyes, dusted the sand from my face, and am ready to confront what should have been confronted long ago. I arrive home after dark and open the door, entering through the kitchen. The lights are off, but the television echoes in the living room amid the amber glow of the side table lamps. It's time to don my lawyer face, the one that reveals nothing. "Hello?"

"In here," Derek calls out.

In the quiet, my footfalls reverberate on top of the wooden floor as I make my way toward the living room. "I'm back."

"I see that," he replies flatly. "How's your mother?"

I glance down a moment, suspecting he has seen through my lie, given his demeanor. "She's okay. The doctor says she's still clear. Any news about Shana? Do the police have any suspects?"

"No. None yet." He shoots me a look. "It's only a matter of time before Detective Langston lets the Nicole Peterson situation leak."

I set down my overnight bag. "Derek, Shana was brutally murdered. You should be thinking about how this affects her family, not you." The irony in my statement is not lost on me as I glance up the staircase. "Is Ben already asleep?"

"Yes," he says, keeping his gaze on the television. "Oh, and by the way, someone left a pig's liver in my desk drawer this morning."

"What?" I take a step toward him. "Oh my God. Who would do that? Why?"

"Good question. Someone who wants me gone, I imagine. Calling me a killer in their own special way. Cops don't know who left it," he replies, stone-faced. "I don't know what to do, Evie."

Standing here, looking at him, I'm furious he's said nothing about Summer. Clearly, he knows who she is, yet he still keeps it a secret from me. I was right about what I saw that night at dinner. They were well-acquainted, and both of them made me think I was crazy.

Even after Shana's death, Derek doesn't see a possible connection to this woman, Riley Dittrich? He doesn't see the need to finally tell me the truth about her?

It seemed possible, for a fleeting moment, after being back in Medford, that Summer came here because her friend was dead. Looking for answers, searching for the truth. I could almost understand that. But I've found out her true identity and how she knows the man who sits here now, his enormous secret hanging between us.

"I'm going upstairs to change. I'll check in on Ben, too." I start up the steps, and Derek says nothing. This isn't how I thought things would go. What will it take for Derek to come clean? He's afraid. For the first time, I see fear in his eyes and hear it in his voice. But apparently, he's only thinking of himself, not the possibility of what Riley Dittrich might be capable of.

Upstairs, the first thing I do is open Ben's door. Shadows play off the window. He's in his bed, his tiny frame outlined beneath the covers. I wonder what will become of us when this is over. Will he respect or hate me? If I'm lucky, he won't remember much of it.

I pull his door almost shut but leave it open a crack. Walking into our bedroom, I drop my overnight bag. Our bed is unmade.

Derek's clothes hang over the chair in the corner. Carrying on into the bathroom, I almost trip over his towel that lies crumpled on the floor. I grunt at the small things that always bother me, knowing they pale in comparison to the real problems.

Changed into pajamas, I return downstairs to see Derek staring mindlessly at the television. I meander over to him, dropping onto the sofa. "Derek, I think . . ."

"Alex." He turns to me, cutting me off. "I think he's trying to screw with us. I don't know if he has the balls to be Shana's killer, but I think he's the one who put that goddam liver in my desk."

He looks at me, waiting for me to say I agree with him. How can I when I know who Summer is? Maybe Alex did do what he said, but why does it matter now? "The police talked to him. If they thought he was a suspect, I'm sure we would've heard."

Derek reaches for the remote and switches off the TV. "But the way he looked at me that morning . . . like I was the devil himself. He thinks I killed her. I mean, for God's sake, why would I do that? I hardly knew her. And I'm no killer."

He could be doing this to shift blame and my attention, keeping me from learning the truth. He wants me to think this is all because of Alex. Maybe part of it is, but I know everything now. Well, almost everything.

And the baby? What about the baby?

"What are you going to do about it?" I ask, trying to see how far he's willing to take this.

"For now, nothing," Derek replies. "I can't let him think he has me over a barrel. What can he do? He has no proof of anything."

"Because there is none — proof, I mean." I lean back on the sofa. "Maybe he's talked to someone at Medford U. Maybe he suspects you killed Shana because of what happened to Nicole."

"That doesn't make any sense," he shoots back, glaring at me. "Just — look — just let me handle this, all right, Evie?

I know what I've done, and I'll figure out how to deal with him. I let this problem follow us here, and I need to stop it from destroying what we're trying to rebuild."

Is this his way of telling me he'll take care of Summer too?

He takes my hand. "Promise me you'll stay out of it?"

* * *

I'm awakened by Ben jumping onto our bed. Light spills in around our window curtains. The clock on my nightstand shows 6:30 a.m.

"You're home!" Ben cuddles beside me, laying his hand on my cheek. "I'm so glad you're home, Mommy."

"Me too, sweetheart." I notice Derek isn't in bed and quickly realize he may have already left for work. I seem to have lost track of my days. "Oh, we need to get you ready for school. I can't believe Daddy let me sleep so late."

"He's downstairs and he made me breakfast."

I sit up on the edge of the bed. "Is that so?" The last time Derek took care of anything for Ben voluntarily . . . well, I can't remember when it was. "Great, then why don't you let Mommy get changed and go ahead and get your shoes on? We'll head out for school in a few minutes."

"Okay." Ben runs off, disappearing into the hall.

I grab my phone from the nightstand and check for messages. I'd half-expected at least a text from Summer since she knew I'd returned last night, but there's nothing. How I play these next few days will determine the course of my son's future, so I take care to ensure I don't slip up.

While the day already fills me with dread, I get ready to take Ben to school. Summer will be there, and maybe I'll see in her face whether she and my husband have come to an arrangement. One that keeps me in the dark. But none of this answers the questions as to whether a child is involved or if Summer had a hand in Shana's murder.

Downstairs, the sound of Derek and Ben talking and laughing surprises me. For a moment, I'm transported back to a time when we were all happy. Or at least, I thought we were.

"Are you ready to go, Ben?" I ask as I enter the kitchen. Derek smiles at me. It's a look I recognize — a smile that begs for forgiveness — for another fresh start.

"Morning. How'd you sleep?" Derek asks.

"Fine, thanks. You?"

"Yeah, pretty good. Woke up early and thought I'd give you a chance to sleep in, so I got Ben ready."

Like he deserves 'Father of the Year' for getting his son ready for school? Of course, I respond with a smile. "I appreciate it, but we should really get going."

"Okay."

I've tempered his expectations. He knows I won't get over any of this easily or quickly. In fact, I won't get over it until I get the truth from him, or from Summer — whoever decides it's worth their while to reveal it.

Ben grabs his backpack, and I usher him away. "I hope things go better for you at work today."

"Yeah, I hope so. I'll see you tonight, hon," Derek replies.

I let out a slight grunt of acknowledgment before stepping outside into the cold air. The sky is gray this morning. Heavy, dark clouds overhead, like it's going to rain.

"Let's get you buckled in, kiddo." I hoist Ben into his car seat and get him strapped in.

On the drive to school, I consider asking Ben if anything happened while I was away. Specifically, did anyone come over to the house? But I'm almost afraid to know the answer and afraid I'll put Ben in a confusing situation. So, I keep my mouth shut as the radio plays.

Upon arriving at school, I park and help him out of the back seat. A few light raindrops land on my shoulders. "Better get you inside before this rain comes."

"Yep. We don't have our umbrella," Ben says.

I take his hand, and we make it to the entrance. Inside, Summer is talking to another teacher, but she soon turns and spots Ben and me. I'd give anything not to be in this situation. Not to know the truth about this woman, but here I am. "Hey, bud. Go ahead and go see Miss Payton. Have a good day."

"Bye, Mommy."

"Bye. Love you." I wave him off, pretending I don't see Summer's approach.

"Evelyn," she calls out.

"Oh, hi, Summer. Good morning."

"Good morning. Did you get back last night?" she asks.

"I did, yeah. It was kind of late, though." I can't help but wonder if she visited Derek while I was away. Does he know about a child? More importantly, is she trying to frame Derek for the murder of Shana Foster? I don't know whether to be angry at her or terrified of her. But my plan is in place. Talk to her. Get to the bottom of what happened in Medford. I'll figure out the rest later. "Listen, um, after taking care of my mom and the traveling and all that, I think I could really use some me-time."

"I'll bet," Summer replies.

"Actually, I could use some friend time. What are you doing tonight?" I study her for a moment. Her face is unchanged. Neither worried, or happy, or anything else. "I mean, if you're available."

"What about Ben?" she asks.

"I'm sure Derek can look after him for a few hours. He's looked after him for the past two days, right?"

"Well, I guess so. Then, yeah. I'll tell you what, why don't you come over for dinner? You cooked for me, now it's my turn."

Even better. No public scenes. But no one to help me either. "That would be great. What time?"

"Six? We'll have some wine, some cheese and crackers, then sit down to a nice dinner."

"I'd love that and could really use it. Thank you, Summer. See you soon."

CHAPTER 24

Derek

Our weekly staff meeting is about to start. I take a seat near the end of the table in the windowless conference room, staring down at the cherry wood like I'm hoping it'll reveal something profound. I'm early, forcing me to fight the urge to leave so I don't have to face them.

At least half my co-workers believe I killed Shana. The other half? I don't know. Maybe they don't give a shit or maybe they know the truth. I swallow hard and tug at the knot in my tie, which now feels too tight. It's not just the room that's airless — it's me, choking on my own thoughts.

I start to wonder why no one else is here yet. They always come in on time. Today, of course, there will be more whispers. More glances flicked in my direction, eyes darting away when I look back. I can feel it, the weight of suspicion pressing down on me. Shana's murder — a week ago today.

Rumors are running rampant, and I've heard my share. Faculty here live for gossip, and this . . . well, this is their feast. *"Derek must know something,"* they'll say. *"She was killed in his office."* Yeah? And who the hell had the nerve to leave that liver

127

in my desk, huh? Who did that? Someone who wants to point the finger in my direction, and I know exactly who that is.

I glance at the door. The room, still empty, still silent.

The door creaks, and I shift my eyes to it. It's James. He nods, but it's a stiff, forced movement, and he's avoiding my gaze. He clears his throat, and for a brief second, our eyes meet. Something flashes there — doubt, fear? I can't tell. I sit up straighter, trying to appear calm, trying to appear innocent.

More colleagues file in, nodding and murmuring greetings, all too careful to keep their distance. And then I see Alex. I'm convinced he must've had a thing for Shana and was jealous of how she looked at me and acted around me. The son of a bitch comes to my house, eats my food, drinks my wine.

I admit, seeing Riley that night at dinner . . . it was all I could do not to come out of my skin. Introducing herself as Summer Burton to my wife? Goddam it. Now this.

I let Evelyn think Alex was the one who left the note on my car. Though I've begun to suspect my wife understands more than she's saying, and what will come of that, I have no idea.

I want more than anything to point Langston in Riley Dittrich's direction. She has, of course, denied having any part in Shana's death, but I can't trust her. I can barely trust her to keep her mouth shut to Evie, so I've agreed to play her game — for now. And I refuse to rule out Alex Murphey. Not yet. He's the perfect distraction.

My world is on the verge of collapse, and what Riley knows will bring about its ruin. I need to find a way to get Langston to look harder at Alex. Just to take the heat off me long enough to fix my Riley problem. And if she did murder Shana, it will be the last person she'll ever hurt.

CHAPTER 25

Evelyn

Knocking on Summer's apartment door, holding a bottle of wine, I work to keep my hands from trembling. I wonder if I'm going about this the wrong way. For God's sake, two women are dead, and she could've had a hand in both. But I'm desperate for the truth about Derek and this baby.

Summer answers the door with a smile. "Hey, thanks for coming over."

It's too late. I'm here, and there's no turning back. "Thank you for hosting." I enter, offering the wine. Looking around, something seems different. Rearranged.

I glance at the bookshelf on the far wall, where I'd seen the electronic frame. But it's gone now. "What's different around here?" I ask casually as though making small talk.

"Well, it's clean, so that's probably the difference you're seeing," Summer says with a laugh. "Let me take your coat."

I hand it over, my eyes scanning the room. The changes are subtle, but it makes the space seem unfamiliar. It's as though Summer is erasing traces of herself and her past, doubling down on her new persona.

In the kitchen, candles flicker on the table beside a cheese-board and glasses. Summer pours the wine with a relaxed hand. "How was your drive over?"

"Fine, just fine." I take the glass and raise it to my lips, watching her over the rim. Does she seem tense? A forced cheerfulness in her smile, or am I imagining things?

"Good. I ate those delicious casseroles you made for me," she continues. "They were fantastic. You're a wonderful cook. Of course, I could see that when I was at your house for dinner last week."

"Thank you. It's kind of you to say." Now that I'm here, I don't know what to do or how to go about exposing what I know.

I take another long sip of wine, trying to steady my nerves. I must tread carefully here — confronting Summer could backfire. I don't want to die in this tiny apartment. "The casseroles were no trouble, really. It's nice to cook for someone who appreciates it," I reply. "Derek has gotten so used to my cooking over the years, I sometimes wonder if he even tastes it anymore." I give a little laugh, watching Summer's reaction, but she smiles in return.

"I'm sure he still enjoys your meals, even if he doesn't say so. It's easy to take the little things for granted after so long together." She takes a sip. "How's he doing, by the way? With what's going on at the university, I can't imagine what it must be like for him to go to work every day."

I nod, thinking she knows exactly what it's like, but I'm not supposed to know that. "Everyone's been on edge, he says. I don't blame them. What an awful thing."

"Have you heard whether the police have a suspect yet?"

I hesitate a moment, hearing a peculiar air in her tone. "No, I'm afraid not. Nothing yet, but it's only been a week. I'm sure the police are doing their best."

"I certainly hope so," she replies.

It's time to wade into trickier waters. "It's funny, when I got back from visiting my mom, Derek seemed . . . I don't

130

know. More attentive, I guess. He even got Ben ready for school this morning."

"Attentive? Really, well, that's nice," she replies.

Do I hear a hint of jealousy in her tone? Is this the road I take for answers — getting under her skin with talk of my wonderful and thoughtful husband? Well, that depends on how deep I burrow.

I grin, tight-lipped, pretending to consider her words. "Yes, it's nice to have his attention again. However, I have to say, I believe part of it is driven by what happened at his work. I think it's forced Derek to reevaluate his life and the life of our family. He sees how important family truly is in times like these." I take a slow sip of wine, letting the statement hang in the air between us, drenched with implication.

Summer's expression remains neutral, but there's a flicker in her eyes that tells me my words have hit their mark.

"Family is the most important thing." She refills our glasses.

The wine is going down quickly. I force a tight smile. "You'll understand one day when you're married."

That got her. A slight raise of her shoulders, a pinch of her lips. She wants to scratch the itch so badly I can see it in her eyes.

"There is one thing, though." I turn sheepish. "I didn't tell him I was coming here tonight."

"Oh?" She sips on her full glass. "What did you tell him? Where does he think you are right now?"

"I told him I was meeting with a partner at a small law firm in town. Thinking, once we get through all this, I might want to go back to work." I'm beginning to see how Derek got so good at lying. Once you start, it only gets easier. But I need her to know Derek has no idea we're together. Maybe she'll open up to me about Nicole, about everything.

We make small talk through the cheese platter, but tension simmers under the surface of our polite conversation. I wonder if she has it in her — to kill for someone she wants. First, Shana Foster, then who? Me? Yet I stay because I have to see this through. I need answers almost as much as she wants to take my husband from me.

Summer gathers the empty plates. "Why don't you relax on the sofa while I check on dinner?"

I move to the living room and sit on the edge of the couch. I'm getting close to something here. I just need to keep chipping away at her veneer. "Hmmm."

"What's that?" Summer calls out from the kitchen.

"Oh, nothing. But I could have sworn you had one of those picture frames on your bookshelf when I was here the other day. I remember thinking what a great idea it was to have one. I don't see it anymore."

Summer returns to the living room, holding full glasses of wine, and hands one to me. She's trying to get me drunk, and with my nerves on end, I don't turn down the liquid courage.

"Oh, you're not wrong. I do have one, but the cord got tangled up in my vacuum. Anyway, I think it's broken now, so I'll have to get another one," she replies.

Bolstered, I move on to my next steps. "May I use your bathroom?"

"Of course." She gestures down the hall with a casual wave. "First door on the left. You can't miss it."

I rise from the sofa, trying to keep my movements steady, feeling the effects of the wine. "Great. Thank you." As I head down the hallway, Summer disappears into the kitchen once more. Do I dare take this chance? Has she gone through the trouble of ridding herself of what I'd seen in her nightstand before? She got rid of the frame. She knows I've seen things I shouldn't have.

Amid the dizziness of the wine and the relentless pounding in my chest, I approach the bathroom door. Stealing a glance back to confirm Summer is still occupied, I continue past the bathroom to her bedroom. The door is closed but unlocked. My palms are clammy as I turn the handle and slip inside.

The room is neat like it was before. I move quickly to the nightstand and pull open the single drawer. There they are — the tiny clothes still folded inside.

"What the hell are you doing?"

Her sharp voice sounds behind me, and I let out a small gasp. I spin around to see her standing in the doorway with eyes raging. This is it — my only chance to confront her. Emily's words echo too loudly in my mind to ignore. "Why do you have baby clothes in here, Summer?"

She steps into the room, her posture rigid, a threatening grin on her lips. "How did you know to look there? It's like you already knew." She meanders closer to me. "How is that possible, Evelyn?"

I straighten my shoulders, meeting her gaze with steady resolve. "Answer the question."

Summer's eyes lock on to mine as if trying to see through me, trying to get to my motive, but I'm the one who deserves answers here. "If there's something you need to tell me, now would be a hell of a good time to do it."

She casts down her gaze, nodding. "I understand now."

"Excuse me?" I ask.

She perches on the edge of her bed, her hands pressing against her thighs. "I wasn't sure until you left to visit your mother." Summer shifts her gaze to me. "I knew then you suspected something."

I say nothing, waiting for her to continue.

"Making the casseroles. Wanting to have dinner together and keeping it from your husband," she adds. "I figured you knew and were trying to make a point about it to Derek. But he must've sold you on a different story."

My knees grow weak, but I fold my arms, determined not to let her see me waver. "Then why don't you tell me your story, Summer, or is it Riley? Who the hell are you, and what do you want with my husband?"

133

CHAPTER 26

Both of us hold our ground, neither wanting to give in. I'm overcome with a desire to scream at her, punch her, shake the life from her for doing this to me. Turning me into a person I don't recognize. Making me believe she was a friend when all she'd wanted was Derek.

The truth irritates the back of my mind. The truth that I'm responsible for my behavior, yet I refuse to let her off the hook.

"How did you find out?" Summer asks in a low, accusatory tone.

"Did you leave me that note?" I shoot back. "How did you know Nicole?"

Summer licks her lips as if the words are too difficult to speak. "She was my best friend."

"Were you sleeping with my husband, too, like your best friend?" My rapid-fire question lands squarely on her shoulders.

Her eyes soften. Her brow relaxes. But her subtle nod is a blow to my gut. No matter how often I've been told, heard, or overheard. Each time, the humiliation never weakens.

"What was the point of the notes, Summer? Why leave them for me to find?"

"It wasn't to scare you, if that's what you think. I assumed you'd tell him, and he would know what I know."

I raise my chin. "Which is what, exactly? Do you think Derek was responsible for Nicole's death?"

Summer's lips quiver as her eyes search mine. "I didn't expect to like you so much. Your son . . ."

"Don't. Don't you talk about my son like you know him." My jaw clenches, unable to bear her mention of Ben. "Just answer the question. Do you think Derek killed Nicole? Even after the police said it was an accident."

She scoffs, shaking her head.

"So you followed us here, making sure he would never be free of what happened." I squeeze my eyes shut. "Then Shana Foster."

"I did nothing to her. I didn't even know that woman!" Summer rises to her feet. "The police were wrong, Evelyn, and you deserve to know the truth. Come with me . . . please . . . I want to show you something."

I follow her into the living room, careful to hide my desperation for the truth. But I'm not afraid of her. I don't feel threatened. Not anymore. Maybe that's by design. Entering the room, I take a seat on the sofa.

Summer raises a finger. "I'll be right back."

A bottle of water sits on the coffee table. Still feeling the effects of the wine, I take a drink from it. I need to sober up — and fast. My gaze is drawn to Summer as she returns with a box in her hands. "What's in there?"

"Nicole's life. At least, what I have of it. Her parents took most of her belongings, of course, but these are things she and I shared throughout our three-year friendship." She takes a seat on the chair across from me and opens the box.

"So, when she arrived at Medford U," I begin. "That's when the two of you became friends."

"That's right."

"But she knew you under the name Riley Dittrich," I say."

Summer takes out several photo frames with pictures of Nicole and her at various locations. Swim meets. Bars. School grounds. She lays them out on the coffee table for me to see.

I study them. Moments of happier times. "Why don't you tell me about your relationship with my husband, and how you came to believe he was responsible for Nicole's death?"

My desire to hear her out surprises me. I'd come here with the sole intention of learning whether Derek fathered her child, a child I assume must exist in some context. Instead, I find myself feeling sorry for her. Is that her intention? Gaining my sympathy? Will she use it against me? Maybe I've become so numb to my husband's transgressions that I've begun to feel guilty for the women involved. As though my husband's actions are my responsibility. But I want to hear her out. I need to for my own sake.

"Derek was an instructor in Nicole's English Lit class at the end of her sophomore year," Summer begins. "She and I had grown closer after she'd been placed on the varsity swim team that spring." The corners of her lips rise in a rueful smile. "I swam competitively in college, which was why she and I clicked, I think. I helped out the coach on occasion, and that was how we initially met. Nicole started seeing Derek toward the end of that year. She told me about him, and I warned her because I'd heard things."

"I'm sure you had," I reply.

"Anyway, once fall semester started, Nicole continued to see him." Summer pauses, glancing at the photos spread across the table. "Derek could be possessive and controlling. He didn't like Nicole spending time with anyone but him. They started fighting more, and Nicole would show up to swim practice with bruises she couldn't explain. She swore it wasn't Derek hurting her, but I had my doubts."

"What?" I feel the wind get knocked from my lungs. "He hit her?"

She shrugs. "According to Nicole . . . no. She introduced me to him at a party. I don't know why he was there, but he was. We had a connection, an attraction, and started seeing each other behind Nicole's back. Maybe I'd wanted to see for myself who he was, if he had hurt her."

So she goes after a man who's seeing her friend. Why? "Did he hurt you?" I press.

"No." Her gaze turns to me, eyes watery. "I thought I was in love with him, and then she wound up dead."

"And you think he did it," I add. "Even though everyone said it was an accident."

She shoots me a look, wiping her tears with the back of her hand. "You can't possibly believe that. Nicole was the best swimmer I'd ever met. She was excited about her meet the next day. No, it wasn't an accident. Not a chance."

I'm torn, unsure of who to believe at this moment. Derek has lied so many times, even keeping Summer's true identity from me. "I have to know. Did you come here to bring all of this out again? To destroy Derek's career and our marriage?"

"I just wanted to know why he did it." She holds my gaze. "But please believe me when I say that I have no idea what happened to that professor at his school. I–I didn't know her, Evelyn. I had no reason to hurt her, nor would I."

That's the only part I believe. She had no motive to harm Shana Foster. But this leaves me to draw the conclusion I fear the most. That Derek killed her for reasons I can't possibly understand.

Confusion swirls in my mind. And then I know I must ask the question that brought me here tonight. Maybe the only question that matters. "Do you have a child with my husband?"

Summer straightens her shoulders and clears her throat. "When you asked me to babysit for Ben, and Derek came home, we — had words."

"Did my son hear you?" I ask, heat rising under my collar.

"No." Summer holds up her hands. "I swear it. Ben was watching cartoons. He didn't hear us. I told Derek he needed to come clean with you and the police. I know he held Nicole underwater until she stopped breathing and that our affair might have been the reason. Despite the coroner's report, he did it, Evelyn. I'm sorry to be the one to tell you."

The wine is making me nauseous. My defenses rise. "How do you know this for certain? Did you see him do it? Were you there?"

"Because, that day, I'd told Nicole I'd been sleeping with Derek." A flicker of anger sparks in her eyes. "That night . . . the night she drowned, she'd been training for her swim meet, so I went to the pool to see how she was doing because it had gotten so late, and I'd expected to hear from her. That's when I saw Derek's car in the parking lot. I was pissed, thinking he was continuing to see her, and so I just sat there." She hesitates a moment. "Anyway, when he came out, he didn't see me. I was going to confront him . . . tell him that he couldn't have us both. But I didn't. I watched him leave."

"And then what?" I demand.

Tears stream down her cheeks now. "I waited a few minutes after he left, trying to calm myself down. Then I walked inside, and I called out to Nicole. I didn't see her. At least, not at first."

"You found her?" I ask.

"No. Someone who worked in Maintenance did. He'd dragged her out of the pool and had taken her over by the far side. That's why it took me a minute. I ran over to her and the guy yelled at me to get help. I guess he'd just gotten there, I don't know exactly. But I called 911."

It made sense now . . . why Derek was questioned by the police. How they'd learned about his affair. Summer must've told them and said she believed he'd killed her.

"And this child?" I press. "Summer, I have to know . . . why do you have those baby clothes in your bedroom? Do you have a child and is Derek the father?"

Her face is masked in guilt, grief, and anger. I'm desperate for her to tell me the truth, but I'm terrified to hear it. And something in her eyes tells me she can't speak that truth. "Please . . ."

"I can't, Evelyn . . ." She trails off and then begins to tremble.

The answer is plain to see. When I arrived here tonight, I'd been fully prepared to confront this woman, Riley Dittrich. I'd been ready to hear her lies, but instead, what I've heard could be the truth. I wouldn't put it past my husband to have used both of those women to his advantage. Even going so far as to pit them against one another in order to use it to discredit them, should the need arise. Derek Moore is a master manipulator. I've known that for years and yet I've ignored it for so long, simply to keep my standing. To keep the facade of a happy marriage front and center.

That facade was destroyed when Nicole died. And now I'm left to ponder a very real scenario — that my husband is a killer after all. And maybe Nicole isn't the only one.

CHAPTER 27

Derek

As I stare at the text message on my phone, I know the truth has come out. Well, Riley's version of the truth, whatever that entails. Evie is with Riley right now. Only moments ago, I received this text from her, telling me exactly what she and my wife are doing.

Now I'm certain Evie's trip away wasn't to see her mother after all. She suspected I knew Riley after dinner that night and went in search of the truth herself. How long before Evie goes to the cops? She'll be certain I had a hand in Shana's death too. If my wife turns against me, the cops will as well.

I trace a restless path across the living room, my phone gripped in one hand. The faint sound of Ben's laughter floats downstairs. The innocence in it breaks my heart. He deserves none of this.

I fear what's being said right now — what Riley is saying to my wife. Little doubt remains that Riley left the notes. No one else knew I'd come here to Beaufort, yet somehow, she found me. It had taken every fiber of my being not to throw the woman from my home when she showed up at dinner. I had no idea she'd pretended to be someone else and befriended my wife.

This is how she intends to ruin me and blow up my marriage right along with it. Could she have murdered Shana? Jesus. If that's the case . . .

A knock sounds on the door, pulling me from my thoughts. I walk to the foyer and open it. "Josie, thanks for coming on such short notice. You're sure this is okay?"

She smiles at me as though she's an ally. "Of course. Stuart is watching television, and we had no plans." She regards me with concern. "Hey, are you all right? Is Evelyn?"

I swat away her worries. "Yeah, of course. She's having dinner with a friend, and I'd completely forgotten something at the office, so I need to head in. It's late, and I don't want to take Ben with me. I'll only be an hour or so."

Josie walks inside, closing the door behind her. "Take your time. We'll be fine. Don't worry."

With a tight nod, I grab my keys and call out to Ben. "Ben, Josie's here. I'll be back soon. You listen to her, okay?"

A distant "okay" drifts down from the second floor.

I bolt out the door and jump into my car. The drive to the school is a blur of headlights and fragmented memories of my affair with Riley. I'd known she and Nicole were friends, and my hubris got the better of me. I'd crossed a line with little regard for the consequences of my actions.

The school is just ahead, and I park near my building. The place should be empty. I swipe my keycard and the door clicks open. My shoes clack on the tile floor. It's cold and dark inside. The heat must be turned down for the night. But I continue on, arriving at Alex's office and flicking on the lights.

I have to find any connection he had to Shana, find evidence, plant it, whatever it takes. There's still hope I can sway Langston unless, of course, he already knows about Nicole. Then he'll be laser-focused on me.

But for God's sake, if I'd killed Shana, would I have left her inside my own damn office? What kind of idiot would do that? Not only do I have to contend with Riley Dittrich, but I also have to prove I didn't murder Shana Foster.

I move quietly through Alex's office. The mousey little man keeps everything meticulously organized, but there must be clues here somewhere. I start rifling through the drawers of his desk, finding stacks of graded papers, office supplies, a half-eaten granola bar. Nothing unusual, but I'm careful to return everything to its place.

I turn my attention to the bookshelf behind his desk. Rows of thick textbooks with titles like *Forensic Psychology* and *Inside the Criminal Mind* fill the shelves. Interesting choices for an English professor. Might that be enough for the good detective? Probably not.

A framed photo on his credenza catches my eye. It's a picture of Alex and Shana, their arms wrapped around each other, smiling happily. When the hell was this taken? I retrieve my phone and capture the image. "What else did you know about her, Alex? Or about me, for that matter."

Detective Langston insisted he'd get to the bottom of who-ever put that liver in my desk drawer. The memory of finding it there still makes my skin crawl, its slick surface glistening under the fluorescent lights. Tests confirmed it came from a pig. It had to have been Alex. Probably has a friend in the Bio department.

Now, I need to leave breadcrumbs for Langston to find. I just need time to take care of Riley. If Alex is innocent, then he'll be found innocent. If Riley killed her, then I will have already solved that problem. After all, Summer Burton doesn't exist.

I reach into my coat pocket and retrieve the earring — a single gold hoop that belonged to Shana. Stepping toward the front of his office, I search for the best place to leave it. A place Alex might not see, but a detective sweeping it would. "Ah, right here."

I bend down, wedging the earring between the rug fibers and the left leg of his desk. It may not be much, but it'll be enough to buy me some time. I hope.

I flick off the lights and close his door, heading straight to my office. Inside, I still feel her presence. I can almost hear her screams.

Shaking off the unsettling feeling, I sit at my desk and open my laptop, knowing what I must do next. It's the first step in ridding myself of the nightmare that is Riley Dittrich.

My fingers hover over the keyboard, and I begin typing an email addressed to Mrs. Babcock, the woman who runs Ben's preschool. With the ease of so many other lies, I fabricate a story about how Summer Burton hit Ben, threatening him that if he told anyone, she'd hurt him again. And without another thought, I hit send. Surely, it'll be enough to get her fired. What happens after that, I can't say, but it's a start.

I turn off the lights and return to the corridor, checking around me to ensure I'm alone. I need to leave now, making sure I beat Evelyn home. God knows what she'll do if I'm not there. Take my son? Leave me for good?

Getting into my car, I speed toward the house. My thoughts are consumed by Alex and Shana. Riley and Nicole. My mind's eye conjures an image of me, standing on the edge of that pool. All my sins staring at me from below the surface, taunting me, telling me to jump in.

The drive goes by quickly, almost unnoticed, and I arrive home. Parking on the driveway, I hope I have enough time to get rid of my nosy neighbor.

Inside, the television is on, but no Josie. I close the door behind me. The lights are on upstairs. Ben must still be awake. "Son of a bitch."

Dropping my keys on the foyer table, I head toward the staircase. I see light spilling into the downstairs hallway. It's coming from my office. My pulse rises as I march on, wondering what the hell I'm about to find. This is the last thing I need right now. Arriving at my office, I see her at my desk. "Josie?" Her wide eyes freeze on me, caught mid-motion like she's been cornered. "What are you doing in here?"

The papers on my desk have been moved. The top drawer of my filing cabinet is open.

"I, uh, I was trying to find a stapler." She bursts out in nervous laughter. "And then I got carried away trying to organize your papers. I'm so sorry, Derek." Josie walks out from behind my desk. "Forgive me, I have OCD, and I couldn't help but try to straighten up."

It's all I can do to keep my hands off her throat. Squeezing her plump little neck until her head bursts. "I appreciate your efforts, Josie, but this is my office. You shouldn't be in here."

"You are absolutely right." She raises her hands. "Again, I'm so sorry."

She brushes past me, and I call out. "Did you find the stapler?"

"What's that?" Josie turns back wearing an awkward grin.

"You said you were looking for the stapler. Did you find it?"

"Oh, yeah. By the way, Ben's upstairs. I did let him stay up a little longer than usual. I hope you don't mind. I, uh, I should get going."

"Let me walk you out." I trail her closely, my eyes boring into the back of her head. Evelyn has mentioned how Josie's curiosity is more than a little disturbing. As we reach the front door, she grabs the handle, but I hold it closed.

She whips around to look at me.

I loom over her, ensuring she knows who I am and what I could do to her if I wanted. "Thank you for bailing me out tonight, last minute and everything."

"Don't mention it, Derek. Really. It's fine." She stares at my hand. "I should get going."

I keep it there just a moment longer to make my point, then remove it and open the door for her. "I trust this will stay between the two of us, should Evelyn ask. I'd hate for her to think I was at the office instead of looking after our son. And of course, I wouldn't want to tell her about your . . . OCD."

Josie raises her lips into a forced smile. "As far as I'm concerned, I was never here."

CHAPTER 28

Evelyn

The number of times I've been lied to is so high, I've lost count. And while Summer's confession weighs on me, I have to know I'm not being used, as I have been so many times before. I absorb all she's told me as we sit in silence, the wine finally beginning to wear off.

"But you didn't see him physically drown her?" I ask, breaking that silence.

"No, I didn't see him do it," she replies. "Evelyn, please believe me—"

"I don't know what to believe right now, Summer, or Riley, or whatever your name is." I lean over, resting my elbows on my knees. "Look, I know who Derek is, the things he's capable of doing, but this?" I shake my head. "Even the police believed her death was most likely an accident. So, why are you here? What did you hope to gain by coming to Beaufort? Do you want him back, is that it?"

Summer's eyes flash with anger at my accusation. "You think I want that monster back in my life after what he did? I came here to warn you, to try to save you from him before it's too late."

"Forgive me, but warning me isn't reason enough for you to pick up your life and move here." I regard her carefully. "Please don't lie to me, Summer."

She straightens her back, composing herself before continuing. "I need you to understand that Derek is dangerous, Evelyn. Nicole discovered that too late. I know you think you're special, that he would never hurt you or Ben. But one day he will turn on you, too."

I bristle at her words. "You know nothing about my marriage. You're just another in a long line of girls he's screwed because you let him." I close my eyes, instantly regretting my words. "Summer . . ."

"No, you're right. I'm just another in a string of affairs Derek's had. But the difference is, I've seen who he truly is. I know who he is, and Nicole, well, she must've made him feel threatened. Like she would say something to you or whatever."

I sit back again, tilting my head. "Derek told the police he was there at the pool with Nicole. The coroner ruled her death an accident. Why should I believe you? You've deceived me just as Derek has." I consider Summer's words carefully, weighing her accusations against my own experiences with Derek. She's right that I've willfully turned a blind eye before, convincing myself he would never betray or endanger me. I think of all the late nights he'd spent at the office, the vague references to past friendships, the defensiveness I've glimpsed when he feels threatened.

Summer's lower lip trembles, her eyes glistening. "You're right. I have deceived you. And I'm so sorry for that. But everything I've told you about Derek is the truth. You have no reason to believe me over him." She grasps my hands in hers. "All I'm asking is that you be careful, Evelyn. Don't let your guard down, not for a second. Derek is ruthless and capable of anything when he feels like he might lose everything."

I stare into her pleading eyes. Doubt still gnaws at me, but something in my gut tells me she's being genuine. "I'll need proof — something concrete I can take to the police. Short of a confession from Derek, I don't know what would convince them to reopen the investigation into Nicole's death."

"I don't have anything concrete," Summer admits. "Just my word against his."

Her voice breaks and she looks away, blinking back tears. At that moment, I feel my skepticism start to waver. As much as it pains me, I have to consider that Summer may be right about my husband. I check the time. "I need to get home."

Summer looks up at me as I get to my feet. "What are you going to do?"

"Take care of my son, first. Then . . ." I sigh. "I'll figure out something. Until then, you have to keep things as they are. Don't go to him. Don't pressure him. Leave it to me because, if you don't, then I'll assume you're the liar." I grab my purse and turn back to her as she walks me to the door. "And if you're lying to me, Derek will be the last person on this earth you'll need to fear."

My head is clear now. Maybe for the first time in years. I leave Summer, letting her believe that I'm on her side, but the only side I'm on is my own. When I get home, I'll say nothing to Derek. Not until I get some facts straight for myself. Because the one thing that I'd asked Summer, she didn't outright answer. And it might be the reason she's here, despite her supposed fear for my safety. The baby. Whoever's baby it is, a baby is in this picture, and I need to know more.

Who is looking after her? Family, friends? My mind boggles at the notion Summer refused to reveal the truth to me. What does she hope to gain by leaving me to wonder whether Derek has fathered this child? It's the one thing that could set me on a completely different path than the one I intend to take now.

I drive home, irrational thoughts swimming in my head. Thoughts that could put me in prison. Could Derek really have killed Nicole? What about Shana? The bodies seem to be piling up. Could he be capable of hurting me or Ben? I think back over our years together, searching for any sign, any hint of darkness lurking beneath his charming exterior.

But my thoughts keep circling back to the baby. Summer's baby. She hadn't denied it when I asked if it was Derek's, so I'm left to assume he is the father. Is that why she's here, out of some deluded fantasy they could be a family? I feel sick at the thought.

As I pull into the driveway, my headlights shine on Josie. She's standing outside, waving at me. "What the hell?"

It's 10:30 at night, what is she doing? I step out. She's walking toward me, her finger to her lips as if insisting I keep quiet.

"Thank God, you're back," she says.

"Josie, what's . . ."

She rests her hand on my shoulder. "Something's going on that I think you need to know."

Oh my God, does she know about Derek too? "What are you talking about?"

"Shhh . . . lower your voice." Her gaze drifts toward our front window where a light still burns inside. "Over here." She pulls me toward the side of the house, closer to hers.

"What is going on, Josie?" I demand.

"Look, I know I can be meddlesome."

I want to say something, but I feel like insulting her might make her stop whatever it is she's about to tell me.

"And I know we aren't that close yet, but I need to tell you something." She darts her gaze around as though someone might be listening.

"Josie, please . . . what is it?" My front door opens, and Derek is standing on the other side. I turn back to face Josie, but she's frozen, staring right at my husband. And then her face changes. She swallows hard, and a small grin appears.

"I, uh, I just wanted to let you know that I'd heard the Parkers were robbed last night. Someone broke into their house while they were out at dinner."

"Oh my God."

"I know, so I thought I'd warn you to make sure you lock your doors, okay?" She glances again at Derek.

"Of course. We do anyway, but I'll double-check to make sure we're all safe and sound. I appreciate the warning, Josie. You should go back inside. You're shivering."

"Yes, I will. Good night, Evelyn."

"Good night." I turn around and head toward the house. Derek's lips are pressed tightly, and all I can do is shrug at him. "She said the Parkers were robbed and that we should lock our doors."

He steps aside while I enter. "All right then." He closes it, makes a point to secure the deadbolt, and turns to me. "How was your meeting? Do you think they'd be interested in hiring you at some point down the road?"

"I think so. The meeting went well," I reply, hanging up my coat.

"Great. Glad to hear it. All quiet here. Nothing to report."

"Is Ben asleep?"

"Of course."

"Then I'll go upstairs and check in on him. After that, I might just crash. You don't mind, do you? I had a glass of wine, and I'm a little tired because of it."

"No, I don't mind at all." He kisses my forehead. "You go on up to bed. I'll be up soon."

I walk upstairs, certain Derek wants to say more but has decided against it. Arriving at Ben's room, I take a peek inside. The sight of him sends worry coursing through me. I don't know who to trust or who to believe. I'm afraid this will come back on Ben in some way, and I can't let that happen. So, for now, I'll do what I need to do to figure out who's the liar — Summer or my husband.

CHAPTER 29

When Derek leaves for work, I drop off Ben at school, side-stepping any chance I might run into Summer. I don't want to see or hear anything more from her until I'm certain of the truth. Right now, the truth is some distant object.

Home once again, I open my laptop as I'm sitting in the kitchen nook. And then, I reach for my phone. The line rings. "Chuck, it's Evelyn."

"Well, hello, stranger," he replies. "Another call from the beautiful Miss Evie?"

I snicker, though it's only out of courtesy. "I wish I didn't need to bother you again, Chuck, but I could use your help."

"Listen, you know I'm always here for you. Tell me what you need. I'll see what I can do."

"Birth records, to start."

"Whose?" he presses.

"Mother's name is Riley Dittrich. Father unknown."

"And the baby's name?"

"I don't have that either, unfortunately. And I have to be honest with you, Chuck, I can't even be sure a baby exists."

"What's that now?" he asks.

I shake my head. "I know, but I have to figure out something and I don't know where else to start."

"Let me take a guess here, this involves your husband, doesn't it?"

"How'd you know?" My marital problems started long before I left the firm. "I need to be sure Derek isn't the father of a baby I believe exists. Can you find birth records with the name of the mother?"

"Christ on a cracker, Evie, that information is usually reserved for family members. I'll have to pull some major strings, and I still can't guarantee you anything." He hesitates. "You sure this is something you want to know?"

"No, but I don't see another way around it," I reply. "How long do you think this will take?"

"Not long. I'll do my best to have something for you by tomorrow. Soon enough?"

I nod as though we're in the same room. "Yeah, thanks, Chuck. Once again . . . I owe you."

"I'm gonna start a tab for you, how's that?" He laughs. "Talk to you soon, kid."

The line clicks and he's gone.

I gaze through the breakfast window again, clutching my coffee mug, watching Josie stroll down the street toward her mailbox. The late morning sun is still shrouded behind gray clouds, and Josie's purposeful gait — slow, deliberate — makes my skin prickle. Especially after last night. What the hell was that even about?

Something about Josie doesn't sit right with me. Sure, she volunteers to watch Ben on a moment's notice, but is there more to it? A reason for her supposed snooping? And there's an undercurrent to her kindness, something that leaves me feeling watched. Studied.

And now, Josie opens her mailbox. A normal enough task, but my instincts tell me it isn't about the mail. Not with Josie. She's checking to see that I'm home — a perfect view of my front window from her mailbox.

My eyes narrow as Josie reaches inside it and pulls out a small stack of letters. She rifles through them casually, like she has no place else to be, but I see her glances this way. And I know better now. Josie isn't just checking the mail. She's checking *everything*.

I stand and pace the kitchen, trying to shake off the creeping suspicion settling into my bones. Maybe I'm overthinking it, and given all that's happened, could anyone blame me? But Josie seems far too interested in our lives. Especially Derek's. I wonder if this has to do with Shana Foster. Does she think Derek murdered the woman? Then again, this started long before Shana's death. This started the moment we moved in.

There's always that one neighbor who has nothing better to do than pry into other people's lives. Maybe she's bored. Her kids are grown. I have no idea what her husband does for a living. I rarely see him. But if she gets too close, she'll discover what happened in Medford. And it won't take long for her to put two and two together.

I recall our first conversation, Josie questioning Derek's late nights in his den. Her eyes had lingered on me a little too long, like she was waiting for my reaction. The question had felt like a hook, baited and waiting for me to snatch it.

Ever since then, I can't shake the feeling that Josie is fishing for something. And now, watching her outside, walking back up the driveway with her stack of mail, my nerves buzz with suspicion. What *does* she know? About me, about Derek. Maybe even something about Shana or Nicole?

I lean over the counter, watching through the window again. Josie's pausing now, staring down at her phone, her fingers tapping across the screen. Is she texting someone? "What is it about you, Josie? Why do you care about us at all?"

* * *

I've become somewhat of an expert tracker in the years Derek and I have been married. He wasn't a cheater at first, though

152

he flirted more than I'd liked. It was his personality, and I had to accept it. And I did, until he began to take it too far.

So, I learned. I watched. I picked up on his tells — signs that he was lying. After a while, years, in fact, I'd stopped looking, knowing it wasn't going to change anything. I kept up our facade, our perfect image. And so it stayed there, the perfect oil painting of our family, hanging over a fireplace for all to see. Until Nicole died. I hadn't known about his affair with her, specifically. Nor had I known about Riley Dittrich, the woman I have come to know as Summer Burton.

I didn't dispute his claim of innocence because I'd never known Derek to be a violent man. A man who rose to anger quickly. So I came to his defense without question, though his whereabouts that night had concerned me. And when the death was eventually ruled accidental, I was confident all of this was over. Even having to move here, I still believed we were past all of it. I don't believe that anymore. Our past has followed us.

But the question remains, do I believe Riley Dittrich? She'd presented a compelling argument for Derek's guilt. Do I take it at face value, ignoring what I know about my husband? I don't think so. While I await Chuck's call about a possible baby in the picture, I must come to my own conclusion about Derek's guilt or innocence in Nicole's death and maybe even Shana's.

For now, I focus on the certainty. Nicole Peterson is dead — they say by accident. If there's more to know, then perhaps her family can help. I haven't seen or spoken to them since it all happened. Did Nicole confide in a family member that she feared Derek, or feared he might end things with her? Did they even know about her affair?

If I'm to move forward — to believe Summer's accusations — I must go to the source, or since the source is dead, her family. The hardest part will be to do this without Derek's knowledge. A phone call? Maybe. Assuming any one of them would speak to me. I can't make another trip. It would draw too much suspicion.

I head into his office. He takes his laptop to work, so I must find another way to retrieve the contact information for Nicole's family. Do I risk a call to the Beaufort detective? Would he ask why I needed to speak to the family? Probably. But I see no other way, and I can't worry about whether the detective might raise a brow because if Derek did kill that girl, I don't give a shit if the cops find out. In fact, I'll be the one to tell them.

Taking a seat at his desk, I open his side drawer. Inside, I find the police statements we'd made. They're the only things I kept of the investigation, hoping none of this would come back to haunt him. Though, I didn't think I would be the one doing the haunting.

Thumbing through the papers, I come across the name of the detective and make the call. "Hello, I'd like to speak to Detective Bartz, please. This is Evelyn Moore."

"One moment, please."

I wait on the line until I hear a click, then another ring. A deep, gravelly voice answers. "This is Detective Bartz."

"Yes, Detective, I don't know if you remember me—"

"Mrs. Moore. Yes, ma'am. I most certainly remember. What can I do for you?"

My throat tightens as the implications of what I'm about to ask settle around me. "I'd like to reach out to Nicole Peterson's mother, if possible."

The line goes quiet, like he's thinking 'What the hell is she doing asking such a question?'

"I'm not sure that's such a good idea, Mrs. Moore," he replies. "May I ask why you'd want to do that?"

The only thing I can think of is . . . "To offer an apology for what happened to her daughter. To tell her how sorry I am about all of it." I close my eyes, praying he can't hear the uncertainty in my voice. "It's just for closure, Detective. I'm sure you can understand that."

"Seems to me, it's Mrs. Peterson who would want closure, ma'am. Not you."

I'm losing my nerve. "You're right. I guess you can call it guilt over the affair my husband had with her daughter. I know it wasn't my fault, but I feel responsible, and I want to try to make amends. Can you help me with that?"

The line is quiet again and I wait.

"All right. I can give you her phone number since she's listed anyway. Doesn't mean she'll talk to you, and if she doesn't, don't try again, you understand? I don't need to reopen this wound with that family, and if you harass them—"

"That's not my intention at all, Detective," I cut in. I wait for a moment, hearing various papers being shifted around. Then he returns. "You got a pen?"

"Yes, sir. Go ahead." I jot down the number. "Thank you, I hear you, and if I don't get a response, I promise I'll back off."

"You be sure to do that, Mrs. Moore. And, uh, if you feel like you need to talk to me, I'm here."

I pick up on his meaning, and it turns out he's more perceptive than I thought. "Thank you, sir. Goodbye."

I enter the number on my phone, staring at the screen, the contact information for Nicole's mother staring back at me. My thumb hovers over the "call" button, and my stomach twists in knots.

But I can't allow myself to believe Summer's accusations without conducting my own research. Derek had been there that night at the pool. Summer saw him, so she says. If Nicole's mother suspected a problem between her daughter and my husband, I need to know.

Taking a deep breath, I press the call button. The phone rings, each tone sending a wave of anxiety up my spine. After the fourth ring, the line answers.

"Hello?" Her tone is soft, weary — older than I expect, and there's a heaviness in her voice that makes my heart ache.

"Mrs. Peterson, it's Evelyn Moore. Professor Derek Moore's wife." My voice comes out strange, almost foreign to my ears.

After a long pause, she replies. "Mrs. Moore. I didn't expect to hear from you."

"I'm sorry to call you like this, out of the blue," I reply. "But I . . . I need to talk to you about Nicole. About her . . . her . . ."

"Accident?" Mrs. Peterson replies, but then goes silent for a long moment. I can hear the faint sound of a clock ticking in the background. The soft drone of a television. "What is there to talk about? Nicole's gone. What good does dredging all of that up do now?"

I swallow hard, knowing what I'm about to say can't be unsaid. "I'm not entirely sure what happened was an accident, Mrs. Peterson."

The words hang in the air, and I hold my breath, waiting for her reaction. For a moment, I think she might hang up. Instead, I hear a soft, bitter chuckle.

"Finally come round to that conclusion, did you, Mrs. Moore?"

My heart drops into my stomach. "What do you mean?"

"I knew from the moment they told me she was dead that my girl didn't die from holding her breath too long. Not when Professor Derek Moore was there. Not after everything that had happened between them."

"You knew about the—"

"Affair? Of course I did. She was my daughter. Nicole called me the night before she died. She was upset. She said she was going to confront Derek. Tell him she would come clean to you about everything — about the affair, about the lies. She was tired of the secrecy, tired of him stringing her along. She said she was going to put an end to it. Course, I begged her to leave it, at least until after the big meet, but that's not who Nicole was."

My eyes sting as I listen.

"And then, the next morning, I got the call from the police that she had drowned. It didn't make sense. My daughter was a strong swimmer — she wouldn't have just drowned like that. And she sure as hell knew her limitations, talking about all this hypoxic blackout nonsense. Not unless . . . not unless someone made sure she drowned."

156

My breaths come in shallow bursts. I'd suspected it from the very beginning, of course. Then, Summer's accusations. But hearing Mrs. Peterson confirm my worst fear made everything real, and it all aligned with what Summer told me.

A long silence persists, and it's heavy with resolve. Finally, Mrs. Peterson continues. "You do what Nicole couldn't, Mrs. Moore. You make sure everyone knows what he did. He doesn't get to walk away from this."

CHAPTER 30

Avoiding Summer has been the hardest part of today. Picking up Ben from school, avoiding her yet again. But I need time to think. To process all that's happened, all that I've learned. Especially from Nicole's mother. I had no idea she felt that way. So now two people think my husband killed Nicole. Do I dare reach out to Detective Langston to find out whether he intends to arrest my husband for murdering Shana Foster?

It's all I can do to stand here in my kitchen, preparing dinner like any other day, when all I want to do is scoop up my son and run as far away from here as I can. I don't know what I'll say to Derek when he gets home. Pretend everything's fine? Maybe. At least until I hear back from Chuck. Then, I'll know what to do — I think.

Headlights shine through the breakfast window. He's home. My shoulders tense, and my back stiffens. I stare at the sizzling beef as it cooks in the pan. *Stay calm. Don't let him see you're afraid.* And for the first time, I am afraid of him — my own husband.

The rumble of the garage door sends my pulse racing. The car's engine echoes as he drives inside. Now, his footsteps sound on the concrete as he nears the back entrance. Finally, a turn of the handle and a click of the latch — the door opens, and he walks inside.

My eyes stay fixed on the stove when I hear his voice.

"Hey, hon. Something smells good. What are you making?" He approaches me, his hand slipping around my waist.

"Oh, hi," I reply awkwardly. If I can't pull it together, he'll know something's wrong. "Tacos. Keeping it simple tonight if that's okay."

"Of course."

He's staring at me as though attempting to read my thoughts. "Why don't you go ahead and get changed? Dinner will be ready in a few minutes."

"All right then." He loosens his tie and gazes out toward the living room. "Where's Ben?"

"Watching cartoons."

"I'll go say hi to him and then get changed."

He walks away, calling out Ben's name. I close my eyes, and my shoulders drop. If I can't get through tonight, Derek will realize I know everything — if he doesn't already. Could Summer have told him about our dinner? Maybe the two of us are simply dancing around a truth that could destroy us both. But I can't afford for Derek to think I might go to the police. My son's safety depends on me pulling this off.

After dinner, I volunteer to give Ben his bath. I'm grateful not to be around Derek. So much has happened that I struggle to wrap my head around it all. Derek has never been the kind of man I thought I'd fear. Never raised a hand to me or Ben. Hardly ever raised his voice. So what could've happened to make him kill Nicole, and how could he have made it look like an accident? Surely, she would've fought back. Scratches or marks on her arms. Bruises. But no, none of that was noted on the autopsy.

And if he'd killed Shana too? My God. The brutality of her murder. I can't imagine he had it in him to do that. Yet now, everything I thought I knew about him has been cast in doubt.

159

"All dry," I say to Ben, rustling his hair with the towel. "Let's get you into some pjs huh?"

"Okay."

As I help him dress, it occurs to me. What if Nicole had been pregnant? Could I have gotten this all wrong? Could the clothes I found in Summer's bedroom have belonged to a child Nicole would've had — had she lived? Emily couldn't be sure of a pregnancy.

That would be reason enough for anyone to want revenge, especially her closest friend. But why would Summer keep that from me? It would be virtually all the proof I needed to convince me of what Derek was capable of doing.

"Hey."

I spin around, startled. Derek stands in the doorway. "Oh, hey." I look back at Ben, pulling the shirt over his head. "There you go, kiddo. All dressed and ready for bed."

"Can I talk to you a minute?" Derek asks.

"Uh, yeah, sure." I look at Ben again. "Why don't you brush your teeth, and Daddy and I will come back and tuck you in, okay?"

"Okay, Mommy."

I raise my index finger. "And remember . . ."

"Sing the Happy Birthday song twice before I stop," he replies.

I grin at him. "That's right." I walk out into the hall, folding my arms as though I'm cold. "What's going on?"

He nods toward our bedroom. "Can we talk in there?"

"Sure." For a moment, my feet refuse to move. I'm frozen with fear. Does he know what I've been up to? I follow him to our room, and he closes the door. "Is everything okay?"

Derek walks to our bedroom window, pulling back the curtain to peek out. "Something is going on with Josie."

Oh, thank God. This isn't about me or Summer. It's about our neighbor, who I already suspect is trying to dig into our past. "What do you mean?"

160

He drops the curtain and turns back to me. "I think she's looking to stir up the other neighbors about what happened at work. Maybe even what happened in Medford."

"She doesn't know anything, Derek. And Shana's death is still under investigation," I say, hoping to convince him I haven't been digging on my own.

"Maybe she does." Derek walks toward me, taking me by my shoulders. "Look, did she say anything to you last night? When you got home, and she practically cornered you?"

I glance at his hands on my shoulders. One wrong word, and he could easily hurt me. I don't want to reveal too much of what I know, but I need to give him something to appease his suspicion about Josie.

"Uh, no. Just about the Parkers and their break-in."

Derek's jaw tightens, and he releases me from his grip. "Right, yeah, okay." He leans in, lowering his voice. "We need to be careful around her, Evie. She's up to something. Fishing for information, and there's no telling what she'll do if she finds anything."

161

CHAPTER 31

The few hours I have to myself, I must put to good use. Chuck should be calling me back today, which will determine my next course of action. I don't know how long I can pretend with Derek. It seems we're already chasing each other's tails, careful not to let the other see.

Outside, I notice Josie returning from her morning walk and wonder whose side she's on. Mine or Derek's. What happened last night was unusual, even for her. And Derek seemed much too interested in what she had to say. So I'll be the one to take the initiative. I'll pay her a visit. Get inside her house. Talk to her. Find out, once and for all, if she's a threat.

Grabbing my keys, I step outside, locking the door behind me. The sun shines brightly this morning, but the air is chilly. The serene neighborhood almost makes me forget what's weighed me down for so long. I'd hoped things would be better here, but I'm not sure they'll ever be better so long as I stay with Derek.

I walk down my driveway and over the sidewalk toward Josie and Stuart's house. He's at work. She stays home. That seems to be the way most of the people around here live — the privileged. I scoff as if I'm not one of them. I may have worked

162

before, but I don't anymore. A decision I'm coming to regret in light of my growing desire to leave my marriage.

I shake off my mood and force a smile as I reach Josie's front door. But before I even get a chance to knock, I hear the deadbolt turn and the door open. "Good morning."

Josie gives me a once-over as if I'm a stranger. "Evelyn. I'm surprised to see you here. Is everything okay?"

"Yeah, of course. I thought I'd stop over to see if you wanted to sit down for a coffee. You could tell me more about that burglary." I thumb back, ready to insist she comes to my house, secretly hoping she'll insist we stay. "I just put on a fresh pot—"

"Oh, don't be silly. I never get a chance to entertain you. Come in. I've got some coffee ready to go, and maybe a muffin or two."

"Sounds perfect." I step inside, realizing I've never been in here before, though Derek has. "What a beautiful home, Josie. It's decorated so perfectly."

"Thank you." She waves at me to follow. "Kitchen's this way. We'll sit down, and maybe later I'll give you the tour."

"Sounds great. Gosh, I'm so sorry it's taken me this long to stop in."

"Well, you're busy, of course, with Ben and Derek. I understand." Josie gestures to the kitchen table. "Take a seat." She opens her cabinet door and retrieves two mugs. "Stuart and I, well, as you know, our kids are grown and with him at work, I don't have much to keep me occupied."

Except snooping around neighbors' houses, I think. "Well, then we should rectify that."

She returns with the coffee, placing the cups on the table, then dashes away to bring over the muffins. "Here you go."

"This is so nice, but you know I was fully prepared to host you, so thank you for doing this."

"Of course." Josie takes a sip and grabs one of the muffins from the plate. "So, how are things going? Are you and Derek settled in? How's he liking his new job?"

Is she intentionally glossing over the fact a woman was killed in his office? "Well, of course, with what's happened, things have been pretty tough at work."

"Oh my gosh, yes." She clutches her necklace. "Do the police have any idea who could've done such a thing?"

"Not yet, or at least, they haven't said anything to Derek or the staff."

"I just can't imagine." Josie takes another bite from her muffin. "And then we had that burglary in the neighborhood. What on earth is happening these days?"

I raise my mug to my lips. "I wish I knew, Josie."

She hesitates a moment, looking ready to say more, so I wait. Moments pass, but it seems she's decided against it. "So the other night, the Parkers. How terrible," I say, hoping she'll come out with whatever it is on her mind.

"Just awful."

"I should probably stop by and see how they're doing."

"Oh, no." Josie waves her hand at me. "I'm sure they'd just be embarrassed by it all. Really."

"Oh, sure. Okay." So she doesn't want me to say anything to the Parkers? Seems odd. I place the mug on the table. "I just want you to know that I'd like us to be friends, Josie. And I want to get to know you and Stuart better. Derek and I both do."

"We'd love that. And you know what? How about that tour, huh?"

"Sounds great." I follow her out of the kitchen. This is my chance to learn more about these people. Maybe something that will shed light on why Josie feels the need to snoop around my home and my family. Why she's lying about the Parkers.

She walks me through the living and dining rooms, decorated in contemporary browns and beiges. I ooh and aah over her choices in upholstery and art, questioning whether I'm laying it on too thick. Finally, we come to a set of double doors at the end of the hall.

"This is Stuart's office," Josie explains as she opens the doors with a flourish.

I peer inside, trying not to look too eager. The office is spacious and clean, with a large walnut desk positioned in front of a bay window.

Josie gestures around the room. "Stuart likes to keep things organized and uncluttered while he works."

My eyes sweep over the desk — no papers or files left out. The bookshelves along the far wall are neatly arranged. Is this nothing more than a dead end? "You know what? Could I quickly use your restroom a moment?" I pat my stomach. "Coffee."

"Oh, I understand." She aims a finger ahead. "Right there. The door on your left. I'll, uh, give you some privacy." Josie disappears around the corner.

I head into the restroom, flipping on the light. My reflection stares back at me in disappointment. "I know, I know. What the hell am I doing here?" I whisper to myself.

I'm not sure what I thought I'd find. And then I hear Josie talking and press my ear to the door. Did someone else arrive? Is she on the phone? The more I listen, the more I realize she's on a call. "Perfect." I slip out of the bathroom and head back into Stuart's office. Again, having no idea what I'm looking for. And as I scan the space, I realize there is nothing to be found.

Until . . .

On the wall, behind the door, I see a degree hanging. A bachelor's degree from the university where Derek now works. "You went to school there? Could that be the connection?" I whisper. Maybe he worked there too at some time in the past? This is the closest thing I've found as to a reason why Josie would be interested in us at all, though I haven't connected the dots just yet.

I can't waste time standing here. I have to get back before she suspects something. I slip out of Stuart's office and head down the hall. As I approach the bathroom, I hear Josie still chatting away in the kitchen. Perfect timing. I duck into the restroom and flush the toilet for effect before washing my hands.

Just as I'm drying them, Josie calls out, "Evelyn, are you okay in there?"

"Yes, sorry!" I shout back. "Be right out!" I take a steadying breath and return to the kitchen, wearing a smile. "Thanks for the tour. You have a beautiful home, and I feel like I've been given a chance to get to know you a little better."

"Oh, I'm so glad you think so," Josie says, beaming. "More coffee?"

"I'd love some, but I should really get going. Lots of cleaning to do before I pick up Ben from school."

Josie nods. "Of course. Well, thank you so much for stopping by. I'm so glad we finally did this."

"Me, too."

"My place next time," I say, heading out the door. As I walk home, I can't stop thinking about that degree on Stuart's office wall. Did their children attend the school, too? How else does it connect to Derek?

Just as I step through our front door, my cell phone rings. Relief sweeps through me when I see the name on the screen. "Chuck. Hey, how's it going?"

"Same ol', same ol', but thanks for asking," he says. "Listen, I wanted to get back to you on that request."

"Yeah?" I make my way to the chair in our breakfast nook and sit down. "What'd you find out?"

"Nothing, I'm afraid. I found no birth certificates, live or otherwise, with the name Riley Dittrich on it."

My shoulders drop, though I'm not sure if this is good news or bad. "Maybe it was Nicole who was pregnant."

"That's the dead girl?" Chuck presses.

"Yeah, the dead girl."

"The coroner's report would've revealed that when the labs came back. Unless she was very early in her pregnancy. But hormone levels would've shown as elevated. So, I'm not sure that's something worth looking into. However . . ."

I rise, anticipating more news. "I'm listening."

"Just because I didn't find a birth certificate with her name on it, doesn't mean she never gave birth."

"I don't understand," I reply, drawing in my brow. "How's that possible?"

"Well, I know you didn't deal with adoptions at the firm, but it's possible if she gave up the baby. Those records are usually sealed. So, that's something you ought to consider."

I lower my head, resting it in my hand. "You're telling me, then, that I still don't have a definitive answer."

"I'm sorry, Evie, really, but . . . no. I can only go by the information that's available to me. You know this—"

"No, you're right," I cut in. "I understand. Listen, thank you for looking into it for me. I really do appreciate it."

"Yeah, all right. I'm sorry, kid."

CHAPTER 32

What's left for me to do except to believe her? Believe Summer, believe Mrs. Peterson. Believe the ones who insist my husband intentionally drowned Nicole. For what reason, I can still only speculate. But he'd done it in such a way as to make it appear like an accident. He even fooled Detective Bartz.

And now I must face Summer once again, this time, insisting that I'm on her side. That I want nothing more than for Derek to pay for what he's done. However, she's still keeping a secret, one that must come to light if I'm to move forward. Riley Dittrich had an affair with my husband, and she may or may not have had a child as a result.

The option remains, of course, to confront Derek. He's my husband, after all, and I should be able to ask him for the truth. But who am I fooling? And if I go that route, am I risking my safety as well as my son's?

I never believed Derek would harm either one of us, but I also never thought he was capable of murder. It's time I consider the real possibility he killed Shana Foster because she knew something she shouldn't have.

Derek had called in favors to get that job. What was the price? Did Shana know? What lengths would he go to keep himself out of prison?

My thoughts have spun for hours with no resolution. Now, it's time to pick up Ben, which means I'll see Summer. I'll tell her I believe her. Then . . . I don't know what will happen.

Grabbing my keys, I head out to my car and drive toward the school. How am I supposed to do any of this with my son at my side? Hell if I know.

The bell rings as I approach the entrance. Kids spill out into the halls, their teachers — not far behind. There she is. Riley Dittrich. With the weight of my actions bearing down on me, I see her differently now. A victim of Derek's manipulation, yes, but also someone who came here to get something from him. Revenge. Money. Acknowledgment. Maybe all three.

"Summer," I call out, raising my hand so that she'll see me over the chaos. Her gaze drifts to mine as she heads my way.

Ben captures my attention and brushes past her straight toward me. "Mommy! Look what I made!" He holds up a sheet of yellow construction paper.

I squat to meet him. "Hey, buddy. What you got there?"

"A picture I drew."

He hands it to me and what I see on it breaks my heart. Even in his rudimentary efforts, he's drawn a family. A mother, father, and child are standing beside a house — a bright sun overhead.

"It's you, and Daddy, and me!" he says.

"Well, this is just perfect, Ben. I love it," I say with a smile.

"Okay." He starts to leave.

"Oh, hang on a minute, sweetheart. I need to talk to Miss Summer."

He stops and returns to my side. I pull him close, afraid I might lose him at any moment.

Summer approaches us. "Hi, Evelyn. Hey, Ben. Love that picture."

"Thank you," he replies.

She looks back at me, waiting for me to give her my answer.

169

I glance at the other teachers and students. None look our way. "We need to talk. I can't do it while I have Ben—"

"I'll take off tomorrow," she cuts in. "We'll meet while he's in school. I take it, you've reached a conclusion."

I pinch my lips, nodding. "I think so, but I still need a few questions answered."

"All right. Fair enough. I'll see you tomorrow." Summer regards Ben. "See you later, kiddo."

* * *

I'd planned for Ben's early meal and bedtime so that Derek and I would be left to eat dinner alone together. The house is unnervingly quiet, as though the walls themselves are holding their breath. No music, no television. The only sound comes from our utensils scraping against our plates — a sharp, grating noise.

Derek's always been hard to read, but tonight, his face is a mask of deliberate neutrality, his eyes vacant. He's playing a part. So am I. I swirl the wine in my glass, the crimson liquid coating the sides. I take a sip, stalling for time. My belief in his innocence wavers like a dying flame. None of what I know — or suspect — is enough to accuse him outright. And because I still love him, I cling to the possibility that I'm wrong.

"You okay, hon?" His voice cuts through the silence, low and smooth. "You're a little quiet tonight."

"I'm fine," I reply too quickly, my voice too high. His lips twitch almost imperceptibly, but he doesn't press. Not yet. Though he must know where I was the other night. Who I'd had dinner with.

"Are you sure?" he asks, his gaze locking on to mine like a predator sizing up its prey. He's not asking out of concern; he's testing me, probing for cracks.

"There haven't been any more incidents, have there?" he continues. "No one's said anything to you?"

"No, none of that," I lie, my voice steadying. "It's just been a lot to deal with. And with my mom . . . well, I suppose it's wearing on me."

170

Derek's knife stills over his plate, his knuckles tightening around the handle. He stares at me for a long moment, the weight of his gaze pressing down on me. "You didn't happen to get any calls from Ben's school today, did you?"

"No. Why?" I keep my tone light, but my pulse quickens.

A flicker of frustration crosses his face, there and gone in an instant. "I guess with everything going on . . . the investigation . . . I want to make sure the school isn't concerned about Ben or his safety."

"His safety?" I echo, my grip tightening on my glass.

"Shana's killer is still out there," he says. "Not that I think Ben is in danger, but the school . . . well, most everyone knows where it happened. So, I thought that if the school believed it somehow involved me, I need to know if they think Ben would be better off at home."

"They've said nothing to me, Derek. So, Langston still has no suspects? No leads?" Since he brought it up, I might as well ask.

"No, I'm afraid not." He fixes his sights on me again, his gaze sharper now, more focused. "Nothing from that woman — Summer? She's leaving you alone?"

It's all I can do to hold my tongue. How he can sit there, straight-faced, and lie about who she really is — it astounds me. It reinforces my plans and reminds me that I must act before he does.

"No. Nothing." I don't bother telling him I'd been to the Brewers' house today and discovered that Stuart had attended his school. That he might have a deeper connection to all this, which could explain Josie's relentless snooping. Somehow, all of that pales in comparison to Shana Foster's brutal murder and Nicole's suspicious death. Both of which could have been the work of the man sitting across from me.

The room seems to shrink around us, the air thick with things unsaid. Derek is the first to look away, his eyes flicking to his wine glass as if it holds some hidden answer. I'd call it a win, in this game of cat and mouse, if it didn't feel so much like a threat.

CHAPTER 33

Derek

Since Evie went over to Riley's house the other night, I've sensed a shift in her behavior. She's become distant. Uncommunicative. Do I need any more proof than last night's dinner to know Riley told her everything?

But did she tell the truth or her version of it? Evie knows more than she's saying, and that's a problem. As if I need another one. But I don't know why she hasn't said anything to me. Is she planning to leave? Take Ben and get away from me? I couldn't take that. I won't lose my son or my wife because of that woman.

Why Ben's school didn't fire Riley yesterday is beyond me. I haven't received a reply to the email I sent lobbing those accusations about her. I would've thought they'd at least reach out to me. So, are they looking into it? Gathering evidence? I need that woman gone. And I need her gone now.

I still have to get Langston back to the university to somehow convince him to sweep Alex's office. The picture I found . . . that could be a start. And, of course, the earring. I must plant the seed of doubt in the detective's mind that Alex and

Shana may have been closer than Alex had let on. Now that Evie knows about Riley, I need time to prove to her I'm not who Riley says I am. I can't do that from behind bars, which is where I'll be if I can't convince Langston to take a harder look at Alex Murphey.

I pour a bowl of cereal for Ben, who sits on the barstool, awaiting his breakfast. Wanting to give Evie a rest, I volunteered to drive him to preschool this morning. But that isn't the only reason I offered. I need to see her — Summer, Riley — whatever the fuck name she's going by in an attempt to destroy my life. I have to know what she said to my wife. And to offer her a gentle reminder that I won't have her anywhere near us again. Not now. Not ever.

"Okay, son, why don't you go brush your teeth and we'll leave in a few minutes?"

Ben eats the last spoonful of his cereal and slurps down the leftover milk. Jumping off the stool, he replies, "Okay, Daddy."

I watch him turn the corner and hear his tiny footfalls up the staircase. I don't want him to wake Evie, though I suspect she's already awake and avoiding me. She's not one to sleep in, even on the weekends. The toaster pops, and my breakfast is ready. I slather on butter and quickly gobble up my piece of toast, washing it down with coffee that I seem to have made too strong. Evie usually makes it, and I can tell the difference.

Ben returns to the kitchen with his backpack over his shoulder. "Let's go, Daddy."

I swipe my keys from the counter and head through the garage door exit. Backing out of the driveway, I see Josie. Jesus, I swear that woman is always around. Watching me, I imagine. At first, she seemed amiable enough. But since I caught her in my office, I have no idea what her angle is. I don't see much of her husband, Stuart. It's almost as if he intentionally stays away. Smart man.

I wave at her, compelling myself to smile. She waves back with severity in her gaze, even from this distance. "Yeah, fuck you too, lady."

"Daddy, did you say a bad word?"

I glance into the rearview mirror. "Sorry, bud. Don't tell Mommy."

He laughs. "I won't."

We head out, my mind swirling with suspicion about what Evie thinks she knows and anger toward Riley. As I arrive at the school, I spot her immediately — Riley is standing outside greeting parents and children, her blond hair shining in the morning sun. My hands tighten on the steering wheel.

"Ready to hop out, buddy?" I ask Ben. I climb out slowly, my eyes locked on Riley. She hasn't seen me yet. After helping Ben out of the backseat, I stride toward her just as she glances up. Our eyes meet, and her smile falters. "Go on ahead, son."

"Okay. Bye, Daddy." Ben runs inside.

I set my sights on her, quickly darting my gaze for onlookers. "I told you to stay away from my wife."

Riley takes a step back but says nothing.

I move closer with every fiber of my being restrained. "You thought you could what? Taunt me by telling me she was at your house?"

She swallows hard but lifts her chin in defiance. "She needed someone to talk to. I care about her."

I laugh louder than I should have. "You don't care about anyone but yourself."

Her eyes flash with anger. "You have no idea who I am or what I've been through." Her voice drops to a whisper. "If Evelyn came to me, it's because she's scared of you. Because she knows the truth about the kind of man you are."

My hands clench into fists, fury pulsing through me. "You know nothing."

She holds my gaze. "I know enough. Enough to help Evelyn when she needs it. She deserves so much better than you."

Red clouds my vision. Without thinking, I grab Riley's arm, my fingers digging into her flesh. She lets out a gasp of pain. "If you come near my wife again, you'll regret it."

She yanks her arm away. "Let go of me! You think you can get away with lying to my boss and sending an email claiming I hurt Ben?"

The eyes of the other staff are aimed at us. The sound of children's laughter drifts over from the playground. I take a step back, inhaling deeply, struggling to rein in my rage.

"You think she wouldn't come to me and ask what happened?" Riley continues. "I told her you'd made an inappropriate advance on me. And when I rejected you, your response was to send that email. That it was all a lie." She straightens her shoulders.

"Stay away from Evie and my son," I say through gritted teeth. "For your own good."

As I walk away, unwanted attention still on me, I step into my car. Closing my eyes, I regret the threat, or at least where I'd issued it. I can't afford for this to come back on Ben, and it will, now.

Heading onward toward the university, I realize Riley is going to feed into Evie's paranoia, and I don't know how to stop it. The two of us can't keep pretending we don't know what the other is up to — the lies we're telling each other.

I'm desperate to end Langston's witch hunt against me. I didn't fucking kill Shana. I press my hands harder against the steering wheel, the tension spreading through my fingers like a slow, creeping ache. Seeing Riley again brings back a flood of memories I've tried hard to suppress. I should have known she would come back to haunt me.

After everything we shared, she wants nothing more than my destruction. The Riley I knew is gone if she ever truly existed. Now there is only Summer — cold, calculating, and ruthless in her quest for revenge.

I've worked so hard to build this life with Evie and Ben. They are everything to me. I won't let Riley and her mind games take that away. If she insists on turning my own wife against me, I will take matters into my own hands. Forget about getting her fired. I won't stop until I completely obliterate her life.

Arriving at the university, I make my way toward the English Department. Langston is several feet ahead, near the entrance, appearing to be waiting for me. My day is looking up. He's exactly the person I need to see right now. "Detective, good morning. What can I do for you?"

He opens the door and gestures for me to enter. "I'd like to ask you a few more questions, if I could."

"Of course," I reply, heading straight to my office. "Can I get you anything? Coffee or water?"

"No, thank you, Professor." He sits down as I walk around my desk.

The metallic smell of blood lingers — Shana's blood. I don't know if Langston can smell it, but I can, and it sickens me. "What is it you wanted to ask, Detective?" Dropping onto my chair, I glance through the window into the corridor, where Alex passes by. I need to recalibrate Langston's sights, turning them toward that man. This is my opportunity.

"I understand you called in some favors in order to get this job," Langston says, crossing his legs casually as though this is a friendly visit.

"Yes, you could say that. I have many contacts in the academic world. I'm sorry, is that a crime?" I probably should've left out that last part. This isn't the time to be an asshole.

"No, sir. Not a crime at all," he replies, a crooked smile on his lips. "In my review of Professor Foster's phone records, I noticed the two of you texted a fair amount. Some phone calls as well. Care to talk about that?"

"She was a colleague," I reply. "I text and call all of the people I work with."

"Sure, sure." He nods. "Since I don't want to waste your time or mine, Professor, I'm just going to come out with it." He locks eyes with me. "Were you having an affair with her?"

It was a question I had anticipated. "Look, Detective, Shana was a friend. That's all. We met a while back at a conference. Didn't really keep in touch until I was looking for another teaching job."

"Because you'd been fired from your last one," he cuts in.

"No, actually," I reply. "The department was downsizing, and they asked me to accept an early retirement package."

"Early retirement?" His brows raise and a smile spreads on his lips. "Wow. At the ripe old age of . . . thirty-six?"

"Yes." I nod as his patronizing becomes blatantly obvious.

"And it had nothing to do with Nicole Peterson's accident?" he presses.

"Of course not. Why would it?" I sit up at my desk, desperate to adjust the direction of this conversation. "Look, Detective Langston, there's something you should know about Alex Murphey." This is my shot. Will he listen, or is he too laser-focused on me, assuming I'm the only possible suspect?

He laces his fingers together in his lap. "Go on."

I show him my phone and the picture I'd taken from Alex's desk. "Here's a picture of Alex and Shana. I don't know when or where it was taken, but it's pretty clear the two were well-acquainted."

"I'm aware," he says. "Despite what you might think, Professor, you're not the only person I've spoken to in this investigation."

Well, that's a relief. Now to bait the line in hopes of a bite. "And I recall Shana mentioning she thought Alex might have developed feelings for her."

"Is that so?" he asks, a look of intrigue on his face as though I might know something he doesn't.

I continue to let him think that as my statement hangs in the air. Of course, it's all a lie, but that'll be up to him to figure out. With a sufficient amount of time having passed, I go in for the kill — metaphorically speaking. "I'm just wondering, Detective, whether it's worth taking a harder look at Alex. I've already told you I had nothing to do with Shana's death. Clearly, if I had, I wouldn't have done it in my office. So, I'm not trying to tell you how to do your job, but Alex has been acting strangely lately."

"Professor Foster called into the station about a week before her murder. Claimed she thought she was being followed. Do you know anything about that?"

"Uh, no, sir, I don't." And that's true. She'd never said a word about it to me.

Langston uncrosses his legs, and then leans closer to my desk. "I'll talk to Alex Murphey again, you can bet on that. But in the meantime, if I discover you and Ms. Foster were more than friends, and you denied it." He leans back again, smiling. "Suffice it to say, that target on your back? I'll make sure to hit it." Langston gets to his feet, aiming a finger gun at me. "Right in the bullseye."

CHAPTER 34

Evelyn

Derek suspects something. Offering to take Ben to school? That only happens when he knows he's screwed up. Is this his way of assuring me of his innocence? That I have nothing to fear, and he's been truthful? That's a lie. The simple fact he'd insisted I cut ties with Summer because she supposedly hit on him is proof of that, let alone the truth of her identity.

I walk outside to check the mail. The brisk air stings my nose as I pull my sweater around me. I glance next door to see if the ever-watchful Josie is peeking through her window at me. Unfortunately, the sun's glare makes it hard to see inside her house. But I imagine she's keeping a close eye out. I know she's a problem, one that must be dealt with, but I have far greater problems on my plate at the moment.

A few pieces of mail lie in the box, and I retrieve them, then head back to the house. Inside, I drop all of it on the foyer table. Beneath one of the envelopes is the cell phone bill. Derek usually handles the finances. It's an old-fashioned notion, but it's how we've always been, even when I was working outside the home.

Nevertheless, peering at the bill, a nagging thought pricks the back of my mind. Was Derek in contact with Shana? When was the last time? I'd checked his emails and direct messages but found nothing.

In the past, Derek did little to conceal his affairs, banking on my trust in him. That's out the window now, of course. So, I wonder if this bill might reveal new information. An affair with the now-deceased Shana? Would he dare after everything we've gone through? Yes, I believe he would.

And what about a possible message or two to Summer? Had she contacted him before arriving here? Warned him to come clean or she would make life hell for him? If she had, she would've done it under her real name. Does she have two phones? The number of ways I could be deceived is disheartening.

But I'm not a fool, and I haven't gone into this blindly believing her. So, I slide my finger under the flap and tear open the envelope. The bill is at least six pages long and covers the past month — before Shana died — before I learned Summer's true identity.

Steeling myself, I walk into the kitchen and sit on my favorite chair in the nook. I steady my hands and unfold the statement. His phone is listed first, and I begin to peruse the calls. I recognize many of the numbers. The university, my phone, his parents' landline. But on the second page, my eyes land on the first of many calls to the same number. It's a number I don't recognize, but I need to double-check to be certain, so I retrieve my phone.

It's not Summer's number, though it could be Shana's. Either way, it offers no great revelation, yet it belongs to someone who matters. The only way to find out is to get his phone from him, and that can be arranged. I consider another option but wonder if it wouldn't be too incriminating. I could call the number myself. Taking a breath, I shake my head. "No. I can't risk it."

I skim through the rest until reaching the section of text messages. No content, of course, just more numbers. There it is again. The same number, over and over.

I toss the bill onto the table, discouraged — wasting my time. All I've accomplished is allowing myself to feel more and more deceived, but by whom?

I catch sight of the wall clock. "Damn it." Pushing off the chair, I prepare to leave to pick up Ben.

The ritual continues as I arrive at school. My daily routine, unremarkable, as if my life is as perfect as the street I live on. But this is what's best for Ben — for the time being. And there he is, smiling, running toward me as though I'm the most important person in the world. I can give him a good life — just the two of us.

"Hey, buddy. Did you have fun today?" I ask him.

"Yeah, it was fun."

"Good. Hey, why don't you go see your friend over there for a minute? I just need to talk to one of the teachers. Is that okay?"

"Okay."

He runs off, brushing past Summer as she smiles at him. And when she reaches me, the bruise on her arm is glaring. "What happened to you?"

She glances at it. "Oh, I didn't realize . . ."

"Didn't realize what?" I press.

Summer glances around as if ensuring no one can hear her. "It was Derek. When he dropped Ben off this morning, he, uh, he sort of . . ."

"What?" I move in closer, lowering my voice. "Did he threaten you?"

She nods, her eyes reddening.

"Jesus. What happened?" Glancing over Summer's shoulder, I catch sight of Mrs. Babcock heading toward us.

"Mrs. Moore, hello," she says. "May I have a word with you?"

I look at Summer, who shrugs as if she knows exactly what this is about. "Yes, of course." Mrs. Babcock ushers me to her office. This is about the bruise. Or is it Ben? The blowback I feared.

"Mrs. Moore, I wanted to speak to you regarding an email I received from your husband," she begins. "I wanted to approach you yesterday, but I had to cover my bases first."

"Cover your bases?" I ask, crossing my arms over my chest. "I'm not aware of any emails my husband sent."

"Frankly, I assumed as much," she replies. "But I must tell you, he's lodged a complaint against Summer Burton, claiming she'd hurt your son, Ben. Physically assaulting him."

"What?" I rock back on my heels. "That can't be true."

"Ben has never said anything?" she asks. "You haven't seen any unexplained marks on him?"

"No, of course not." Why would Derek say such a thing? But then it occurs to me . . . the question he'd posed at dinner . . . it makes sense now. He's trying to get her fired. "Mrs. Babcock, I am confident Ben has suffered no injuries from anyone at your school. I — my husband's under a tremendous amount of pressure at work—"

"I do know what's happened there, and it's a true shame. But, Mrs. Moore, that doesn't excuse these lies he's told."

"No, it doesn't. Please, let me handle this from here. Summer and I have become friends. And whatever Derek thought he was doing, it was obviously misguided."

"Yes, and there's the matter of his threats to Summer this morning. Again, I don't know if you're aware."

The bruises. Derek's lost it. He's out of control. "Mrs. Babcock, I assure you, my husband will not come here again."

"She has every right to press charges . . ."

"Yes, of course." I raise my hands. "I'll talk to Summer."

"Please be aware that Mr. Moore is no longer welcome here on school grounds," she adds.

All I can do is nod. I return to the hall and make my way to Summer again. Ben is still talking to his friend, though his mother is looking at me. I smile at her, raising my index finger, silently begging for one more minute. And when I reach Summer, she must see on my face that I know.

"He threatened to have me fired if I didn't stay away from you and Ben," she says. "He got angry with me and grabbed my arms."

I stare at the marks, realizing Derek has reached the end of his rope. His secrets and lies have taken their toll, and he knows he's about to lose everything. With fresh resolve, I pull her aside. "Listen, give me a couple of days, all right?"

"For what?"

I plant my hands on my hips. "I'm going to bring this to an end, but I can't do it on my own. You were in the parking lot that night when Nicole drowned. You saw Derek come out of the pool building. I'm on your side, Summer, okay? We're going to get answers, but I need some time to put it all together. Can you give me that?"

"What . . . what are you saying, Evelyn?" she asks, wiping away a tear.

"I'm saying, the time's come to get to the truth. I won't let Derek hurt or intimidate you. We'll get answers, and we'll do it together."

* * *

Going through with a plan to hold Derek accountable will have significant consequences. Financial, legal, all of it. But without his confession — about Nicole — about his relationship with Summer — hell, maybe about Shana too, I simply can't go on. And seeing the bruises on Summer's arm. How dare he threaten her when he's the guilty one.

I'm walking a razor's edge, and I have to go about this the right way. Coming out and asking Derek to tell me the truth will only yield more lies. No, I must confront him head-on and demand the truth. And I can do that — if he's weakened.

I've arranged a special evening tonight. Josie and Stuart are finally joining us for dinner. Might as well get to the bottom of Josie's intentions while I put Derek in the spotlight. The two could yet be connected.

I texted Derek only an hour ago, giving him no choice but to agree, even if he did so reluctantly. I need Josie here. I need to know how her husband, Stuart, plays into this, if at all. Somehow, I'm certain this is tied to Shana's murder, too, I just don't know how yet. And I need to make Derek squirm.

I arrange the table with the precision of a surgeon prepping for an operation. Every plate, every fork, every wine glass is aligned just so. The candles flicker, casting enough shadow to make the room feel intimate but not too dark. I want everything tonight to feel perfect. Almost too perfect.

I pause for a moment, my hand resting on the neck of the bottle of Bordeaux. Derek has always loved this one. It's hard to tell if tonight he'll appreciate the gesture or if he'll feel it like I intend — as the start of something more.

The doorbell rings and I take a deep breath. I can't afford to be anxious. Not tonight. Tonight, Derek needs to be the one who feels the pressure.

Josie and Stuart stand on the other side of the door, smiling. They provide the perfect cover. Josie has been poking her nose into our business. I poked around theirs.

"Mmm, something smells amazing in here," Josie says, glancing toward the kitchen. "I told Stuart we're in for a treat."

"Just a simple dinner. Come in, please." I give her my warmest smile. "But I did open a bottle of red. Thought we'd spoil ourselves a little."

Stuart laughs as he glances around. "If this is simple, I don't even want to imagine what your idea of complicated is." He offers his hand. "It's nice to finally meet you, Evelyn. Josie's told me a lot about you. Where's your husband?"

"Oh, he should be here any minute." Stuart seems pleasant. I don't know why I expected him to be different — even standoffish. Instead, he's unpretentious. A large, middle-aged man with a kind face. Funny. I guess what they say is true that opposites attract.

I see headlights in the window and smile. "In fact, there he is now. Why don't you two take a seat in the living room? I'll bring in some drinks while we wait for Derek."

I return to the kitchen and fill their glasses when Derek enters through the garage side door.

"Hi."

I glance over my shoulder. "Hi. You should get changed. Josie and Stuart are already here."

He moves toward me. "I gotta say, Evie, I'm surprised you invited them, and for tonight? Don't you think we have enough on our plates right now, especially considering how Josie is? You're only giving her more ammunition."

"Well, we need to know why she's so interested in us. Something's off, and it's time we find out what that is." It's only a partial lie because I do want to know what's behind Josie's keen interest, and I'm certain the other night, when she stopped me as I stepped out of my car, she'd wanted to say something more, but then Derek appeared. What is she hiding?

"Maybe you're right. I'll go change. Where's Ben?" he asks.

"Watching a movie in the living room with our guests," I reply.

Derek checks his watch. "Should I put him down for the night?"

"That's a great idea. He's eaten dinner, and it won't harm him to skip his bath tonight. Thanks. I appreciate it." I express my gratitude, as always, when he offers to do something most fathers would find second nature rather than as some sort of kind gesture to his wife.

"No problem. I'll go say hi to the guests and take care of Ben."

He starts to walk away when I call out to him. "Oh, hang on. Take these with you?" I hand him two glasses of red wine.

"Sure thing."

I watch him leave the kitchen. The table is set. The guests are here. "Time to start the show."

CHAPTER 35

As I step into the dining room, Derek is already seated at the head of the table. His smile is tight, controlled. There's tension around his eyes that I see. After years of blindness, I'm beginning to see everything.

We sit down, and I pour the wine, making sure to save Derek's for last. His hand reaches for the glass, shaking with the smallest tremor. It's slight, almost invisible, but it's there. He's already tense. Does he know the school confronted me about his lies? Did something happen with the investigation?

I settle in my chair and look at Josie. "I'm so happy you both could make it on short notice. Thank you."

"Of course, our pleasure," she replies. "It was so nice having you over the other morning for coffee."

Derek's stare bores into me because I hadn't told him I'd gone over there. "So, Stuart, we haven't had much chance to get to know you. What do you do for work?" Looking at him, I'm surprised he's married to Josie. He seems the laid-back type. A little older than she is. Possibly closer to fifty? Full around the mid-section, thinning hair. But a handsome, rugged face with deep brown eyes and nice lips. I can't tell if he's a friend or foe, but I suppose that depends on his answer.

"Well, I'm the assistant principal at the high school," he replies, taking a sip of his wine.

"Really? I didn't know that." My gaze drifts to Josie. An odd expression masks her face. Irritation, anger? Hard to read. "Josie, you never mentioned that."

"We haven't had the pleasure of spending much time together," she replies. "Unless it's been babysitting Ben, which I've thoroughly enjoyed. But, uh, yeah, Stuart works at the high school." She turns to him. "You used to work at the university, right?"

"That's right," Stuart replies.

His jaw tightens as though he wasn't prepared to reveal this news. Looking at Derek, I say, "Oh, were you aware of that, honey?"

"No, I wasn't." He eyes Stuart. "What department?"

Stuart's cheeks redden a little, though it's hard to say whether it's due to embarrassment or resentment. "Well, uh, the English Department. I got let go a few months ago. Seems they were looking for a more dynamic personality."

There it is — the connection I was certain existed. And the revelation strikes not just me, Derek sees it, too. He must've taken Stuart's job. Is it any wonder why Josie's been so nosy? Watching us, like she's been waiting to find something to use against Derek so Stuart might get his old job back? I thought Alex was the one who'd been slighted, but it seems I was wrong.

Derek takes a long drink from his glass, almost draining it because it's clear he doesn't want to respond. Finally, he sets down his wine glass. "I had no idea, Stuart. Man, I gotta say, that's surprising. Hey, I'd love to see if I can do anything, you know, put in a good word if something opens up."

Stuart fixes his gaze on Derek. "I appreciate it, but I wouldn't go back there after all that. No, I'm happy at the school." He stabs a piece of butternut squash and shoves it into his mouth. He doesn't look happy.

While this is the information I'd hoped to learn, this night is far from over. Time for a change of topic. "You know,

I read a fascinating article the other day," I jump in. "It was all about murderers — first-time killers, specifically. Apparently, they almost always make a small mistake that gives them away. Something trivial, like forgetting to delete a text message or leaving behind a trace of something at the scene."

I say this casually like we don't all know Shana Foster is dead with no suspect in custody. The effect is immediate. The mood in the room darkens. Josie lets out a shaky laugh, shooting a glance at Stuart as though the topic came out of left field. Admittedly, it did. But I keep my focus on Derek. His hand freezes halfway to his mouth, just for a second, but long enough.

"Really?" Josie asks, clearly doing her best to hide her unease. "That's wild. What kind of mistake are we talking about?"

"It's almost always something psychological," I reply. "They think they've covered everything, but guilt or maybe overconfidence makes them careless. It's usually something tiny, something they believe no one would ever notice."

Derek takes a slow sip of what's left of his wine. I watch the way his throat moves as he swallows, the slight paleness of his cheeks as though they're draining of color. "Maybe you should rethink your reading material," he says, offering a half-smile. "Seems a little morbid under the circumstances, don't you think?"

The way his fingers tighten around his glass — I've rattled him. "Exactly why it occurred to me. It's shocking that the police still have no idea who took that poor woman's life. Maybe whoever did it is more experienced than they know." I swat my hand. "Sorry. I just thought it was fascinating how even someone as careful as, say, a surgeon could overlook something small."

Stuart chuckles in much the way Josie did — nervous and uneasy. "Let's hope my next surgeon isn't multitasking murders with medical procedures."

At this, everyone laughs, including Derek.

As the dinner continues, I steer the conversation back, again and again. Guilt, mistakes, the things people think they can get away with when they assume no one is looking. Each time I bring it up, Derek plays along, but I can see the cracks forming. His smile is a little slower. His responses are a little colder. And the wine — he's drinking more than usual, but then, so am I, and it's filled me with audacity.

"Well, we should probably head out." Stuart lays his napkin over his plate.

"Already?" I say, trying to be polite. "Well, it is a weeknight. School and work tomorrow for this guy." I jerk my thumb at Derek.

"Yes, Stuart's right," Josie adds. "Thank you for the wonderful meal, and . . . stimulating conversation."

They get to their feet and head toward the foyer. Derek and I follow though I keep my distance from him. I've ruined the night, that much is evident. And I also know that Stuart worked at the university, in the English Department, of all places. That's no coincidence, and I'm not the only one to see it.

"I'm so glad you both agreed to come over this evening," I say while Derek opens the door. "We should do this again soon."

Stuart outstretches his hand. "Derek, nice to finally get to know you better. Thank you."

"And you." He returns the gesture. "Listen, I was serious when I said if there's anything I can do with the university . . ."

"No, we're good," Stuart says, swatting away the idea. "Like I said, I'm happy where I'm at."

"Yeah, sure. That's good to hear." Derek slips his hands into his pants pockets.

I offer a light embrace to Josie and feel a stiffness in her body. She doesn't return the gesture. "Good night, Josie."

"Good night, Evelyn. Thank you again for a lovely evening."

Derek closes the door.

The house feels different to me now. Quieter. Colder. I head back into the dining room and gather the wine glasses when I sense Derek's presence behind me. I don't turn around, but his reflection in the window stares at me. The way he stands in the doorway, half in shadow, unnerves me.

"That was quite the conversation you steered us into," he says, his voice steady. There's something beneath the surface, something sharp.

I shrug. "I just thought it was an interesting topic."

He walks toward me while my hands are full of dishes, defenseless. "Did you really think that was appropriate considering?"

"Considering?" I ask as if the idea never occurred to me.

He looks away. "Jesus, Evie. Considering what happened to Shana. Stuart must have known her, too. He could be hurting. It was completely insensitive to go on like you were."

I intended to rattle Derek, to let him know he can't get away with murder. I accomplished that, as evidenced by his current stance. But I had no idea about Stuart. It was an unfortunate coincidence, though it did reveal the truth about Josie.

"We wanted to know why Josie's been snooping around our house. Guess what, Derek? It's because you took Stuart's goddam job." He's standing before me as though I'm unaware of what he's become — a liar and a killer. "When you got this job, you said you had to call in favors. Who granted those favors, huh? And what did it cost you?"

He scoffs and turns away. "Fuck you, Evie."

CHAPTER 36

The gulf between us grows ever larger and deeper. After last night, it was all but destined to happen. Derek is already gone, out the door this morning without so much as a goodbye.

Last night's dinner brought about the end of my marriage. Part of me regrets the loss, the life I've known for so long. The other part of me knows it has to be this way. Two women are dead and the person who could have killed them has been lying to me for longer than I can tolerate.

Today, I will take the necessary steps to get my desired answers. There will be no going back after this. The idea frightens me, and I'm not sure I can go through with it.

"Mommy?"

Ben is standing at the door, ready to leave for school. "Can we go now?"

"Yes, sweetheart. Let's go." I look around my home, a place I never wanted to move to, and see it differently. Josie is standing on her front porch as we step outside. She waves at us, and I return the gesture. Finally, I understand her behavior, though I wish she'd come clean at the outset. Still, I'm not sure I would have if it was me.

I go through our usual routine, except Summer isn't here at the school today. She's taking the day off so that we can meet later and do what must be done. Guilt weighs on me for Ben. His father is going to go away for a long time. Probably forever. But the alternative? Yeah, well, maybe I shouldn't feel so guilty.

After dropping him off, I head out, wondering where Ben and I will go after this. I suppose I'll rejoin the workforce, probably having to take on a junior role at a law firm at first. That's okay. I'll earn enough to support the two of us.

My first stop is the pharmacy. I walk inside, and the cashier regards me with a smile. "Good morning."

"Good morning," I reply, disappearing into an aisle.

I scan the shelves where they keep the sleeping aids. Everything from herbal remedies to over-the-counter nighttime headache medicine to essential oils. All are designed to help one fall asleep and stay asleep. Well, I want him to fall asleep. It's the only way to ensure his compliance. I need him helpless and unaware.

I look at something non-prescription that could knock him out. As I hold the box, I sense eyes on me, like everyone in the store is watching. Can they see the guilt infecting my thoughts?

I've been married to Derek for eight years, eight years of stability and safety because I've chosen to ignore the truth. Now, the truth has clawed its way to the surface after whispers I could no longer ignore. And then Nicole. Her mother was right to blame Derek. Nicole was the best swimmer on the university's team. She didn't drown, not by accident. She didn't kill herself either. I'm not certain about Shana, though I will get my answer from him about that, too.

My stomach turns with growing nausea at the thought of what I'm about to do. But justice won't come unless I take matters into my own hands. I've heard his version of events — his fake alibis, the charm that had won me over for years. And I've heard Summer's. I know who's telling me the truth now. Derek never should've come after her like that.

My fingers tremble as I take a box of sleep aids. Too obvious? It's not like I'm looking to kill him. I just need him defenseless and weak. I put back the box, moving to the next shelf. Muscle relaxers. No, that wouldn't be strong enough.

I sense a presence next to me and glance over to see an elderly woman, bent over a cane, staring at the products on the shelf. I offer a polite smile.

"Trouble sleeping?" she asks.

My throat tightens. "Yes. Well, not me. My husband's been . . . restless lately."

The old woman's eyes soften with understanding. "Happens to men. Always something on their minds." She nods toward the shelf. "That one there works wonders. A couple before bed, and he'll be out like a light."

I manage a tight smile and take the box of nighttime tablets. "Thanks."

When the old woman disappears around the corner, I make my way to the cashier. Placing the item on the counter, I reach for my wallet.

"Is this all, ma'am?" the cashier asks.

"Yes, thanks."

She scans it over the barcode reader and peers at the screen. "That'll be twelve eighty-five, please."

I prepare to swipe my credit card but stop. "Um, actually, I think I'll pay cash for this." Luckily, I find a twenty in my wallet, as I don't usually carry cash. I figure cash is the safer bet. "Here you go."

She hands over the change and the box she's placed in a plastic bag. "Thank you and enjoy the rest of your day."

"You, too." I take the bag and offer her a smile. Upon returning to my car, I slip behind the wheel and stare at the box. I'm not looking to kill Derek. Just incapacitate him for a while until Summer and I can force the truth from him. Will it work? I have no idea. And if it doesn't, well, I'll at least get the truth about whether Derek fathered Summer's child. That's something even she hasn't confessed to yet. Not directly.

The idea seems solid, yet do I really think he'll come clean about murder? Doing so will destroy his life, and mine too, but he won't be thinking about that. So I must consider what will happen if he refuses to talk. Refuses to confess. What will I do?

* * *

I've chosen a neutral location to meet with Summer. Neither one of us has the upper hand. I can't dismiss the notion she was the one texting and calling Derek in the month leading up to now. She has a new identity; is it so far-fetched to think she has a new phone? Did she plead for Derek to take her back? Tell him he's the father of her child? I don't know, but the circumstances linger in the back of my mind. Trust will never come easy for me again.

She enters the diner. I raise my hand to garner her attention, and she sees me. Anticipation builds, as does fear. And when she slides into the booth, indecision etches itself in her features.

"Hi," she says.

"Hi." The bag of sleeping pills rests on the vinyl bench next to me. I rest my hand on it to remind me of what I intend to do. Glancing past her, I'm relieved the diner isn't busy. An older couple sits at the breakfast bar. A couple of young mothers with their toddlers sit in a booth on the other end. Okay, enough stalling.

I return my gaze. "So, I'm going to need your help. If you really want to prove Derek was responsible for Nicole's death, I need you with me on this."

Summer licks her lips and swallows her hesitation. "What's the plan?"

"I'll drug him with sleeping pills. You'll come over once he's out. We'll get him into the basement and tie him up." I stop for a moment, hardly believing the words coming out of my mouth. "With you there, he'll know he's been exposed. That I know who you are and your relationship with him."

"Then what?" She shrugs. "He's just going to confess to drowning Nicole?"

I pull back and study her a moment. "I thought you wanted the truth as much as I do?"

"Of course I do, but this?" She leans in, lowering her voice. "Will this even work?"

"It will if he thinks he'll be hurt." The words come out easier than I expect. "I plan to have a baseball bat with us for effect. I don't want to hurt him, Summer, but he needs to know that we're serious."

A server approaches our booth. "Good morning, ladies. What can I get for you?"

I take a quick peek at the menu. "I'll have the yogurt parfait and a cup of coffee, please. Cream and sugar."

"And you, miss?" she asks Summer.

"Oh, uh, just a cup of coffee, please. Thanks."

"All right then. I'll be right back."

We're quiet for a while. I don't know what to say to her, and she doesn't know what to say to me. The situation is too surreal — too unbelievable to be true. But this is my life, and this is where things stand.

The server returns, setting down our cups of coffee, placing my yogurt in front of me.

"Thank you so much," I reply.

"Yes, thanks," Summer adds.

"Of course. Enjoy."

Summer's eyes are glued to the server as she walks away. Finally, she returns her attention to me. "I'm not sure I can go through with this."

My brow creases, and I cross my arms in defiance. "What do you mean? I told you all you need to do is help me get him secured in the chair, and when he wakes, we'll talk to him. I'm not really going to hurt him, Summer. He's my husband. I

195

still lo . . . never mind. He'll do what we ask. For God's sake, I'm doing this for you."

"What are you talking about — for me?"

Heat rises under my collar. "Of course. Look, we're just going to talk to him in a way that makes him think he has no choice but to answer our questions."

"And if he overpowers us? How pissed do you think he'll be?" she presses.

"He won't. Not if we do this right, understand? I don't get this. I mean, you've been texting him, calling him, whatever else, and I have to assume it's because you wanted him to come clean." I raise my chin. "Unless you were trying to get him back. Is that it? Are you trying to make him leave me, Summer — Riley, whoever you are?"

She glances around and lowers her tone. "No, I don't want him. I tried to get him to admit to what he'd done, okay? That was why I called and texted him. I want nothing to do with him, I swear it."

"Then what?" I ask. "You want the truth about Nicole to come out, don't you? You want him to take responsibility for fathering your child?"

Summer leans back. "What are you talking about?"

I sigh. "I'm not stupid. You should know that by now. The baby clothes in your room you never answered for? They didn't belong to Nicole. And you refused to answer me when I asked why you have them, so I'm left to assume they belong to you."

She hesitates, appearing defiant. Her chest rises and falls with growing intensity. "You want to go through with this, fine. He needs to pay for what he's done, and if this is how we go about accomplishing that, then that's what we'll do." Her eyes redden. "And I'll give you the answers you need about a child. I'll tell you everything, but not until we get what we want from Derek."

"Okay." I nod. "I need more time to set things up. So, we do this tomorrow. Got it? Tomorrow night."

CHAPTER 37

Derek

The polished wood of my desk blurs beneath my gaze. The soft hum of the overhead lights in my office cuts through the stillness. As I sit here, where Shana died, a surreal circumstance, it is clear to me that something has shifted — irrevocably. Too many lies have slipped from my lips, too much damage done. Now, the last threads of trust between Evie and me have snapped.

Hosting that dinner — that's when I knew. I don't know what clicked in her, but something did, and now, I'm left to wonder not if but when she will leave me. Her long, calculating glances she thinks I didn't notice. She's studying me, wondering what else I'm keeping from her. Figuring out how much longer she has to pretend everything's fine before . . . before what?

She knows. She has to know. And soon, she'll know about Shana, too. Langston will see to that. But the fact remains, someone murdered her, and it sure as hell wasn't me. The detective says he'll look into Alex, but will he? Will he find the earring I left there and connect the dots I pray exist? Shana's

197

presence surrounds me — taunting me, telling me I deserve all this.

What will happen when I get home tonight? Will Evie say something? Will she tell me to leave, pack my bags, and get the hell out of the house? I don't know because it all depends on what she knows. And I have to think, whatever that is, this is Riley's doing. Maybe she killed Shana, trying to frame me for it. I regret ever meeting Riley Dittrich. She's the one responsible for bringing all this down on me. Evie, Shana. I should've done what was necessary to be free of her.

My only option is to confront Riley. Not at the school. That was a mistake. She did something to clear her name after I'd sent the email, and it could yet backfire on me. No, this has to happen before I see Evie again and before I go home tonight.

So I leave the office, not bothering to explain my abrupt departure. They've all but erased my existence anyway. My career is ruined right along with the rest of my life.

I drive to Riley's apartment and wait for her to get home. I admit that I've been here before. Before all this shit started rolling downhill, I'd tried to convince her to leave. That's when I'd had my chance and squandered it. Of course, I had no idea she'd taken on a new name, gotten a job at Ben's school, and then introduced herself to my wife as Summer Burton. Jesus. She's fucking insane.

Now, I wait, forced to think about all the mistakes I've made. All the lies I've told to protect myself. Evie was right to be suspicious. I never should have gotten involved with Riley. That was the beginning of the end. And not just for me.

I check my watch again. School's been out for over an hour. Where the hell is Riley? I grip the steering wheel, playing out the confrontation in my head. I'll demand she stop poisoning my wife against me. I'll threaten to go to the police if she doesn't leave us alone. And if she doesn't agree? Well, Summer Burton doesn't exist anyway.

The sun sinks lower in the sky, blanketing the building in shadow. Still no sign of Riley. Where could she be? Evie will be expecting me home soon. God knows what she'll think if I don't arrive on time. I can no longer bank on the trust she had in me. It's gone.

The longer I sit here, the greater the risk of arousing suspicion. I've been here for too long already. If I don't leave now, things will grow worse for me. "Goddam it." I press the ignition and pull away from the curb, the apartment building shrinking in the rearview.

I race home, rehearsing excuses in my head. As I step through the front door, I hear Ben's laughter coming from the kitchen. Relief at the sound of him offers a sense of normalcy even though this is anything but.

Evie is sitting with Ben as I enter the kitchen. They're playing a board game in the breakfast nook. "Hey, guys," I say, trying to keep my voice steady.

Ben leaps from the chair and runs into my arms. I scoop him up, holding him tighter than I have in a long time, feeling his small heartbeat against mine. Evie is sitting in the shadow of the early evening light. She's smiling. Not at me, but at Ben. "Hey, hon."

She stands, inhaling deeply as if gathering strength from the instinctive action. "Hi. I hope you don't mind, I ordered pizza tonight. Didn't feel much like cooking dinner. After last night's dinner party, I'm a little worn out."

"I don't mind at all. Pizza sounds great." The words come out easy, relaxed, and for a moment, it feels like we're still okay, but I can't let myself be fooled. Evie's made up her mind. Now it's up to me to change it.

I lower Ben down again and look at her. She glances at me only a moment before turning back to clean up the game pieces scattered on the table. "I'll go change and be back down in a minute."

"Okay," she replies.

This time, she smiles at me and touches my arm lightly — a gesture that speaks of an attempt at peace — I hope. I take my bag and head upstairs, relief enveloping me like a cool breeze on a stifling day. She's said nothing about me having left early this morning or how my day went or anything about Shana. The thing is, I'm not sure if I should be worried or relieved, so I force myself to think the latter.

As I change, I decide that whatever happens next starts tonight; this is where my atonement begins, if she'll accept.

I return minutes later, reaching the landing when the doorbell rings. "I'll get it." Jogging down the steps, I open the door.

"Evening, sir." A teenager holding a large pizza box smiles at me. "One large pepperoni with extra cheese. That'll be twenty-four ninety-five, please."

"Of course." I hand him a twenty and a ten and he offers me the box. "Keep the change."

"Thank you, sir. Have a good night."

"You, too." I close the door on the pimply-faced kid and walk into the kitchen. "Pizza's here."

Ben shouts his excitement from the living room. I place the box on the kitchen island, where Evie stands, peering at her phone. She quickly sets it down. "Food's arrived, hon," I say.

"Perfect timing. I'll grab the plates." She snatches her phone from the counter, tucking it into her pants pocket.

I pretend not to notice that she's keeping her phone so close. Instead, I open the lid of the pizza box. A waft of melty cheese and greasy pepperoni fills my senses. "Oh, man. We haven't had this in a while. It smells delicious."

Evie returns, holding the plates and setting them next to the food. "I thought it would be a nice treat for us. Thought we could use one."

The corners of my lips curl in a smile. "Great idea, I agree."

We all sit around the living room coffee table, Ben on the floor, eating over his plate. The pizza goes quickly. We laugh, tell jokes, talk about our next family trip. My God, I feel like I'm in heaven and everything that's happened has simply melted away. Wishful thinking, I know, but I'll take it while I can.

After Evie puts Ben down for bed, she returns to the living room. I'm watching the news. My feet, propped up on the coffee table, I look at her. "Did he go down all right?"

"Oh yeah. A belly full of pizza and a nice bath, he'll sleep through the night, no doubt." She glances into the kitchen. "Hey, you want a cup of tea or something? It's so cold today, I kind of feel like I could use a hot drink."

"That sounds great. I appreciate it, babe. Thanks."

"No problem."

It's been a long time since we've been this comfortable around each other. Evie has always forgiven me. Maybe she's chosen to do so again. She soon returns with a piping hot cup of tea. "Thank you." I wait until she sits next to me with her own cup. "I mean it, hon."

She turns toward me. "Sorry?"

"Thank you," I repeat. "For sticking it out with me. I know . . . believe me . . . I know it hasn't been easy. But I feel like maybe we've turned a page."

"I hope so, Derek," she replies. "I really do."

CHAPTER 38

Evelyn

He suspects nothing. Last night, I'd been doting, loving, engaged. I'd been the wife I used to be. This morning, he kissed my lips softly, slowly, in a manner he hadn't in a long time. He kissed me like I meant something to him.

The cup of tea, a rare offering, was intended to build trust. And it worked. We had our hot drinks, watched the news, chatted about current events, then went off to bed — together, I might add.

I admit, it felt good. It felt normal. But it changes nothing. I know too much now. And I'm prepared to move forward with the plan. That starts with a visit to my neighbor, Josie, who I've now come to have a great deal more respect for, sympathetic to her snooping.

With Ben already at school, I walk over to Josie and Stuart's place, knocking on the door. She quickly answers and I offer a pleasant smile. "Good morning, Josie. Hey, I don't suppose I could ask for a huge favor?"

She steps outside, still dressed in her robe, crossing her arms in a serious manner. "Of course. Anything you need. What is it?"

"Could Ben come over for a few hours this evening? I completely forgot about an appointment Derek and I have, and he won't be able to come with us."

"An appointment with the both of you?"

Her interest is piqued. Good. "Yes, well, I'm sure you must know how hard it is to keep a marriage healthy and happy. Derek and I work hard at it. Sometimes that work involves a little therapy."

"Oh, I see," she replies with an air of superiority as if she has the perfect marriage. "Well, yes of course. I'm happy to look after him. I can come over if that would be easier for you."

I raise a preemptive hand. "No, no, that's fine. I don't want to put you out any more than I already am. I'll bring him by."

"Well, okay then. Should I plan on feeding him dinner?" Josie asks.

"That would be great." I touch her arm to reinforce my appreciation. "You're so kind to bail us out again. Thank you. I'll bring him over at around six."

"Sounds great. See you then. I look forward to it." Josie steps inside and closes her door.

I head back to my house, relieved that the hardest part is over. Keeping Ben away from all this is the only thing that matters.

* * *

The first part of the plan is in place. Now, to confirm my partner in this operation remains on board. Without her, this whole thing falls apart.

I arrive at school to pick up Ben, my thoughts consumed by whether Summer will back out. I'm doing this for her as much as for myself. She's already expressed reservations, and I can't afford for her to waver again.

There she is. I capture her attention and see her slight nod of acknowledgment. She walks toward me, looking anxious.

Goddam it. She better not renege on our deal. I don't like this. I can't do it alone. After the damage that's been caused, I hate admitting that I need her.

Summer's arms are folded over her chest, and her gaze darts around like she's guilty of something. "Hey."

Ben appears in the corridor with the other students. "Hey," I say to her. "Ben's coming. I don't have much time. You need to be at my house tonight. Seven thirty, okay? Don't be late."

She swallows hard. "Yeah, I get it. I'll be there."

The more I study her, the more convinced I am she's going to bail on me. Her eyes flicker with uncertainty, and it gnaws at my insides. "Summer, stop second-guessing this, all right? We're going to get to the truth. That's what we both want."

"You're right. I hear you, Evelyn, I do." She thumbs back toward the school entrance. "I gotta go. See you tonight."

Fuck. She walks away, leaving me stranded in my own plan's enormity. I have no idea if she's going to show, and all I can do is press on.

"Mommy!" Ben rushes toward me, clutching my waist.

"Hey, buddy. You ready to go home?"

"Uh-huh."

My sights are drawn to the entrance again as I see Summer. Just a wisp of her blond hair trailing as she disappears. Was she watching me? Gauging my temperament? Wondering if she'd be better off calling the cops to alert them to my plan? That'd be one way to get me out of the picture. I have no idea whether I can trust her, but I'm about to find out.

* * *

Ben and I arrive home after killing as much time as I could. Spending these past couple of hours with him, eating ice cream, visiting the bookstore, reminds me that I'm still his mother. Even while I plan to do everything in my power to force a confession from his father, to see him go to prison, Ben still needs me. Will he forgive me for what I'm about to do?

Stepping out of my car, my gaze is drawn to Josie marching toward me. "For God's sake, what now?" I say under my breath. "Afternoon, Josie." I open the back door and help Ben out of his car seat.

"Evelyn, hi, listen, I'm so sorry. I–I can't watch Ben tonight."

"Oh? Why is that?" I ask, doing my best to sound breezy while my chest tightens.

"Stuart about chewed my head off for forgetting we're supposed to see his parents tonight. They just moved into a senior living facility and invited us to come see the place. We're joining them for dinner. I completely forgot that was tonight."

"Oh boy." What can I say to convince her to make up an excuse? I need her almost as much as I need Summer. "You don't think you could convince Stuart to reschedule? I really hate to miss our therapy session."

She's already shaking her head, hands on her full hips. "I would if I could, Evelyn. Believe me. I hate letting you down like this. But his mom has already bought the food and started cooking hours ago." She raises her hand. "That's how she is — overdoes everything. But maybe you could reschedule your session? I'm sure it must happen all the time — people who can't find childcare and whatnot."

I swat away her concern. "Yeah, no, you're probably right. Don't worry about it, Josie. I'll figure it out. I can always ask the Parkers' daughter. It's not a problem, really."

"Are you sure?"

Of course it's a problem, a big one. But what more can I say to her? "I'm sure. Don't think twice about it. Go on and enjoy dinner with your in-laws." I rest my hand on Ben's shoulder. "I should get him inside."

"Oh, yeah, sure." Josie takes a step back. "But you know, any other time . . ."

"Got it. See you later, Josie. Have fun tonight." I unlock the front door and quickly close it behind me. "Shit."

"Mommy . . . language!"

Something I've said to Derek a thousand times. "Sorry, sweetie. Go wash your hands. You've got sticky ice cream all over them."

"Okay."

Everything has just been thrown into disarray. Ben can't be here tonight. He can't see what I'm about to do to his father. Panic clutches my ribs, squeezing so hard I can't breathe. What do I do? Put it off a day or two? I don't dare, not with how spineless Summer seems to have become. If she's out, then this whole thing goes out the window. No, I can't risk it. It has to be tonight. I'll just have to occupy Ben upstairs. Put him to bed early. Something.

We'll be in the basement anyway. He'll be fine.

CHAPTER 39

Derek

My co-workers have gone out of their way to avoid me. And now, as I head to my next class, passing by students, they avert their gazes, too. I'm a pariah once again. At least, last night, I was offered a small glimmer of hope after Evie and I enjoyed a pleasant evening. In fact, I can't recall the last time we've gotten along so well.

That feeling is what will carry me through this swamp of suspicion over Shana Foster. I only hope Langston is looking into Alex. But the more I think about it, is it too far a stretch to consider Riley played a part? Means and motive are a big driver in murder. But that would mean I'd have to come clean to Langston about Riley, and if I do that, God knows what conclusions the detective will draw about Nicole. No, I have to let him find the killer, even if I might know who it is.

When I enter my classroom, not a single student has arrived. With only five minutes before class starts, I don't like where this is headed. Yet it only takes a moment for me to see the reason no one is here. There it is, scrawled in red marker across the entire whiteboard.

Killer.

"For God's sake." I whip around in search of a culprit, but I'm alone. It's just me and the accusation scribbled on the board. I snatch the eraser and wipe away the slanderous remark with quick, angry strokes.

No one's coming. Not today and probably not until they find out who killed Shana. Maybe not even then. I'm ruined.

"Fuck this." I march out of the room, ready to confront Alex. I can't be the only one they're looking at. I don't give a shit what this does to Alex. For all I know, he did play a part. That's what I tell myself, no matter the glaring neon sign burning in my head that reads "*Riley.*"

I brush past everyone, bumping into a student by accident. When I push on, I hear him call me a prick. I've been called far worse; it barely registers as anything more than background noise.

Returning to my building, I continue through to Alex's office, barreling through my colleagues, who part like a school of fish around a predator. Doesn't matter because none of them utter a word. Standing in the doorway, I look inside. Empty. I peer down at the leg of his desk where I'd left the earring. It's gone. Goddam it. Did the cleaners find it or Langston? Shit. Where the hell is Alex?

I spin on my heel. Alex isn't here, but he's somewhere, and I'm going to find him. My footsteps echo off the marble floors as I storm down the hallway.

The faculty lounge is quiet, save for the faint hum of the vending machine and a half-empty coffee pot exuding a burnt aroma into the air. I clench my fists, my patience thinning like a rubber band about to snap.

I'm halfway back to my office when I hear it. His voice.

Alex.

It's faint but unmistakable, coming from the courtyard. I veer toward the sound, shoving open the glass doors to let in the crisp fall air that pricks my cheeks. There he is, standing near one of the stone benches, talking on his phone, oblivious to the storm brewing in my gut.

"Alex!" I shout, my voice cutting through the chilled air.

He startles, whipping around to face me and lowering his phone. Something flickers in his expression. Guilt? Annoyance? Fear? It's an unreadable mix of emotions that only fuels my anger.

"Derek, what the hell?"

"You don't get to walk away from this." I close the space between us with determined strides. "Did you write that word on my whiteboard? You know something about Shana, and you're gonna tell Langston. Now."

Alex stiffens under my gaze as his lips curl into something that's not quite a smile. "You've lost it, man," he says. "And you need to back the hell off."

"Back off?" My voice rises. "You've been lying through your teeth since the second they found her body. You think no one sees that?"

"Don't blame me for your mess, Derek. You're the one everyone's whispering about." His words hit like a slap across my face, stinging more than I'd care to admit, but I don't stop.

I step closer, our faces now inches apart, my breath mingling with his in the cold air. "Say that again."

He doesn't. Instead, his hands press against my shoulders, shoving me back.

It happens fast. Instincts take over. I grab the front of his shirt and yank him toward me, sending us both stumbling over the brick pavers. He swats at me, trying to push free, but I land a fist on his jaw. My knuckles crunch against his bone, sending a bolt of pain up my arm.

"Derek, stop!" Alex yells, his voice tinged with panic. He swings wildly, connecting with my shoulder. Pain flares, but it's drowned out by the adrenaline coursing through me.

"You know what happened to her!" I shout, my grip tightening around his shirt.

He claws at my hands, trying to shove me back with more strength than I expect. Somewhere behind us, footsteps echo against the stone path, but I'm too far gone to care. Alex snarls something under his breath — words lost to the chaos — then throws a fist that clips me across the cheekbone in a flash of white-hot pain.

"Enough!"

The voice cuts through the haze of our skirmish. I'm yanked backward, a strong hand grabbing the collar of my jacket and pulling me off Alex. I stagger back, breathing hard as Detective Langston steps between us. His face is a mask of irritation and authority, leaving no room for further argument.

"What the hell is going on here?" Langston demands, his gaze darting between Alex and me.

Alex straightens his shirt, his expression smug despite the red mark growing on his jaw. "He came at me out of nowhere!"

Langston sets his steely gaze on me, his jaw tight and eyes narrowing. "Professor Moore. Care to explain why you're assaulting one of your colleagues?"

I wipe the blood from my mouth with the back of my hand, glaring at Alex over Langston's shoulder. "Because he's hiding something about Shana."

Langston sighs, pinching the bridge of his nose like he's staving off an impending headache. "You both look like idiots right now. And if you don't want to spend the night cooling off in a holding cell, I suggest you keep your hands to yourselves."

"But—"

"I said enough." Langston points at Alex with conviction. "You. Go back to your office." Then he turns to me. "And you — we're going to have a little chat."

Alex smirks as he brushes past me, his voice low enough that only I can hear: "Nice try, Derek."

I grit my teeth so hard it feels like they might crack under pressure; my fists curl at my sides.

"Let's go," the detective says, gesturing toward the building. I follow him, my face burning with humiliation. But one thing is clear — I'm not letting this go easily or quietly. I need Langston's sights set on another. And Alex is as good a target as any.

"In your office. Now," Langston says, standing in front of it.

I walk inside, my chest still heaving from the adrenaline. "Why are you here?"

He enters behind me and closes my door. "Sit down, Professor." The detective makes his way toward the guest chair, dropping onto it, leaning back like he hasn't a care in the world. "I'm here because Shana Foster was murdered in this very spot." He aims his finger at the floor.

I take a seat behind my desk. "You know I didn't do it, Detective. This has to do with Alex Murphey. He has a picture of Shana and him on his desk. Did you even search his office like you said, or just mine? And the pig's liver? Jesus . . ."

He raises a preemptive hand. "Just take a breath, Professor, all right? I'm here because you're right."

I freeze, wondering if I heard him correctly. "I'm sorry, what did you say?"

"I said, you're right. I know you didn't kill Professor Foster."

I let his words settle over me, soothing the pain radiating from my body. "So you found the person who did?" My words are calm and relaxed.

"No, not yet. But DNA tests came back. None of the samples matched yours."

Just as I'm about to interject, he raises his finger.

"And it doesn't match any of your co-workers either, including Alex Murphey."

I lean back, exhaling my relief. Not for that asshole, Alex, but for me. Will this change anything? I don't know. It might be too late for that. But at least I can go home to my wife and tell her I'm no longer a suspect. Yet I know who should be, and I can't say a word.

CHAPTER 40

Evelyn

My nerves are frayed. I sit in the kitchen nook, sipping on a cup of coffee that will only rattle me more. It's all I can do not to crawl out of my skin. The plan runs through my head, over and over again. Each step, playing out in agonizing detail. I'm not sure I have the stomach for it, but it's too late now.

Derek will be home any moment. He called me earlier, but I couldn't answer. He didn't leave a voicemail, so I assume he'll be home at the usual time.

Ben is in the living room, surrounded by his toys. I can't believe Josie backed out on me like that. I needed this one thing from her, and now, I have to do this with Ben in the house. Maybe I'll give him something to help him fall asleep. "No. I'm going to drug my kid, too?"

Tears prick my eyes as I cover my mouth. I've lost my senses, but how else to find out the truth? This is Derek's fault, not mine. He did this. He made me this way.

I think of Nicole Peterson. Shana Foster. Might Summer have been his next victim? "Not anymore. Not if I can help it."

The garage door opens, and my pulse races. This is it. Showtime. I smooth my blouse and force a smile as Derek walks in.

"Hi," he says.

I rise from the chair. "Hi." His expression is different. Happy. Relieved. "Everything okay?"

He grins. "More than okay. Detective Langston came to see me today at the school."

I step back, tilting my head. "And?"

"He got the results of the DNA tests. Evie, he cleared me." Derek drops his laptop bag on the floor. "I mean, I knew I was innocent, but now, everyone does. I called you earlier to tell you, but I got your voicemail."

"Uh, yeah." I glance at my phone. "I was making Ben a snack and missed your call. So, what does this mean, exactly? Does he know who killed her?"

"No." He peers down a moment. "But he says the results clear not only me, but everyone in my department."

"Alex?" I ask, hesitantly.

"Yes, Alex, too."

He looks as though he might cry. The news stuns me, sending waves of relief and worry throughout. What does this mean? What do I do?

"It's over, Evie," Derek says, taking my shoulders. "My part is over and that's all that matters to me. We can focus on us again. I feel awful for Shana's death, but I didn't do it. They all know that now."

His brow narrows. He must see the uncertainty on my face. "This is good news, baby."

"Yeah, no, I see that. I'm just — I'm surprised. Grateful, but surprised." I've heard this line before. He's been cleared before. Now, I don't know what to believe.

He takes a step back. "I'm sure you struggled to see I was telling the truth about her. I can't be angry with you for that. Not after what I've put you through." He looks around. "Where's Ben?"

213

"In the living room, playing," I reply.

Derek nods. "Good, good. Listen, I–I feel like I need a shower. Take a moment to process all this. Then, we'll order some takeout, okay? We'll have a nice dinner as a family. And then, you and me? We'll try to figure a way to start again."

* * *

The DNA results cleared him. Derek is innocent, at least of Shana's murder.

I picture Nicole's face and hear her pleading for the truth. I still believe Derek is responsible for her death in some way. But now . . . if he didn't kill Shana, can I be so certain he killed Nicole?

Doubt floods my mind. All my carefully laid plans, all the risks I've taken to get to this moment, suddenly seem rash and misguided. Derek's warm smile and obvious relief at being found innocent have cracked my resolve.

Upstairs, I stand outside Ben's room. He's asleep. His soft snores are a comforting rhythm. The sound pierces my heart. What was I thinking, planning to drug my own son? Derek is right, we need to try and be a family again. There are still unanswered questions, but maybe it's time to have faith. To give Derek the benefit of the doubt.

Summer is due here in just over an hour. Do I call it off? If I do, it means I believe Derek is innocent of Nicole's death, despite Summer's words, despite the words of Nicole's mother. And despite his knowledge of Summer's real identity, which he kept from me. And this child? Summer promised to reveal all when she gets here tonight.

A text message arrives on my phone. I retrieve it from my pocket, glancing down the stairs to be sure Derek doesn't see me.

I'll be there, just like I said. But I won't be alone. You'll understand when you see me.

It's Summer. She's coming after all. Apparently, not alone. What does that mean? The child? Does she have his child?

214

All my resolve returns in a rush at the thought of it. This is it. I'll get the answers I need and Derek will provide them. She's bringing the baby. He won't be able to talk his way out of this one. This goes on as planned. Nothing changes. Not now.

I pocket my phone. Now's the time to offer Derek his tea. I've been the devoted wife tonight, just like last night, playing my part to perfection. I need him to continue to trust me. And his mood is now markedly improved with the weight of Shana Foster off his shoulders.

Returning downstairs, I walk into the living room. "You know, I enjoyed that tea last night. Think I'll make another. Care for one?"

He begins to rise from the couch. "How about I make you one?"

"No, no," I insist. "I'll do it. So is that a yes from you?"

"Sure. I'd love one, honey. Thank you." His focus drifts back to the football game on TV, the flickering screen casting shadows across his face.

He's different. Almost like he used to be. But I won't let myself be fooled again.

I head into the foyer, my heart pounding as I reach into my purse hanging on the hook. I take out the box of sleeping pills. Glancing back, I note that he's paying me no attention now as I disappear into the kitchen's dim light. I fill the kettle and set it on the stove.

As it heats up, I open three of the capsules with fumbling fingers, dumping their contents into his mug. Sweat forms on my neckline, and doubt gnaws at me like a persistent itch. Can I go through with this? But Summer is on her way, so there's no point in asking myself that question any longer. A quick check of my phone shows no new messages from her. She could still yet turn up with the cops. Maybe that's what she meant by not coming alone. I might find myself in handcuffs before the end of the night.

The kettle whistles, snapping me back into the moment. I take it off the burner and pour the steaming hot water into

215

both mugs. Little white flakes float to the top of Derek's cup but dissolve quickly as if they were never there at all. Now, to make sure I don't mix them up — I laugh silently at myself, knowing that would be something I'd do in this bizarre situation.

All this underhanded, deceitful behavior isn't me — but here I am anyway, standing on the precipice of transformation with no turning back.

I take hold of the mugs, steadying my hands, and carry them into the living room. *Right hand. Right hand.* "Here you go, sweetheart." I extend my right hand.

"Thanks so much, honey." He takes it, carefully placing it on the side table next to him.

I join him, taking a sip of mine. "Mmm. Even better than yesterday." Am I being over the top? Maybe. But I need him to drink his tea. Quickly.

"Oh?" he asks. "Did you do something different tonight?"

"I added a dash of cinnamon. Really brings out the flavor." I'm talking out of my ass now because I'm not usually a tea drinker, and Derek is aware of this.

"Sounds delicious." He wraps his fingers around the handle of his cup and draws it to his lips. Taking a slow sip, he nods. "Oh yeah. I can taste it. Very nice."

For God's sake, just drink it. I watch Derek take another sip, willing him to drink it faster. He sets the mug down and turns his attention back to the TV. Come on, I urge silently, pick it up again. The minutes tick by slowly as he watches the game, oblivious to my rising tension.

Finally, he lifts the mug again, taking a long drink this time. I exhale, trying not to seem too interested. Just a little bit more now.

A commercial break comes on and Derek reaches for the remote to flip the channels. My heart sinks. "Not going to finish your tea?"

He shrugs. "In a minute. I just want to see what else is on."

I nod, trying to hide my impatience. I glance at the time on my phone. Summer will be here in forty minutes. Derek needs to be out cold by then. If not, things are going to go south pretty goddam fast.

"Well, I'm glad you're enjoying it," I say. "I'll have to make it like this more often."

"Mm-hm," Derek murmurs, focusing on the TV.

I look at his mug. He's barely downed half. I need to get him to finish it.

"Oh, hon, your show's back on," I say, pointing at the screen.

Derek's attention snaps back to the TV, and he reaches for his tea. As if on cue, he drains the rest of it.

"Ready for another?" I ask, reaching for his cup.

He waves me off. "No thanks, I'm good."

I nod. Now, it's just a waiting game.

Several minutes pass, and Derek's eyes begin to droop. His head bobs forward, and he jerks it back, blinking hard. "I didn't realize how tired I am. I think I'll head up to bed early," he mumbles.

"Of course, honey. After all that's happened today, I can't imagine you have much energy for anything else right now." I help him to his feet and walk beside him as he shuffles upstairs.

He practically falls onto our bed, and I stand over him, waiting, watching. Within minutes, he's snoring. I can't believe it worked.

On my way down again, I stop at Ben's door, peering inside. He's asleep too. And as I descend the staircase, my phone vibrates in my pocket. Pulling it out, I read the message on the screen. Summer is here. She's standing outside, but who is with her? I walk toward the front door, glancing back as if I might find Derek standing behind me. But he's out. Ben's asleep. Everything is going as it should.

Quietly, I open the door. Summer's face is pale, looking like a frightened child. But it's what I see in her arms that frightens me. "Oh my God." I swallow hard.

"You wanted to know about a child. Here she is," Summer says. "And Derek's her father."

CHAPTER 41

This tiny baby Summer holds in her arms . . . I can't stop looking at her. Her curious blue eyes, taking in her surroundings. Her tiny hands gripping the blanket in which she's wrapped. My eyes sting with tears; my heart swells with both pain and love. She's part of Derek, but not part of me. The baby girl I'd always wanted.

I've been staring for so long, I'd forgotten how cold it is outside. "Oh my God. Come in. Come in."

Summer enters, clutching the baby that can't be older than three months. I secure the door and turn back to them, unable to find the words. "Summer, I'm — I wish you'd told me sooner. Why keep this from me?"

"None of this was supposed to involve you, Evelyn."

"Of course it involves me. Derek's my husband," I reply. "Come sit down." I usher them to the sofa, glancing upstairs to ensure we haven't disturbed him. Although after three of those pills, I doubt we could disturb a horse. Now, however, I don't know what to do about this child. She springs this on me now. "Why did you bring her here tonight? Where has she been?"

"I've been working to get her out of foster care. I gave her up." Summer peers down at the baby, a tender smile on her face. "When I moved here, and I met you, I thought, maybe I could get her back and try to make Derek see that she's his responsibility too . . ."

I sit down next to them, letting the baby wrap her tiny hand around my finger. "Maybe you're right to do this now. Maybe it will get him to see the consequences of his actions. Get him to realize he needs to atone for what he's done."

I glance upstairs again. "Look, Ben's asleep. We need to get Derek downstairs, so maybe the best thing to do is put the baby in my room once we get Derek out. Do you have the car seat? We can put her in there. She'll be safe."

"Yeah, I do." She hands me the baby. "I'll go get it."

Summer walks out, and I can't help but stare at this perfect little baby girl. She's so beautiful, so innocent. To think she's been in foster care breaks my heart into a thousand pieces. I should be angry, incensed at Derek's actions, but how can I be when I gaze into this child's eyes? She doesn't know the kind of life she was brought into. But I can make it better. When Derek's put away, I'll help Summer raise the child. After all, she's Ben's sister.

My attention turns to the door as Summer enters with a car seat in hand. I rise from the sofa. "Do you have a diaper bag? We should change her now."

"Uh, no. I–I don't have anything like that right now."

"Oh, okay." It's not like I can run to the store. "We'll figure it out later." I walk toward her as she sets down the car seat and places the baby inside. "You haven't told me her name." I buckle her in and look up. "Summer, what's her name?"

"Jenny."

"Jenny. Very sweet." When I'm sure she's safely in the car seat, I return my attention to Summer. "What about your family? You said you gave her up. Did your parents agree with your decision?"

"They don't want anything to do with me. Since Nicole died and I told them how I got pregnant, they turned their backs on me. They said what I did with a married man was disgraceful. I haven't spoken to them since."

"Oh my God, I'm so sorry." I lay my hand on her forearm. "So you've had no support from anyone. I see why you felt you had to give her up. I'm ashamed to be Derek's wife right now."

"It's not your fault, Evelyn."

We're silent for a moment, the baby cooing a little. And then I take a deep breath. "It's time. We need to get him into the basement. I have a chair with some rope. We'll secure him so he can't leave." I catch myself saying these awful words, wondering if they're really coming from my mouth. But they are.

I pick up the car seat and take the baby into Derek's office. On my return, I stand at the bottom of the basement steps. "We'll have to do this as quietly as possible. We can't risk waking Ben."

"And if he does wake?" Summer asks.

"I'll figure it out if that happens. For now, we get Derek downstairs. He'll be out of it, hardly able to walk on his own . . . I hope." Apprehension masks her gaze, and it mirrors my own.

Climbing the stairs, Summer trails me. The stairs creak under our weight, and I curse the sound but press on. When we reach the top, I glance at Ben's room. His door rests against the frame, and a faint sliver of light slices through the crack. A nightlight.

Summer's hand touches my shoulder, and I glance back. "I'm scared," she whispers.

"Me too." I offer her no comfort because there's none to give. We're about to restrain my husband, who I've drugged. I'm pretty sure we'll have broken several laws. So, I'd better be right about this.

Summer and I quietly make our way to the master bedroom. My heart pounds as I slowly turn the knob and peek inside. Derek is sprawled out on the bed, softly snoring. The pills have done their job. I gesture for Summer to follow me into the room. We stand over Derek's sleeping form, exchanging nervous glances.

I lean down to shake Derek's shoulder. "Derek, wake up. You need to come downstairs with me." He stirs slightly but doesn't fully wake. I shake harder as Summer looks on. "Derek, get up now," I say a little louder.

Finally, his eyes flutter open, glazed over and unfocused. "Wha . . . Evie? What's going on?" he mumbles.

"I need you to come to the basement with me. Can you get up?"

He blinks in confusion. "Basement? Why?"

"I'll explain everything, just come with me." I grab his arm and start tugging. He slowly sits up, swaying unsteadily. Summer comes over to help me pull him to his feet.

With Derek barely awake and leaning on us, Summer and I take care to guide him out of the bedroom and down the hall. He's out of it, not even realizing Summer is here. My heart is pounding as we pass Ben's room, praying he doesn't wake.

We make it to the top of the stairs, and I glance at Summer. "Ready?" I whisper. She gives a solemn nod.

I wrap my arm tighter around Derek and we begin our descent, his feet dragging on each step. About halfway down, his head lolls, and he mumbles incoherently. I freeze, glancing up in panic, but the movement doesn't seem to have roused him fully.

"Almost there," Summer says under her breath.

We reach the first-floor landing, and I lead the way to the basement door. Flipping on the light, we guide Derek down toward the wooden chair I placed there earlier.

"Get the rope," I tell Summer. She hurries to retrieve it from the shelf where I had left it coiled up and ready. My hands are shaking as I take it from her.

"Help me sit him down," I say.

We lower Derek onto the chair. He slumps down without resistance. His eyes are barely open now, his whole body limp. I bind his arms and legs. He doesn't resist at all.

Once he's fully secured, I step back, my heart racing. What now? This man tied up here is my husband, the father of my child. What the hell am I doing?

CHAPTER 42

Derek

My eyes crack open, and everything swims in a sickly haze. My head feels like someone packed it with wet cement, each throb echoing painfully in my skull. Slowly, the world comes into focus, and confusion grips me as I take in the familiar gray cinder blocks of the basement walls. My basement.

I try to move, but my arms are dead weight. Ropes bite into my wrists and ankles, keeping me secured to a chair. Panic rises, raw and electric, cutting through the fog of whatever drug entered my body. I didn't take anything. But then I remember the tea. The tea my wife gave me.

"What the hell?" My voice comes out rough, a gravelly rasp, painful in my throat. "What is this?"

I blink hard, focusing on the two figures standing in front of me. Evie, her arms crossed over her chest as if she's cold, her eyes shadowed with something unreadable. And beside her — God, I'm not seeing this, am I? Riley, shifting her weight from one foot to the other, looking anywhere but at me.

"Just stay calm, Derek," Evie says, her voice sounding uncertain and fearful.

It only makes my panic grow when I see the baseball bat next to her. "What . . . what are you doing?" I try to twist against the ropes. "Evelyn, untie me right now. I don't understand what's happening here."

"We need answers, Derek," she replies, this time with firm resolve. "I'm sorry, but this is the only way I knew we could get them."

Riley's gaze flickers down to me for a split second before darting away again, her lips pressed into a tight line. She looks nervous — her skin pale and drawn like she's seen a ghost. "Riley?" My voice cracks under the weight of desperation and disbelief. "Riley, come on. Tell her to let me go. Whatever this is about, it's gone way too far."

But she doesn't respond. Instead, an uneasy silence stretches between us. Evie steps closer, and I see sadness mingled with determination in her gaze.

"We need the truth, Derek," she insists. "I'm sorry to have to do this to you, but there's no other way."

"The truth? About what? Jesus, Evelyn," I say, my words tinged with an edge of anger. "You have to tell me what the hell is going on." And then realization strikes like lightning. "Where's Ben? What have you done with my son?"

"*Our* son," Evie corrects me. "He's our son, and he's fine. He's upstairs asleep in his bed."

"Look, I clearly fucked up, all right? I know that. It's obvious you know who Summer is, and I should've told you when you brought her over for dinner that night. There's no excuse . . ."

"Yes, you should've told me," Evie replies. "But that's not what this is about, Derek. It's time you told us the truth . . . about everything."

"What truth? What the hell are you talking about? You know about Shana. I didn't kill her." I nod at Riley. "She's a liar. She let you believe she was your friend. Following us to Beaufort like a goddam psychotic bitch. I ended things with her long ago, and yet she's here, manipulating you, Evie. She's

223

the one who left the notes. She tried to scare you. Come on."
I sigh, feeling more and more hopeless as I try to convince
my wife of the reality we both now face. "Please, baby. Please
untie me, and let's talk through this like a husband and wife
who still love each other."

Her eyes well. I'm getting through to her.

"I know it was you, Derek," she says. "Summer saw you
there that night at the pool. You drowned her, didn't you?
Nicole? Did she threaten to tell me about your affair? Threaten
to go to your department head? Is that why you killed her?"

My shoulders slump and I close my eyes. "Oh my God,
you can't be serious. Is that what she told you? That I killed
Nicole? For God's sake, Evie. I was there that night. Yes." I
narrow my gaze. "But you knew that. The police knew that.
And when I left, Nicole was very much alive."

"Now who's lying?" Summer cuts in.

Anger balls in my gut. I can't believe Evie trusts this
woman more than she trusts me. None of this makes sense.
The ropes cut deeper into my wrists, and I try to break free.
I'm not sure if they intend to kill me, but I can't rule it out.

I home in on the bat that rests near my wife. Breaking
free from these ropes is doable. The chair is light enough. I
can do this if I try. But then what? *Kill her.* Riley Dittrich is
the cause of all of it. From the moment the police knocked on
my door about Nicole to this very second. She's the reason my
wife is doing this. She's the reason my life has been ruined.

I must find a way to break free. Convince Evie that Riley
wants her to kill me. It was her plan all along. I take a deep
breath and look my wife in the eyes. "Listen to me," I say as
calmly as I can. "I did not kill Nicole. I swear on our son's life.
Riley is lying to you, can't you see that? She's manipulating
you for her own twisted reasons."

Evie blinks quickly, uncertainty flickering across her face.

"Think about it," I press. "Why would I kill Nicole? We
were having an affair, yes, but I broke it off. I chose you, I

chose our family. Nicole was upset, but she accepted it. There was no reason for me to hurt her."

Evelyn glances at Riley, who shifts on her feet, eyes narrowing.

My gaze darts to this nightmare of a woman who stands there, stone-faced. Rage bubbles up inside me. "Tell her the truth!" I shout. "Tell her this is all some sick plan for revenge against me. That it was you who left the notes, you who lied about your true identity. That you want my wife to do your dirty work for you because you were jealous of Nicole."

Riley doesn't even flinch. "Don't try to pin this on me," she says. "I'm not the one who's been lying to his wife for years."

"Please, Evie," I beg. "Don't let her poison come between us. I love you and Ben so much. I won't do anything ever again to jeopardize that. You have to believe me."

She's quiet for a long moment. Finally, she turns to Riley. "Is it true? She was your friend. I imagine you must've been jealous she was sleeping with him, too."

Riley shakes her head emphatically. "Of course I was jealous, but that doesn't change the fact she was my best friend. I saw him come out of the building that night. It was all over his face, the guilt. He killed her, I know he did."

"What about Nicole's mother?" Evie turns back to me. "She believes you killed her daughter, too."

"Of course she does," I say, exhaustion weighing me down. "She's her mother, and she needs to blame someone."

Growing more desperate, I thrash against the ropes, the chair creaking under my efforts. "Dammit, I am telling you the truth! I slept with Nicole, yes, but I did not kill her!"

My voice breaks as I look at Evie again. Her body seems rigid and defensive, but I see another flicker of doubt in her eyes.

"Evie . . ." My tone softens. "You know me. You know I couldn't—" I stop and raise my eyes to the ceiling at the sound. "What the hell was that?" My gaze sweeps between

them. "It sounds like a crying baby. Is that Ben? Evie, go . . .
go check on him—"

"It's not Ben," she cuts in.

I don't like the look between them, like they know something I don't. "Well, what the hell is it?"

Evie licks her lips, glancing down a moment. "It is a baby,
Derek." She sets her gaze on me. "It's your baby."

CHAPTER 43

Evelyn

He doesn't know. Derek truly doesn't know about the child he fathered with Summer. I see it in his eyes as clearly as I see my own hand. I'd suspected she came here to force him to take responsibility for his baby girl, but he had no idea. "That's why she's here, Derek. To hold you accountable for your actions. But now I see that there's more to it, isn't there? You fooled the police. Just admit what you've done, Derek."

"Jesus, Evie, you drugged me, tied me to a goddam chair in our basement and now you're telling me this woman is here because I fathered her baby?" he scoffs. "You're both out of your fucking minds."

"I should go check on her," Summer says.

I nod. "Go. I can handle things down here." I wait for her to head upstairs and then return my gaze to Derek. "My God, why didn't you just own up? She came to you. She told you she was pregnant. Was this before or after Nicole died?"

His head sinks below his shoulders. "Evie, for God's sake. I didn't kill Nicole, all right? And Riley never said a damn word about a baby. She's lying to you. We moved, what two months ago? How old is this baby, huh? Do you even know? She didn't have a baby when Nicole died. She wasn't even fucking pregnant."

"I see desperate words from a desperate man," I say, raising my chin. "Just tell me the truth, Derek. Own up to your actions. Nicole deserves better than that. That baby upstairs deserves better."

Footfalls sound on the basement steps and I see Summer returning. "Is she okay?"

"Fine, yeah."

"What — I don't get to see this supposed kid of mine?" Derek asks, sarcasm tainting his words.

My nerves are on end. We've been down here for too long and still have no answers. Once the pills are fully worn off, Derek won't have much trouble breaking free from his confines. That may be why he's stalling. He knows this, too.

"This isn't working." I turn to Summer. "He's not going to admit to anything."

She frowns, hands on her hips. "So what do we do?"

I glance at Derek, his eyes burning into mine, still denying everything. Anger and hurt well up inside me. I have so many memories with this man — our wedding day, bringing Ben home from the hospital, lazy weekends spent curled up together. Were they all lies? How could I not have known? I wrap my fingers around the bat.

"Evie, please, you don't have to do this," he says, his voice cracking. "I'm telling you the truth. This woman is unstable, she's trying to destroy our family."

I take a slow breath, steadying my nerves. "I don't want to do this, but you've left me no choice."

"What? What are you going to do, Evie?" he asks, almost taunting me to act.

"Tell the police I lied," I reply. "That I have no idea whether you were home that night Nicole died or when you got home. I'll take it all back, Derek. I swear to God I will. And with what Summer has said." I unleash a heavy breath. "They'll reopen the case."

228

"Bullshit." He raises his chin in defiance, but then stops and squeezes his eyes shut. "Fine. You want to know what happened when I went to the pool?" He shoots a look at Summer. "I'll tell you exactly what happened."

* * *

I slip out of the house, praying Evie doesn't hear me. The goddam stairs creak so loudly, I have to fix them. She's been sleeping in the guest room again, making it all too easy for me to make my escape.

I'm on my way to see Riley after receiving a text message from her. After what happened with Nicole earlier this evening, she probably wants to talk about it. I broke it off with Riley months ago, but the two are friends. I can't risk Riley opening her mouth. I'll have to do my best to soothe her.

What I don't get is why she wants to meet at the pool. Maybe because she has a key, and it'll be empty in the middle of the night. I don't know, but she didn't take our breakup well. Especially when I was seeing Nicole, too. I'll need to keep up my guard around her. God knows what she has planned.

As I head into the parking lot, I see Riley's car near the entrance. Good. She's already here. I can't be gone too long in case Evie wakes up. So, I'm glad not to be wasting time waiting around.

Inside, the faint sound of water lapping against the tiles is the only thing breaking the silence. It's dimly lit; only a few of the lights are on. I see Riley standing on the pool's edge. "Hey," I call out.

She turns to me. Then a figure emerges from the shadows, just steps away. "Nicole?" She's in her swimsuit, like she's just changed. I'm surprised we aren't alone. "What the hell?"

I continue my approach, sensing something is terribly wrong. As I near, Nicole appears just as confused as me.

"Now that we're all here," Riley begins. "We can get all this out into the open."

I lock eyes with Nicole. She's afraid. I don't know why she's here, but I sense it wasn't her choice. "What's going on, Riley?"

"Well, I thought since you were fucking both of us, Nicole should probably know that, right?" Riley asks.

"What?" Nicole replies. "What is she talking about, Derek?"

My heart drops into my stomach. What the hell is Riley doing? Why is she telling Nicole about us? But I remain fixed in place, my eyes never leaving them.

"Nicole, I had to do it," Riley says. "I had to get him away from you. He broke it off with you, too, right? That's why he was here earlier today?"

"Did you see him or something? Were you here?" Nicole asks.

"I followed him when he left his office."

I rub my temple. "You followed me?"

"Look, I–I needed him to leave you alone," Riley continues. "I'm sorry. I didn't want it to be this way, but I did it for you."

"What do you mean, for me?" Nicole asks. "What are you talking about? You told me to meet you here tonight for a final lap-time check. I don't understand any of this. How could you betray me? You knew how I felt about him. And today? I've got the most important meet of my career tomorrow, and you do this now?

"I'm sorry." She takes Nicole's shoulders. "I did it because I'm in love with you. I needed you to see that."

Nicole pulls back. "What the fuck?"

"I needed Derek out of the picture so I could tell you how I felt. How much these past three years have meant, having you in my life."

"Yeah, as a friend, Riley." Nicole shakes her head. "Nothing more. I'm sorry. I don't mean to be harsh, but I don't feel the same about you. So, you tried to sabotage my relationship with Derek?"

"Relationship?" She scoffs. "He's a married man who fucks any female student he can, including me."

I shrink back, ashamed of myself.

Nicole sets down her towel. "So you made sure you were one of them. Great. My supposed friend."

"I love you," Riley says. "He isn't the one for you. I am." Her voice drops. "Derek's just a pawn in this game. It was always about us."

"I'm — I'm so sorry, Riley, but I just don't feel that way about you. I love Derek. I knew what I was getting into with him, and I fell in love anyway. I just can't understand why you'd want to hurt me like this. What's the point of all this?"

I keep my mouth shut, her words piercing my chest like daggers. Only now do I see the pain I've caused.

"I wanted you to see who he really was. He doesn't love you, Nicky, you must see that now." She turns to me. "I mean, look at him. He's a piece of garbage."

Riley looks back at Nicole, reaching out for her. Nicole flinches, and steps back, her heels teetering over the edge of the pool. I feel my stomach twist as I watch, a part of me wanting to rush out, to pull her back, but my body's frozen. Riley takes a step closer. I see her arm shoot out, fingers curling around Nicole's wrists.

"Let go of me!" Nicole's voice trembles.

"Not until you hear me out," Riley says.

Before I can process it, Riley pushes her into the pool, falling in with her. The water explodes with sound, a chaotic, desperate thrashing as Nicole surfaces, gasping, her arms flailing against Riley's grip. But Riley holds her down, pushing her head under with a force that seems impossible. I watch, horrified, the splashes growing weaker, quieter. I can't look away.

An eternity slips by before I finally come to my senses and lunge forward. "Stop! Riley, stop! Get off her!"

She spins around, eyes wide with shock. Before I can get close enough, the air fills with an eerie calm. Nicole's movements cease, her body still beneath the water. Riley stands there, breathing hard, droplets of water streaming down her face, her expression calm.

It takes a moment to register what I'm seeing, but then I immediately jump in and grab Nicole, pulling her up to the surface and dragging her onto the side of the pool. "Call 911!" I yell before starting chest compressions.

"You're too late, Derek," Riley says. "She's gone. If she didn't want me, then I guess I don't want her."

"What? You're fucking crazy. Why did you do this? I'm calling 911 right now." I reach for my phone.

"If you do, I'll tell them you killed her," Riley says.

"Not if I can bring her back." I push on Nicole's chest, firmly, methodically, praying I can feel her pulse. "Come on. Come on. Wake up, Nicky. Come back to me."

231

Riley moves toward me. "Derek, stop. She's gone. You'll say nothing. Believe me, I've thought this through. Even down to making sure she's in her swimsuit. I'll tell them I came here after getting worried I hadn't seen her today, knowing she had an important meet tomorrow, but I found you, holding her underwater."

"So I'm just supposed to let her die?" I shout.

"She's already dead. If you do as I say, the only person who will be blamed for Nicky's death is Nicky. But I swear to you, Derek, one word out of your mouth to the police, and I'll put the blame all on you. You were fucking both of us. Who do you think the cops will believe?"

* * *

"And so I left. Left like a goddam coward. And the price I'm paying is having this bitch come back into our lives to destroy us. To destroy me once and for all," Derek says.

My mind spins, and my stomach churns. "But the police came to you anyway."

"She sent them to our door, Evie. A reminder that she was in control of the situation," he replies. "Riley told them about the affair, that was why they came."

I look at Summer, searching her eyes for the truth, but all I see is emptiness. I forget for a moment that my husband kept his mouth shut, knowing the truth of what happened. "My God, Summer. Is this true? Did you kill Nicole?"

CHAPTER 44

Josie

The dinner with Stuart's parents lasted much too long. We're finally home, and I couldn't be happier. We toured their small apartment, then went off to see the dining facility, the games room, and the pool. The indoor heated pool was a nice touch. I'm happy his parents found a place where they can retire. I know it's a load off Stuart's mind.

As he turns down our street, I notice Evelyn's and Derek's cars are in the driveway. "That's odd."

"What is?" Stuart asks in his gruff tone.

"The Moores. They're home. I had to back out of babysitting Ben tonight, but I thought Evelyn arranged for another sitter."

"Maybe she did and they're already back." He points. "Whose car is that along the curb?"

"I don't know. It's not that late, but I suppose they could've come home early. Even so, who does the other car belong to?"

"Josie, you don't have to know everything that goes on in this neighborhood," Stuart says. "Maybe they're having company over."

233

He pulls onto our driveway, and I scoff. "Doubt it. Evelyn said they had a therapy appointment tonight. Guess all isn't so peachy in the Moore household."

"Just leave it, all right?" Stuart cuts the engine. "They're nice people. They had us over for dinner."

"Which was weird with that whole murder conversation, right?" I ask, recalling the strange tension that had settled over the table.

He sighs, opening the door. "Let's just get inside."

I follow him into the house, my thoughts clinging to the notion that Evelyn lied to me. That she needed a sitter for another reason, like going out with other friends. And when I backed out, she opted to have them over. That has to be it.

I wait until Stuart goes upstairs before I head into the living room and peek through the window. The curtains are drawn tight across the Moores' house — an unusual sight that fuels my suspicions further. Evelyn's been off lately. That dinner was clear evidence with her forced smiles and Derek's evasive answers. But why? Why the change, and why ask me to look after Ben tonight, specifically at my house?

They shouldn't be here, the Moores. And they wouldn't be if her husband hadn't elbowed Stuart out of his job at the university. Six years, and then poof — gone, just like that. I got rid of our last neighbors for taking advantage of my husband — the wife, having gotten a little too cozy with him. I'll get rid of them, too.

I keep my eyes on their home, studying it. I need more than speculation to get Derek out of the English Department and get Stuart back in. Derek had threatened to tell Evelyn about my snooping in his office, but I'll bet I can find something to use against him. We've been humiliated by them; everyone knows that Stuart was replaced by a younger version of himself — a good-looking guy with charisma and charm who seemed too perfect from Day One. "Wait another ten years, pal, and we'll see what happens to all that charm."

Why did they leave their big, fancy school in Medford? I bet they think I don't know where they came from, but I'm not stupid. As if I wouldn't do my own digging on the new neighbors. Maybe they have some dirty little secret lying in wait — something lurking beneath their polished exterior like rot under fresh paint. I've been in their home enough times to sense Derek's not who he claims to be.

You don't move from a large school to a smaller one, not when I'm sure he must've had tenure. It doesn't happen unless you've done something terrible — a scandal buried deep enough to avoid public scrutiny but not in-house whispers.

"So what is it? What did you do?"

I glance upstairs. Stuart must be in the bathroom. The faint hum of the exhaust fan drones through the walls, a reminder that he's occupied. I slip on my coat and walk outside, the chill of the evening air nipping at me. No one is around, so I continue down the sidewalk and casually stroll next door. The street is quiet; the only sound is my footsteps on the concrete sidewalk.

I look inside the car parked in front of Evelyn's home. Nothing seems unusual — just a couple of empty coffee cups and a bottle of water on the floor of the passenger side. But then I notice out-of-state plates. That's interesting.

An idea strikes, so I walk toward their mailbox and take a peek inside. They haven't checked their mail yet today. Envelopes sit, waiting for someone to claim them. With a swift glance around, I snatch them up and tuck them into my coat, feeling the adrenaline course through me as I hurry back to the house.

Inside, I find Stuart on the stairs, his brow furrowed in mild curiosity. "What are you doing?" he asks. "Why were you outside?"

"Oh, I left my phone in the car," I reply, always a quick thinker. "Went to go get it."

He grunts, accepting my explanation without much thought, and moves past me into the living room to turn on the television. The familiar buzz of voices fills the air as he settles in to watch the evening sports show.

I hurry upstairs without another word from Stuart. He's too invested in whatever is on the screen before him to notice me.

Reaching my bedroom, I lay down the mail on my dresser and begin to sift through it. The usual stuff: an electric bill, a cable bill, a few pieces of junk mail . . . but then something catches my eye.

"Hold on. What's this?" My fingers brush against a letter-sized envelope addressed to no one — no return address, and it's not post-marked either. "Someone put this in their box."

I walk to my doorway and peek around the corner, ensuring Stuart is still downstairs. His occasional cough punctuates the steady drone of TV chatter. I glance again at the letter.

I wonder . . . do I open it?

CHAPTER 45

Evelyn

Derek's words replay in my mind, a story so horrific that doubt creeps in. After all, my husband has lied to me throughout most of our marriage. Why should I believe him now? He's tied up, vulnerable, and desperate enough to spin any tale if it means I might free him.

I fix my gaze on him, searching for cracks in his facade. "Why didn't you tell this to the police? If she's responsible, why let them consider you a possible suspect?"

He glances at Summer, a knowing look passing between them that I can't decipher. "Derek, answer me. If the school had known the truth, they might've overlooked the relationship you'd had with Nicole."

"Because she was right. The cops would've believed her over me." His gaze meets mine again, pleading for understanding. "I had a motive for killing Nicole. I was sleeping with Riley and—"

"You had every reason in the world to kill both of them," I say, feeling the weight of my words.

"Yes. And Riley would've said as much." He shoots her a look. "But she's lying about a baby. I swear to God. She would've told me she was pregnant."

"I was afraid to," Summer jumps in. "I was afraid you'd hurt me, like you hurt Nicky."

"What the hell are you talking about? I never hurt her. And you're telling me when you held Nicole's head underwater, you were nine months pregnant? For Christ's sake, Evie, can't you see . . ."

"Stop!" My mind spins as I rub my temple. I don't know who to believe. My husband of eight years, or this woman who's come to me with a sob story about how she'd been lied to and betrayed by him. How her best friend was murdered by him. Yet Derek tells a completely different tale. Emily said Riley claimed to be pregnant, yet she couldn't tell either way. Do I trust Derek to have been so observant? They'd already broken up. Could she have been so good at hiding it from him, from Nicole?

But what if he's right, if she's a killer, then I've bound the wrong person. "Summer . . ." Locking eyes with her, the icy gaze confirms my worst fears. Her face twists into a snarl as she stares at Derek. The chilling certainty settles over me. Derek is telling the truth — this woman murdered Nicole.

Summer's lips curl in contempt. "You just had to run your mouth, didn't you, Derek? I warned you what would happen if you told anyone. All you had to do was fucking leave your wife. You cost me the love of my life with Nicole. I gave you the chance to make it right. To care for me and your daughter, and . . . Ben."

My instincts kick into overdrive at the mention of my son. It propels me backward from Summer, whose entire demeanor has transformed into something feral. "No. You don't get to keep my son."

She regards me with contempt. "Oh, Evelyn, sweet naive Evelyn. You've been lied to for so long, you don't recognize the truth when it's being spoken, do you? Did you really think we were friends?" She steps forward slowly, deliberately. "I

238

thought if you heard it from me, you might actually leave him. But you didn't. You're too afraid. You have no idea what a life without Derek would be like. You're weak."

"I'm weak?" Betrayal churns in my gut. All this time, Summer has been using me, worming her way into my life under false pretenses while poor Nicole paid the ultimate price. "Riley," I say, trying to keep my voice steady despite the tremor of fear, "why don't you sit down, and we can talk about this?" I am now keenly aware that a killer stands next to me, and my son is upstairs, defenseless. Yet I have a weapon. Am I prepared to use it?

She whirls on me, eyes flashing. "Don't call me that. Riley died the day he took everything from me. I go by Summer now."

I hold up my hand in a placating gesture. "You're right, Summer. I'm sorry. I just want to make sure you're okay and your daughter is okay."

She laughs. "How can I possibly be okay after what Derek's done to me? That man" — she points a shaky finger at him — "seduced me and got me pregnant all while sleeping with Nicole, too."

"But you knew that," I say. "It was you who wanted to make sure Derek slept with you so you could later tell Nicole what a piece of shit he is." I glance at Derek as shame masks his face.

Tears fill Summer's eyes as her voice catches. "Nicole was everything to me. The only good thing in my life."

Before I can react, Summer lunges, her fingers closing around my throat like a vice. Panic explodes through me as I raise the bat, but as I try to swing it, it strikes a column and slips from my grasp.

I claw at her hands, but her grip is unyielding. Derek thrashes in the chair, desperate to free himself. His shouts echo around me. "Let her go, Riley! Let her go!"

My lungs burn as the world starts to blur. Black spots swarm in my vision, growing larger with every passing moment. "Stop," I rasp, the words barely escaping my lips. "The baby."

I feel her grip loosen a little, just enough for me to bend back her fingers and free myself. I gasp, drawing in precious air. She offers only a moment of respite and then smiles, casting her gaze upstairs.

Oh God. The children.

Summer pushes me to the ground, racing toward the stairs with a terrifying determination. I shoot a look at Derek, his eyes wide, mirroring my own panic. We both know what she intends to do.

"Go!" he yells. "Stop her before she hurts Ben!"

Hurrying to my feet, I stumble toward the stairs, regaining my balance as I dash up them as fast as I can. She's several paces ahead of me, and when I see her reach the second-floor landing, dread coils in my stomach. "Summer, don't!"

The only light in the living room comes from a side table lamp near the sofa, casting just enough light for me to see. And then I realize. "The bat. Goddam it." I left it down there, but there's no time. She's almost at Ben's door.

My heart pounds in sync with my footsteps as I take the stairs two at a time to reach the top. Summer's hand rests on Ben's door. My heart plummets.

I meet her gaze and see nothing but darkness. This is how she'd intended for things to go all along: incapacitate Derek, leaving me vulnerable.

"Don't, Summer," I plead, my voice trembling. "Ben has nothing to do with any of this. Don't you dare touch him."

She turns the handle with slow deliberation, a crooked smile crossing her face. "No? I think he has everything to do with this." Summer opens his door and vanishes inside.

"No!" I scream, sprinting after her into his room. In the dim light filtering through the curtains, I see her outline — a dark silhouette against the blue-gray walls — and then Ben. She holds him in front of her like a shield, hand clamped over his mouth.

I gasp, locking eyes with my son's terrified gaze — those innocent eyes pleading for help, tiny arms and legs flailing, desperate to escape. "It's okay, Benny. You'll be okay. Mommy's here."

Summer unleashes a guttural laugh that echoes throughout the room — a sound devoid of humanity.

"Let him go, Summer."

"Why? So he can grow up and turn out just like his daddy?" Her words drip with malice. "Don't you think you should end this vicious cycle, Evelyn? Stop it right in its tracks? I can do that. It's the most humane thing I can do for this boy."

Tears prick my eyes as Derek's desperate screams reach us from downstairs. "He's the one you want. Derek did this, not Ben! And not your daughter. Have you forgotten about her? She needs her mommy. She needs you, Summer."

For a moment, Summer's face softens as I mention her daughter. Her grip on Ben appears to loosen just a little.

"You're right," she says quietly, almost to herself as if waking from a nightmare. "My little girl does need me."

A wave of relief relaxes the tightness in my chest. Maybe I can appeal to the mother in her, the part that still has love and compassion.

"Let Ben go," I say. "He's just an innocent child. Take your hands off him, and we can talk, just you and me."

Summer hesitates, conflict flickering across her features. For a moment, I think she might release him. But then her expression hardens once more, the softness vanishing as quickly as it appeared.

"No. Men like Derek destroy everything they touch. Their sons grow up to be just like them." Her arm tightens around Ben again, hand clamping back over his mouth more firmly. He squirms in protest, his muffled whimpers penetrating the air.

"I have to end this. I have to," Summer insists, her voice at a manic pitch.

Desperation knots my gut. I have to keep her talking, distract her somehow. My eyes dart around the room, searching for anything I can use to stop her. There's no time left for strategy or negotiation — just raw instinct driving me forward. Fuck it.

I charge toward her, colliding with both of them as we all tumble to the ground in a chaotic heap. "Ben, run!" I yell, my voice cracking with urgency as I try to pin down Summer's thrashing arms. "Go next door! Run, baby, run!"

But he's too young to understand — too afraid — and he simply stands there, frozen in place, tears streaming down his cheeks as he calls out my name.

"Mommy! Mommy! Make her stop!"

Summer struggles beneath me with surprising strength, her movements wild and desperate like an animal caught in a trap. I catch sight of Ben scuttling toward his bed and crawling underneath it for safety, and at that moment, Summer pushes me off her and crawls away.

I pull myself along the thick carpeted floor inch by inch as she draws closer to the door. Reaching out with every ounce of strength left in me, I clutch onto her pant leg. She kicks and kicks at me, trying to force me to let go, but I cling on for dear life. I can't let her escape. I have to stop her.

My elbows burn from dragging along the rough carpet fibers as I inch closer to her calf. Just when I'm close enough to pull her back from the brink, her right leg shoots out with terrifying precision, connecting with my forehead in a blinding flash of pain. My neck snaps back — and then . . . darkness.

CHAPTER 46

Josie

The envelope bends in my hands. I slip my index finger under the flap and rip it open. The noise echoes in my bedroom, and I freeze, wondering if I'll hear Stuart climbing the stairs to check on me. But who am I kidding? Even if he heard it, he doesn't care. He doesn't care about any of it. Losing his job seemed to have meant nothing to him. But it means something to me.

Our argument the other night . . . the Moores had heard it. I'd finally tired of Stuart letting things happen to us. The incident with our old neighbors. Now, refusing to act against the man who took his job. Derek Moore ruined everything.

I'd destroyed our priceless china, blaming it on him when I saw Evelyn. She couldn't have known it was about her husband. But it's been about Derek Moore since the day he arrived.

Of course I'd wanted to see inside their house. To find whatever it was that brought him and Evelyn to my neighborhood. To my school, which my husband and children attended. Where he'd worked for years. But this?

I pull out the letter, glancing back at my bedroom door as though I'm doing something illegal. Then again . . . I let out a stifled laugh. I unfold the letter; the words are handwritten in messy cursive.

I murdered Nicole Peterson.

The words stare at me. My breath comes in short and quick. "Oh my God. What is this?" I whisper. I have no idea who Nicole Peterson is or who killed her, but no doubt it has everything to do with Derek Moore.

The ink is smeared on the next line — the obvious mark of a left-handed writer. Is Derek left-handed? But would he have written out this confession only to place it in his own mailbox? I read on.

The police called it an accident. They talked to my husband, Derek Moore, who had been having an affair with Nicole. I found out about the affair, and when I told Nicole to stay away from my husband, she pushed me to the brink, refusing to stop. I was left with no choice but to end her life so that mine could carry on.

Evelyn — a killer? My eyes widen, darting over the words again as though I must have mistaken their meaning. But it's all here, in indelible blue ink. Nicole Peterson — dead. And Evelyn . . . a murderer?

I don't understand. Did she write this and leave it in her mailbox? Why? A confession or a cry for help? I tilt back my head, drawing in air as the weight of this knowledge suffocates me. I knew there was something wrong with them. I just didn't know it was her.

I leap from my bed and rush to the window, pressing my cheek against the glass to get a glimpse of their house. I see a faint light burning through the living-room window. All three cars are still there.

I knew something was off with them. I sensed it, but this? No. Not in a million years would I have believed this. When I peer through the window again, nothing looks out of the ordinary. No screaming or shouting. No noise whatsoever. "What is going on over there?"

With the letter in hand, I jog downstairs and see Stuart on the sofa, eyes glued to the television. "I have to tell you something." As I move closer, he doesn't look at me or acknowledge my presence. "Stuart? Stuart, are you listening?"

"What?" He finally turns toward me. "Honey, what is it?"

I hand him the letter, my hand shaking. "I found this in Evelyn and Derek's mailbox. It's . . . it's a confession letter."

Stuart's forehead creases as he takes the paper from me. "You took this from their mailbox? For Pete's sake, Josie, that's a crime, you get that, right?"

"Just read it. Please."

His eyes scan back and forth across the page, widening with each line he reads. His mouth falls open. "What the hell?" He looks up at me, disbelief stamped on his face. "Is this for real?"

I nod, perching on the edge of the sofa next to him. "I think so. I mean, I don't know Evelyn's handwriting, but what else can I think except that she's written it?

"Dear Lord," Stuart says under his breath. "Have you talked to her? Or called the police?"

"No. I just took this. I thought something felt off, you know? When we got home?" I glance down sheepishly. "So, I went and looked in their mailbox, and there it was, mixed in with other envelopes. I wanted to show you. I just . . . I can't believe it." I gesture toward the window as though their house is within arm's reach. "Who the hell is Nicole Peterson? Is that why they moved here? Were they escaping some awful, horrible thing Evelyn did?"

Stuart scrubs a hand over his face, as though trying to wipe away the confusion and disbelief clinging to him. "This is insane." He glances down at the letter again, brow furrowed.

"Why would she leave something like this in her own mail-box, though? She want someone to find this? Derek, himself, maybe? Who else would check their mail?"

"But why not just tell him directly?" I bite my lip, gnawing on the uncertainty and fear that twists my stomach into knots. "Do you think it's a cry for help?" And then it hits me. "If Evelyn murdered this Nicole Peterson, what about Shana Foster? Stuart, could she have done that, too?"

CHAPTER 47

Derek

My wrists burn from the ropes as they dig deeper into my skin, each twist and pull sending a fresh wave of pain shooting through me. Blood drips down my hands, falling onto the gray rug beneath me. I don't hear them anymore — only the oppressive silence that fills this room. I don't know what's happening. Whether my son is safe, or my wife. All I do know is that I have to get free of these ties, to break loose from this hellish nightmare. How could I have let this happen? I knew Riley was crazy, and I did nothing to stop her.

I was so certain they all loved me, the girls I slept with, and I used that love and admiration to build up my ego. Now, my wife and son might die because of it.

My arms are tied around the back of the chair — a sturdy, solid oak relic from my grandmother's house. My best option is to tip it over, hoping the impact will be enough to break it apart. But if I can just free my arms, the rest is easy — untie my legs, grab the bat, and rush upstairs to protect my family from the psychotic bitch I unleashed on them.

Only now does it begin to make sense — Shana's death. I suspected Riley could be the culprit, but almost hoped it was

Alex. That he'd grown jealous of her attraction to me. Now, I know that the woman upstairs, the woman I watched murder Nicole — she killed Shana. God knows why or how she knew anything about Shana, but it had to be her.

I close my eyes, tears welling. "I have to help them." As I shift my weight side to side, preparing for the inevitable fall, a new sound pierces through the silence — voices. They're muffled and indistinct, and I can't make out what's being said. Panic surges again in my chest. "Hey!" I yell out, sharp and jagged. "Hey, Riley! I'm the one you want, you bitch!" The words echo off the walls like a plea and a challenge all at once.

The voices fall silent. What's happening up there? I peer at the ceiling as though I might see through the crisscross of beams and wires tucked between the floors. But there are no footfalls. Nothing.

Inhaling deeply, I fill my lungs with the stale, dusty air that hangs in the room. We still have unpacked boxes down here. We've barely started our new lives, and now this. Never mind. My family needs me.

I throw myself sideways. The chair tips over, sending me crashing onto the unforgiving concrete floor with a jarring thud, the thin rug doing nothing to soften the blow.

A groan wrenches itself from my throat as pain flares through my shoulder. The chair has splintered and cracked under my weight but refused to break apart. "No. No, please, God. Get me out of here."

The voices return, growing louder and more frantic. The piercing wail of a child cuts through the noise. Ben? God . . . what are they doing? "Help!" The word tears from my lips. My hope rests on Josie — our nosy neighbor with an insatiable curiosity for neighborhood gossip. I need her to hear me. "Help!"

Anger bubbles, and I let out a guttural roar. "Don't you dare lay a finger on them!" My voice reverberates around me.

Their cries and screams grow louder. I thrash on the ground, impotent to do anything else. Please, for the love of God, let Josie hear us.

248

CHAPTER 48

Evelyn

By the time I come to, Summer is standing at the door. She's going to escape. The door opens and she flies out. Ben is crying from under the bed. My head is clouded with fear. Pain radiates through my entire body from my struggle to stop this woman. Cuts and scrapes. Bruises, already forming.

"Oh God." I scramble on my knees toward Ben. "Come here, baby. It's okay. You're okay." I grip his arms and slide him out, pulling him into an embrace.

What do I do? I have to protect my son. Will we make it downstairs and outside? We need help. My head is spinning, and I don't know what to do. Then I hear the cries — sharp, piercing notes that cut through my panic like a knife. Is that . . .? I look at Ben, holding my finger over my lips to try to silence him as he quietly sobs against my shoulder. Where the hell is she?

There it is again. It's the baby. She's crying. But it's not just any cry. No. I recognize a cry for food or to be changed; this is different — urgent, desperate, filled with a rawness that sends panic through me. That's not the cry of a tired baby. She's in pain. She's hurt. No. It's not possible. Summer wouldn't hurt her own baby, would she?

I search Ben's room as if a solution will magically appear amid the toys scattered across the floor. But I know what the solution is — a decision that twists my heart into knots.

"Benny?" I raise his chin, holding his gaze with all the strength I can muster. "Baby, I need you to go into your closet, okay? I need you to stay there and be as quiet as you can. Only for a little while. Will you do that for me, sweetheart? I'll be right back."

"No, Mommy. Don't go." He grips my arm with surprising strength, his tiny fingernails digging into my skin as the baby's cries grow louder.

"I'm going to lock your door, okay? I have a key, don't worry," I whisper, struggling to keep my voice steady. I can't let him see my fear. "But I need you to stay in your closet and be quiet as a church mouse. Please."

I help him up and take him to his closet. "I know it's dark in there," I say, smoothing back his hair. "I know, sweetheart, and I promise I won't be long. Don't unlock your door for anyone. I have a key to open it, and I will be back. I promise you."

Lying nearby is his beloved stuffed tiger. He clutches it tightly against his chest as tears stream down his cheeks. I close his closet door, muffling my own sobs with my hand. Leaving him alone is the last thing I want to do, but I have to end this. And it has to be now.

I have no idea what she's doing to that baby, but the mere thought fills me with a primal fear that rips my insides. I have to stop her. A terrible certainty grips me — if I don't act, she will kill that child. And then . . .

I charge toward my bedroom, the baby's cries growing louder with each step. I burst into the room, and I'm confronted with the unthinkable. Gasping, my hands fly to cover my mouth.

Summer looms in the center of the room, holding her baby upside down by one leg, the infant's head dangling precariously above the floor. Her expression — a dark, twisted smile and empty eyes — the definition of evil.

"Put her down! You're hurting her! Stop!" The words spill out, fractured and uncertain, a frantic plea.

The baby's face is flushed with blood rushing to her head. Tears blur my vision as I see her little arms flail. She needs help. She needs someone to protect her. To save her. "Summer, please . . ." I'm out of breath, terrified for this tiny baby. If she falls to the floor . . . she's so little . . . "Please, put her down. Please. My God, this is your child. Why are you doing this?"

Without a word, Summer walks to my bedroom window, still clutching the baby's leg. As she opens it, panic rises in me like a tidal wave. "Don't," I beg, every syllable infused with raw desperation. "Don't do this. Please."

"Why not? She's a bastard," Summer replies, almost mechanically. "Why would you want the child your husband fathered with another woman to live?"

"Because I'm a human being! Because I'm a mother!" I snap back, my anger flaring hot and bright. But I need a new approach. She must see reason. Yelling at her only makes her push harder against me. "It doesn't have to be this way, Summer." My voice softens. "I'm begging you."

The baby screams as the cold from the open window wraps around her. I take a step closer.

"Don't!" Summer demands. "Don't come any closer, or I will drop her from this window." Suddenly a soft thud echoes outside, and her attention is diverted.

I don't waste a moment as I charge toward her. The baby is within my reach, I snatch her from Summer, thrusting one hand against her chest. Summer stumbles back, dropping to the floor.

I've got her. I've got the baby. "It's okay. You're okay," I whisper.

Within seconds, Summer scrambles toward the door, disappearing into the hallway. "Ben." With the infant still in my arms, I dash into the hall, but she's gone. I grip Ben's door handle, checking it's still locked. Thank God.

251

A flash of light on the stairs draws my attention. I glimpse Summer's blond hair as she runs down them, disappearing again. "Oh, no. Derek." Her plan is clear to me now. The baby was a distraction. She knew I'd never let anything happen to the child. Now, she's going after my husband.

I glance back at Ben's door, then again at the stairs. I need to keep these children safe at all costs. If I leave them again, she will come for them. She will kill them — both. Summer will do anything to destroy everything I love. Everything Derek loves.

There's only one answer. The only way to protect the children, to protect my husband, is to end her. A gun rests inside a locked metal case on top of our closet. I yank the blanket off our bed and drape it on the floor. Setting down the baby, I run into the closet and peer up. There it is.

Standing on tiptoes, I stretch, my fingers searching for an edge to grasp. Relief washes over me when I wrap my fingers around it. It's heavy, but I pull at it, and it teeters on the edge of the shelf. I only have moments — I'm certain Derek's life is in danger.

Stretching as far as my arms can go, standing as tall as I possibly can, I balance it on my fingers, lowering it down. "Oh, thank God."

I return to the bedroom. The baby is quiet for now. Ben is quiet, still in his closet. God — how terrified he must be. I can't think about that now. I can't afford the distraction. Placing the box on the bed, I eye the combination lock. "What the hell is it?" I rack my brain, trying to recall the numbers. Panic surges. I can't remember. "Fuck!" My hands tremble, and tears spill down my cheeks. "Come on. Come on! What is it?"

I hear muffled voices through the floor. She's with him. *No.* She's there with Derek. I look back at the case and begin to press the keypad, praying I remember. I know this number. Derek's told me before, but it was so long ago.

The box clicks. The door swings open.

I gasp in surprise, then quickly reach in and retrieve the gun. A box of ammunition lies beside it. I pop out the clip and snatch several bullets from the box, fumbling to load each one. It's harder than I remember — pushing them in. I pull back the barrel and release a bullet into the chamber. I guess I remember more than I thought.

I lock eyes with the infant. She smiles, and my heart shatters. "I'll be right back. I swear it." I rush out into the hall, stopping at Ben's door. No sounds emerge, but I have to go. I have to leave him there.

Running down the stairs, I catch sight of my cell phone on the living-room side table. I need to call the police, but a loud thump startles me. "Derek!"

I brandish the gun, my hands shaking so hard that I might actually drop it. I head toward the basement stairs. My breaths come in short gasps. My throat is dry and my pulse echoes in my ears.

Down the steps, one at a time, I hear a sound that can only mean one thing. "Please, God, no," I whisper. Reaching the bottom, a low, thick scream claws from my throat. "No!"

Summer, splattered in blood, her face burning red with rage, brings down the bat onto Derek. Over and over, shattering his body, smashing his head while he lies on the floor, helpless to stop her. Tied up — because of me.

"Stop!" I scream, my finger on the trigger, taking aim.

She looks up — Derek's blood dripping down her face, soaking through her shirt — and smiles at me. "It's over, Evelyn. Our problem is gone."

"Not yet, it isn't." I squeeze the trigger and fire off a shot. The bullet slices through her throat.

Her eyes widen as she clutches her neck.

I watch in horror as everything moves in slow motion. Summer sways, looking at me with wild eyes. Derek lies motionless on the floor. I can't breathe. Time has stopped.

She falls to the ground, and I pull myself from my stupor. "Derek!" I run to him, but I'm too late.

He's dead.

They both are.

CHAPTER 49

Josie

Standing outside, I wait again for the sound. Stuart stands next to me, both of us scanning our usually quiet street. "What was that?"

"I don't know," he replies.

"Something tells me that it came from the Moores' house. Especially after reading that letter." I look over at their home. It appears otherwise quiet. "Stuart, we need to call the police." I don't want to tell him what I believe the sound was because it doesn't seem possible. I swear it sounded like a crying baby. "I'm going over there."

"Josie, wait," Stuart calls out. "Let's go back inside. We'll call the police, all right?"

"I'll just check real quick," I yell back.

I swear it was a crying baby. But not just any cry. It sounded like the infant was screaming in pain. My children are grown, but a mother always recognizes the cries.

I stand in front of their home. Only a faint light in the window, just as I'd seen from my house. The cries have stopped, replaced by an eerie silence hanging in the frigid night air. My breath floats above me and I shiver. "What on earth is going on over here?" My imagination races with possibilities.

A flash of movement catches my eye. There, in the upstairs window, a shadow passes by. It's too quick for me to make out any details, but it looks to be an adult.

That car is still here. And I didn't see a car seat or the base of one inside, so where did this baby come from?

A gunshot rings out. I jump. "What the hell? Oh my God." I glance back at my house, wondering if Stuart has called the cops. There's no time to waste. I'll have to do it myself if he hasn't. I snatch my phone from my pocket and dial.

"911. What is your emergency?"

"I heard a gunshot come from my neighbors' house. You have to send the police. Now."

CHAPTER 50

Evelyn

Summer lies sprawled out on my floor. Her lifeless eyes stare blankly at the ceiling. Blood trickling from her neck. Derek, bound to the splintered chair, lies still. His face, unrecognizable. His body, in tatters. No matter how hard I try, he won't wake up. There's blood everywhere — thick and dark, staining the rug with the violence that occurred before my eyes.

My body is shaking as if trying to purge me of this trauma. My husband is dead. The room spins, each rotation bringing fresh waves of nausea. What do I do? "Call the police," I tell myself, though my voice comes out fragile and cracked, barely audible over the pounding in my ears.

I peer up the staircase, my heart clenching. "Ben." Scrambling away, I slip on the blood, my hands landing in the pool around Derek's body. The sticky warmth clings to my palms. Fear fills my lungs. I can't breathe; each gasp is like it'll be my last as panic threatens to consume me whole.

I somehow find the stair railing, gripping on to it for dear life. I have to get to my son. As I reach the first floor, the doorbell rings. I freeze, my legs refusing to move.

Outside, there's no sign of anyone. No headlights. Nothing. But I have to go upstairs. I have to tell Ben he's safe. And the baby . . . oh my God . . . the baby. What do I do? I killed her mother. Her father's dead too.

The doorbell rings again. "Shit. Shit. Shit." I peer upstairs. "No. Just get Ben." Who is at the door at this hour, I have no idea, but if it was the cops, they'd say as much.

I run up to Ben's room, unlocking his bedroom door and rushing toward the closet. I yank it open and see my boy, curled up in a ball, clutching his stuffed tiger. "It's okay, sweetheart. Everything's okay now." I reach down for him, but he recoils.

I knit my brow in confusion but then glance at my bloody hands. "Oh, no. No, it's okay, baby. I'm okay. I — everything's fine. Don't be scared. I'm not hurt." I can't tell him about Derek. Not yet. He seems to relax, so I reach down and scoop him up in my arms. "I'm so sorry, baby. I promise I'm okay. Are you okay?"

His face wears fear. He's terrified of the blood all over me. But then, he nods a little. "Good. Okay, good." I set him down. His clothes have blood on them now, too. "Stay here. I'll be right back."

"No!" He curls his fingers around the bottom of my shirt. "Don't go, Mommy. Don't leave me."

"Okay. Okay. Come with me, then." I usher him through the darkened hall and toward my bedroom.

There she is. The baby is still on the floor, now asleep on the blanket. I walk toward her when the doorbell rings again. "Dammit." I quickly realize whoever it is has no intention of leaving.

I squat low to meet Ben's gaze. "Honey, how about you stay here with the baby for a minute, okay? I could really use your help right now. Can you watch her, like a big boy?" I have to find a way to keep him occupied, and this is the best I've got. "I just need to go see who's at the door. But don't say anything, all right? Stay up here, keep an eye on her, and just sit tight. No noise. No talking." Guilt weighs on me as I'm asking my

257

four-year-old son the impossible — again. "I'll be back in just a minute. We'll figure all this out and get cleaned up, okay?"

He nods.

"That's my boy." I rise again and kiss the top of his head, then march toward my bedroom door and stop to look back. Ben's sitting on the blanket with Summer's baby. I pull the door closed and cut across the hall to the bathroom.

I gasp, my reflection startling me. I turn on the water and wash the blood from my hands. Nothing I can do about what's on my clothes. Downstairs, my phone rings. "For God's sake." And then I realize whoever's at the door is probably trying to call me now. I stop, no longer able to keep my composure as tears stream down my face. I struggle to catch my breath. I can't stay here. I have to go downstairs. The police will come. They'll arrest me and take my son and the baby.

I reach the bottom of the steps, and a voice calls out on the other side of the door.

"Evelyn? Derek? Are you guys okay? I heard a gunshot."

It's Josie. "Coming," I choke out. *Coming?* What the hell am I saying? Do I tell her? She's heard the gunshot. Did she call the cops?

I wrap my fingers around the door handle and pull it open. Josie's eyes scan me. Her brow tightens, and I don't know what to say. I don't want to tell her my husband is dead, along with a woman I thought was my friend. "Josie."

"Oh my God, look at you. The police are on their way," she says. "I already called them, Evelyn, what happened?"

I stand frozen in the doorway, unable to form words as Josie stares at me with dawning horror. The wail of sirens cuts through the night air, jolting me back to the present.

"You need to leave," I say with a surprising calmness. "The police will be here any second."

Josie shakes her head, her eyes searching mine for answers. "I'm not going anywhere. Tell me what's going on!" Her gaze drifts over my shoulder, searching for the truth of what happened.

I grip the door handle tightly, blocking her view with my body. "Please, Josie, you can't be here. Just go." I'm begging now, desperation making my voice tremble as I attempt to shield her from the horror inside.

"Evelyn, please talk to me." Her voice brims with fear. "Is Derek . . . is he . . ."

"Go!" I shout, before attempting to close the door on her.

She thrusts out her hand and inserts her foot, blocking me. "I found something, Evelyn. You need to see it." Her voice is steady now, determined.

Josie unfolds a piece of paper. It's a letter. She holds it up to my face with trembling fingers.

"Read it."

I don't grab it, only taking in the first few sentences — enough to know what this is. "Where did you get this?"

"It was in your mailbox."

I crease my brow in confusion. "What the hell were you doing checking . . ." I wave my hand dismissively. "Never mind." It occurs to me then that Summer must've written it. "She'd planned on killing me," I say. "She'd planned on killing all of us, blaming me in the process by leaving this note. She wanted to make it look like a murder-suicide." I look at Josie, her eyes widening at the revelation.

"Who, Evelyn? Who are you talking about?" She tries to peer around me. "Is she here? Is she . . ."

The sirens grow louder. I don't trust Josie. I can't tell her all that's happened.

"The police will be here any minute," she continues. "Did you do this, Evelyn? Did you murder your husband?"

259

CHAPTER 51

For a moment, I stand frozen, wondering what to tell Josie, who, up until now, I believed had been after Derek for what happened to her husband.

Looking at her now, fear in her eyes, I'm aware she has no idea what's happened. I glance over at the gun lying on the coffee table. And now, she sees it too. "I–I tried to save them all."

She peers over her shoulder toward the basement stairs as if drawn by morbid curiosity. "What am I going to find if I go down there?"

"Something you can't unsee," I reply with a composure that surprises me.

"This letter." She waves it in front of me. "You confess to killing Nicole Peterson in this letter."

"I didn't write it," I snap back. "It was her. The woman in my basement — Summer, I mean, Riley. She's — dead. So is Derek." Red and blue lights flash through my front window, reflecting off the wall behind Josie. The lights cast a strange glow across her face as she stares at me, seemingly uncertain of whether my words are true. "They're here, Josie. My time's up."

The baby upstairs begins to cry — a sharp wail cutting through the tense silence — and Josie's gaze snaps back to me.

"Whose baby is that?" she asks.

I close my eyes for a moment, feeling trapped. "I know why you were snooping around our house. It was Derek, wasn't it? You thought he was responsible for getting Stuart fired. You think he killed Shana Foster, don't you? But it wasn't him, Josie. The police finally cleared him as a suspect."

"He threatened me, Evelyn. I tried to tell you, but . . ."

The cries grow louder.

"Whose baby is that?" Josie demands.

CHAPTER 52

Josie

I don't know what horrors occurred in this house, but I'm not afraid. Something in her eyes tells me she's speaking the truth. The pieces don't yet fit together, but Evelyn Moore needs my help. I came here tonight, certain Derek was the enemy. Stuart's career was ruined because of him. And I was certain he murdered Shana Foster. Am I wrong about that, too?

"The woman . . . who was she?" I ask again.

Evelyn wipes a tear from her eye, clearing her throat. "Derek had an affair with her. She confessed to doing something back in our old town. She followed us here, Josie. That baby you're hearing? It's hers. Hers and Derek's."

"Oh my God." I glance at the front window where I'd seen the patrol cars, but the lights are gone now. "Where'd they go?"

Evelyn turns around.

"I don't see the lights anymore." I walk to the window and pull back the curtain just enough to peek through. "What in the world?"

"What is it?" Evelyn says.

"The cops. They're not here anymore. They're at my house."
I spin around to her, dropping the curtain panel. "What's going on? Did you do this? Did you call the police too and send them to my house?"

"No. Why would I — I don't understand."

I hurry to the door and step outside. "Hey!" I call out, running toward my house. "I live here. What's going on?"

An officer grips the sidearm in his holster as I draw near. "I'm going to need you to stop right there, ma'am."

I halt in my tracks. "I don't understand. That's my house. Tell me what's going on."

"Are you Mrs. Josie Brewer?" he asks.

"Yes, I am. I called you minutes ago about a gunshot I heard at my neighbor's house." I feel my pulse quicken. "What are you . . ."

"Is your husband, Stuart Brewer, home?"

"Of course he is."

The officer waves at his colleagues, and three of them approach my front door. In the distance, a detective is leaning on a black car, observing the scene. I glance back at Evelyn's house. She's standing in the doorway, just inside.

"For God's sake, will someone please tell me what's happening?" I march toward the detective. "Excuse me. I'm Josie Brewer. What's going on? Why are you here, and why aren't you next door? Do you have any idea what's happened over there? I called—"

"Ma'am, why don't you stick close for a few minutes, all right?"

"No. It's not all right." I head back toward my house when I see the door open, and Stuart stands there.

At that moment, the officers brandish their guns, screaming and shouting . . . "Get down! Get down on the ground, now!"

I freeze in place. My gaze darts between the cops, Stuart, and the detective. When I finally find my footing, I race toward them.

"Stay right there, ma'am!" One of the officers strong-arms me as I try to reach Stuart.

"That's my husband!" I shout. "Leave him alone!" They force him onto his stomach, the cops twisting his arms behind his back. "Stuart! It's okay. Just do what they tell you." He raises his head and sees me.

Two officers pull him to his feet. Stuart's a big man, and they're struggling.

One of the officers stands in front of him. "You're under arrest for the murder of Shana Foster."

As I lock eyes with him, my head grows light. What did they just say? Murder? "Stuart?"

He says nothing — completely stone-faced. They lead him to a patrol car, shoving him into the backseat. I run to the vehicle. "Stuart! Stuart! Wait, you're wrong about this. He didn't do this."

The detective steps toward me, his hands gently gripping my shoulders. "Ma'am. Ma'am, please. We have evidence that proves your husband murdered Shana Foster. I'm sorry."

His words land, sharp and heavy, like a slap across my face. "What did you just say?" I aim my finger next door. "Do you know what's happened over there?" He says nothing. "Look, my husband's done nothing wrong—"

"I'm afraid that's not true, Mrs. Brewer," he says. "We found the murder weapon used to kill Ms. Foster. Your husband's prints were on it."

I falter. "I don't understand. Why? He barely knew her."

"She worked at the university at the same time as your husband, correct?"

I nod, almost imperceptibly.

"And your husband was let go recently?"

"Yes." My voice comes out in a whisper.

"We discovered evidence that Ms. Foster had threatened to come out with a story about your husband — that he'd assaulted her — if he didn't voluntarily retire his position."

"Why? I don't understand. He said he was fired."

"That may be what he told you." The detective glances at the Moores' house. "Ms. Foster had known Derek Moore intimately in the past. According to emails we discovered in Shana's possession, she'd offered to help him get the job after leaving Medford under dubious circumstances."

The patrol car pulls away from our curb. Stuart looks at me, a slight raise of his lips. A shrug of his shoulder. He did it.

"Weeks after he started, Ms. Foster contacted the police about being followed. More than once. She was scared," he continues. "Two days later, she was dead."

"This is Derek's doing. I know it is." I shoot my gaze toward Evelyn, still standing in her doorway. "She killed him. Just now. She murdered her husband in cold blood." I shout over to her. "Stuart is innocent! Tell them, Evelyn! Tell them the truth!"

CHAPTER 53

Evelyn

Josie's words echo around me. I don't know what's happening, but Stuart just got hauled away in handcuffs. What the hell is going on?

The baby's cries grow louder, and I look upstairs.

"Mrs. Moore?"

I recognize the voice and return my attention to the front porch. "Detective Langston." His gaze roams over me, my blood-stained hands and clothes. He rests his hand on the butt of his gun. This is it. I have to tell him.

"What happened in here, ma'am? Where's your husband?"

The baby keeps crying, and Langston raises his gaze, then flicks off the snap of his holster. "Mrs. Moore, I need you to tell me what's happening right now. Mrs. Brewer called 911 and claimed she'd heard a gunshot over here."

"Then why did you go to her house? What happened with Stuart Brewer?"

He looks beyond me, toward the basement where the light shines. "He killed Shana Foster, ma'am. Not your husband."

My lips tremble and I close my eyes a moment, tears spilling over. "He's dead," I whisper. "She killed him. And I killed her."

Langston widens his stance and brandishes his gun. "Who is she? I'm going to need you to stay right here, you understand?"

"The baby," I say. We both hear her crying now, and it's only a matter of time before Ben walks downstairs. "I have to check on the children."

He tosses a nod. "Go. I'll follow."

I walk upstairs and head into my bedroom.

"Mommy!" Ben runs to me. "She's crying, Mommy. The baby's crying."

I lift him into my arms. "It's okay, sweetheart. Everything's going to be okay." I turn back to Langston. "Downstairs, in the basement." He seems to know what I want to say, but I can't form the words, not in front of my son.

"Bring them down. Let's go," he says, his gun at his side.

With Ben next to me and the baby in my arms, we descend the steps once again.

"Mommy, I'm scared." Ben tugs at my shirt.

"It's okay, baby. It's the police. They're here to help us."

Langston presses on a radio that's hooked on his belt. "I need some help in here. Now."

As we reach the living room, two more officers arrive.

"Step outside, please," Langston says. "And stay with Officer St. Claire."

I nod and we do as he asks.

Several more officers rush inside my home. What they're about to see, an unspeakable, horrific scene I can hardly comprehend myself, they won't forget. I have no idea how I'll tell Ben what's happened to his father.

Langston soon returns, gun holstered. "Where's the firearm?" he asks, approaching us. "Where's the gun, Evelyn?"

"On the coffee table," I reply in a whisper.

"And did you fire the weapon?" he presses.

"I did, yes."

He looks at one of his officers. "Get your kit. Test her residue. Now."

"On it." The officer darts away.

I remain on our porch, shivering in the cold. Ben is shaking as well. The baby is wrapped in a blanket. "Excuse me?" I ask one of the officers.

She turns around. "Yes, ma'am?"

"I need someone to look after them while the police talk to me. Can you arrange that?"

"Of course."

I go through the process of fingerprinting. They take swabs of my fingers, they say, to check for gunpowder residue. But I have no intention of lying to them about what I've done.

Josie is standing in her yard, watching, as has become her trademark. I'm in shock over Stuart but enraged because, if he hadn't killed Shana, maybe Derek wouldn't be dead right now. Maybe I wouldn't have been pushed over the edge, fearing my husband was a killer, and going to lengths I never thought possible.

When she approaches, her face is red, eyes swollen.

"I'm so sorry, Josie."

She nods. "Me, too, Evelyn. They said Derek had known Shana — intimately. She'd arranged to make Stuart leave or come up with some story about him assaulting her."

"Oh my God. I had no idea." I close my eyes for a moment. "So Stuart . . . killed her?"

She looks away, wiping her eyes. "He was so humiliated, and he kept it all in. But Derek knew. He knew what Shana did so he could get the job. A job he needed because of what happened to Nicole Peterson."

"Josie, I couldn't have known what Stuart would do. I'm so sorry. I'm so sorry for all of this."

Langston walks toward me. "Mrs. Moore?" he asks, standing next to Josie. "Your children . . . do they have a place to go tonight?"

I realize in that moment his words and their meaning. *My children*. I look at Josie. Only she knows the baby isn't mine. But there's something in her eyes. Something that makes it okay for me to do what I'm about to do.

I nod, turning back to the officer. "Yes, sir. My children have a place to go."

EPILOGUE

The basement is clean, like nothing ever happened down here. The rugs were replaced. The concrete — scrubbed with an acid solution to remove the blood stains. The detective who'd investigated Nicole Peterson's death was made aware of Summer Burton, aka Riley Dittrich. He went back and reviewed the evidence, asked the coroner, based on new information, to review his findings regarding Nicole's autopsy.

A minor bruising of her hyoid bone was noted but had been considered an insignificant finding at the time and glossed over. While it wasn't fractured, which would automatically lead to the notion of manual strangulation, in light of revelations, the implication of the finding became clearer. A hand had been wrapped around her neck, pressure applied to her head to keep it underwater.

With Derek gone, he couldn't relay to Langston the story he'd told me. Nor could Summer refute it. So it was my word against — well, no one's.

I was shown the evidence on Shana's email proving she had known my husband from before — a conference held a couple of years earlier. One of the many times Derek had attended them. No one could've known the lengths Shana would go to help Derek pull the strings he'd so desperately needed pulling in order to get the job.

Stuart must've felt he'd lost everything as he'd watched Derek gain the attention and admiration of a staff he'd once been part of. Still, what he did to Shana was — shocking and horrific. He'll spend the rest of his life behind bars as a result.

I shut off the light in the basement and return to the first floor. Everything is packed. The moving truck is loaded and outside, waiting for me to sign off. Josie is looking after Ben and the baby, who I've named Nicole. She's Derek's daughter, and I killed her mother. So I'll be the one to take care of her now. I'll be the one who will give her the life she deserves. Her and Ben, both.

Josie walks toward me, the baby in her arms. "Are you ready?"

I sweep my gaze around the house once more. I never wanted to move here in the first place. I loved my home in Medford. But I'm not going back there. No. Too many painful memories.

Instead, Ben, Nicole, and I — we're starting over. "Yeah, I'm ready."

THE END

THE JOFFE BOOKS STORY

We began in 2014 when Jasper agreed to publish his mum's much-rejected romance novel and it became a bestseller.

Since then we've grown into the largest independent publisher in the UK. We're extremely proud to publish some of the very best writers in the world, including Joy Ellis, Faith Martin, Caro Ramsay, Helen Forrester, Simon Brett and Robert Goddard. Everyone at Joffe Books loves reading and we never forget that it all begins with the magic of an author telling a story.

We are proud to publish talented first-time authors, as well as established writers whose books we love introducing to a new generation of readers.

We won Trade Publisher of the Year at the Independent Publishing Awards in 2023 and Best Publisher Award in 2024 at the People's Book Prize. We have been shortlisted for Independent Publisher of the Year at the British Book Awards for the last five years, and were shortlisted for the Diversity and Inclusivity Award at the 2022 Independent Publishing Awards. In 2023 we were shortlisted for Publisher of the Year at the RNA Industry Awards, and in 2024 we were shortlisted at the CWA Daggers for the Best Crime and Mystery Publisher.

We built this company with your help, and we love to hear from you, so please email us about absolutely anything bookish at feedback@joffebooks.com.

If you want to receive free books every Friday and hear about all our new releases, join our mailing list here: www.joffe-books.com/freebooks.

And when you tell your friends about us, just remember: it's pronounced Joffe as in coffee or toffee!

www.ingramcontent.com/pod-product-compliance
Lightning Source LLC
Chambersburg PA
CBHW011453170626
46814CB00009B/3037

* 9 7 8 1 8 0 5 7 3 1 3 7 5 *